RAVENSCLAW

The Edinburgh Vampires, Book I

Maggie MacKeever

Vintage Ink Press

ISBN: 978-0-9889799-6-3

First publication September 2005 by Kensington Publishing Corp

Vintage Ink Press print publication January 2016

Books By Maggie MacKeever

THE DULCIE ADVENTURES:
Dulcie Bligh
The Baroness of Bow Street
Bachelor's Fare
The Right Honourable Viscount
The Ghosts of Greenwood

THE EDINBURGH VAMPIRES:
Ravensclaw
Vampire, Bespelled
A Judgment of Vampires

REGENCY HISTORICALS:
The Purloined Heart
The Tyburn Waltz

REGENCY NOVELLAS:
The Loversall Novellas
Point Non Plus
Quin
A Respectable Female

TRADITIONAL REGENCIES:
Cupid's Dart
Love Match
Lover's Knot
An Extraordinary Flirtation

Lady Sherry and the Highwayman
French Leave
Our Tabby
Sweet Vixen
An Eligible Connection
Strange Bedfellows
Lady Sweetbriar
A Notorious Lady
Fair Fatality
The Misses Millikin
Jessabelle
Lady Bliss
A Banbury Tale

Maggie MacKeever

Lady in the Straw
Lord Fairchild's Daughter
Merrie

GOLD RUSH ROMANCES:
El Dorado
Outlaw Love
Caprice

Who could resist his power?
His tongue had toils and dangers to recount...
He knew so well how to use the serpent's art ...

Excerpt from *The Vampyre,* by John Polidori, first published in the April 1819 edition of the *New Monthly Magazine.*

Chapter One

When an ass climbs a ladder we may find wisdom in a woman.

It was a dark and dreary night— or, rather, drizzly late afternoon— when a small shabby cart rattled along the rutted, little-used track that led from Morpeth to the coast of the North Sea. The driver was as shabby as his vehicle, the collar of his coat pulled high around his chin to combat the damp.

On the seat beside him perched a wee snippet of a lass. Large gold-flecked brown eyes peered inquisitively through the gold-rimmed spectacles that rested precariously on the bridge of her freckled nose. Frizzy tendrils of orange hair had escaped their tight braid to curl around her vivid little face. If no one would call the lass pretty, she had a fey quality about her. Willie spat over the side of the carriage, and discreetly crossed himself. He wadna hae been surprised to discover her ears were pointed at the tips.

The old road wound through wooded valleys and springy turf fields, past an old stone church and several abandoned cottages, and ended abruptly at the base of a desolate cliff. The young woman pushed her spectacles back up where they belonged, the better to survey the grim battle-scarred tower that stood harshly silhouetted against the gloomy sky, surrounded on three sides by deep water, the fourth approachable only by a steep slope. "Are you certain this is the right place?"

Of course Willie was certain. Wasna he Morpeth born and bred? Corby Castle this was, or what was left of it, after Robert the Bruce pulled three of the great towers down to near ground level, and Oliver Cromwell blasted open the gatehouse with a mortar piece.

1

All that remained intact was the three-story keep, which held the Lord's Hall and private apartments, not that Willie had seen them himself, nor did he care to, for the place 'twas said to be haunted, and Willie had nae more desire tae be meetin' up wi' gravestane-gentry than wi' the grey folk.

His passenger allowed that the ruin looked haunted. She said, nonetheless, "I'm going inside."

Willie gaped at her. "G'wa! Haeno' I been tellin' ye aboot the ghaisties?"

"So you have." She turned to look at him. "You *will* wait for me?"

Willie scowled. Was it no' just his luck to be oot in the middle of nae place wi' a fashious female (not to mention ghaisties and gropies and wirriecows), and the gloaming comin' on? "If it's castles ye're after visitin', there's Traquair and Drumlanrig and Sterling. Come away, noo, and I'll take ye someplace better on anither day."

Miss Emily Dinwiddie grasped the handle of her umbrella and refrained, barely, from giving her driver a good poke. Those other castles weren't said to house a creature old enough to remember fabled Sarmizegetuza, once perched atop a crag in the Orastie Mountains in Romania, or the Dacian god Zalmoxis, or the powerful night goddess Bendis, whose cult involved curious orgiastic rites. Emily produced a gold coin, which she brandished in front of the driver's nose. "You'll wait."

He snatched the coin from her. "Aweel."

Emily stood up, shook out her shirts, snatched up her furled umbrella, and climbed down from the cart. Gingerly, she made her way past the stone nesting-boxes where doves and pigeons had once been bred—pigeons being especially tasty cooked in a pastry pie—to provide a source of fresh meat in winter or during times of siege. Green moss spread like a slippery soggy carpet over the broken stone steps that wound upward to the castle. Emily trod carefully, lest she slip and fall and join the other wraiths wandering the ruins.

At the top of the stair stood a small side entrance, its door long since rotted away. Emily moved down the arched walkway, skirting the murder hole through which castle defenders had once spilled boiling oil, hot sand or sharp rocks through the ceiling onto unwelcome guests. Such light as the dreary day provided filtered down from the winching room on the second floor.

She followed the passage into a courtyard. The battlements on the west side were missing, and holes gaped in the outer wall. Courtesy of Cromwell's mortars, no doubt. Here would have been the stables and kitchens, guardrooms and vaults. Bake house, brew house, chapel. The deep pit where criminals—and any uninvited visitors who had survived the murder hole—had been thrown and left to rot.

Yes, well. Hopefully, a creature old enough to remember fabled Sarmizegetuza would be more enlightened as regarded uninvited guests. To the left of the gate, the tower Emily had glimpsed from below rose three stories high, its domed roof miraculously intact.

A strange stillness hung over the courtyard. Not even a bird sang.

No good sign, that. Emily gathered up her courage and strode briskly toward the tower's ancient door. She lifted the rusted iron knocker, which was formed like a dragon eating its own tail, and let it fall.

There came no response. Emily rapped the ebony handle of her umbrella briskly against the weathered wood. Still no reply. Frustrated, she gave the door a good kick.

With a groan of unoiled hinges, the door swung slowly inward. Half expecting to encounter one of Willie's ghaisties, Emily stepped across the threshold, umbrella thrust out before her like a broadsword.

The lower floor of the keep was one great empty room, separated from the entry by a wooden screen with a minstrel's gallery above. The vaulted hall was damp and drafty, bare of furniture save for a couple carved chests. A raised dais stood at the chamber's upper end. The plaster walls behind it still bore faint red lines, representing large masonry blocks, each decorated with a flower. A hooded fireplace was set into the far wall.

Broken wooden shutters hung drunkenly at the windows, some of which still held cracked cobwebbed panes of greenish glass. *"Buna seara!"* snarled a voice from the shadows, startling Emily almost out of her skin.

She spun around, umbrella at the ready. A small shrunken man hobbled forward to plant himself, arms akimbo, smack in her pathway. Bright beady eyes squinted up at her from a face as wrinkled as a raisin. Strands of dark hair had been combed carefully across his gleaming pate.

Surely this wizened little man was not he whom she sought. "This *is* the residence of Count Revay-Czobar?"

" 'The earthen pot should keep clear of the brass kettle'." His nose was impressively long for so short a fellow. He gave it a good twitch.

Emily looked down her own nose at him. "That's as it may be, but I'm not budging one inch until I've spoken with the Count. Meanwhile, you may build up the fire."

The old man regarded her sourly for a moment, then limped toward the doorway, muttering under his breath.

Emily exhaled. Her breath ghosted in the chill air. Timeworn tapestries hung here and there around the chamber: a giant gnawing on the leg of a bear; three archers shooting a duck; a dead woman standing in her shroud while worms gnawed her entrails.

Memento mori: remember that we all must die.

The old man returned, carrying an armload of kindling. In almost the same moment, a huge brownish gray canine padded through the arched opening of the wheel stairway that had been built into one stone wall. Emily snatched up her umbrella and fell back a step. The creature's triangular ears were alert. His slanted, black-rimmed yellow eyes fixed on her with unnerving intensity. Lupine lips parted to reveal gleaming white teeth.

The old man dropped his kindling into the fireplace. "Drogo, behave yourself."

Emily moved prudently behind a dusty carved chest. "Drogo looks like a wolf."

" 'A wolf knows a wolf as a thief knows a thief'." The old man tossed the last twig onto the fire and then limped toward the spiral stone stair. Did he think she'd come to steal the silver? The wolf-dog settled on the hearth, his pale stare still fixed on Emily.

Drogo seemed content to remain where he was for the moment. Emily pulled off her damp wool cloak and draped it over a rusty candle stand. Impatiently, she tucked a tendril of carrot-colored hair back behind her ear. Difficult to look brisk and businesslike when curly tendrils frizzed out about one's head in all directions, like Medusa and her snakes.

She edged toward a deep-set window. Other than swiveling one pointed ear in her direction, the wolf-dog didn't move. There was little enough to see outside, save for the darkening sky and the wind-tossed waters of the sea.

Dusk was nigh, that hour when, according to her studies, the exanimate emerged from their graves, not being prone to perambulate about beneath the sun's lethal rays. Emily touched the chain from which she'd hung a crucifix, the seal of St. Benedict, an evil eye from Greece, a tiger's eye, a crescent-shaped charm, and a brass finger ring. Lest those precautions prove insufficient, she had also splashed herself liberally with holy water and garlic oil. Would Count Revay-Czobar be a blood-sucking fiend so foul she couldn't bear to look at him, let alone ask his help? Would he see her as a tasty tidbit, and thereby force her to defend herself?

A reflection appeared behind her in the clouded window glass. The hair on Emily's neck rose. A chill crawled up her spine. Even her elbows tingled, and in her admittedly limited experience, elbow tingles were almost always a bad thing.

Clutching her umbrella, Emily turned to face the man standing by the fireplace. He was rumpled, tousled, as if recently roused from a well-used bed. *Coffin*, she reminded herself. His shirt was half-unbuttoned. Tight breeches molded to his strong thighs. Emily realized she was staring, and where, and hastily elevated her gaze to his face.

And what a face it was. No mortal sculptor had the talent to chisel such exquisitely formed bones. Eyes the blue of the most precious sapphires, mouth a shamelessly sensual delight. Pale perfect skin and a slanted slash of eyebrows. Thick auburn hair tumbled loose over his shoulders, gleaming in the firelight.

He reached down to rub the wolf-dog's ears. "You asked to speak with me?"

His voice was smoky, dark, seductive, with the faintest trace of an accent. Emily attempted to collect her scattered wits. "Count Revay-Czobar?"

"Call me Ravensclaw. It's easier on the tongue."

If here was no graying skin or deathlike pallor, no stink of putrefying flesh—'Ravensclaw' looked to be no more than five-and-thirty—the Count was definitely preternatural. No mere mortal could be so magnificent. Emily was grateful for her umbrella's sharpened tip.

The sensuous lips curved. Ravensclaw's gaze caressed her face, skimmed her forehead, the slope of her cheek; kissed the tip of her nose; lingered on her lips; nuzzled an earlobe.

Emily's knees trembled. Sweat popped out on her brow. A strange drugging sensation stole over her senses, as if those elegant fingers stroked her flesh instead of Drogo's thick fur. As if his lips were warm against her ear, whispering of her hunger to be consumed by something greater than herself. She longed to touch him in turn, to slide her hands over the smooth skin hidden beneath his linen shirt, unfasten his snug breeches, and—

And what? She wasn't certain. Ravensclaw made her feel things she'd never felt before.

Made her feel them. Irritated, Emily said, "Stop that!" She was a sensible, bespectacled spinster, not at all the sort of female this man would have noticed when he was still alive—and if Ravensclaw was this potent now, what had he been *before?*

He had moved, somehow, without her noticing, and now stood so close she might have reached out and touched him, had she wanted to touch him, which she did, very much. Emily locked her traitorous knees together and thrust out her crucifix.

Ravensclaw plucked the thing out of her hand. "Excellent workmanship. Solid gold. Byzantine. The sort of thing a Crusader might have worn."

So much for the literature. The Count hadn't cringed or blanched or hissed at sight of the holy relic; he'd touched it with no sizzle of burning flesh. Moreover, he was—despite the experts' assertions to the contrary—standing in what remained of the daylight without any ill effect. Emily found herself fascinated by the length of his eyelashes, which were thicker and darker than her own.

He leaned toward her and sniffed. *"Eau de garlique.* Is this a new fashion of which I'm unaware?"

"Garlic doesn't disturb you?"

"Quite the contrary. I especially like garlic with chicken, forty cloves and two bay leaves." Ravensclaw reached out one graceful finger and pushed Emily's glasses back up to the bridge of her nose.

The Count was toying with her as if he were a cat and she a witless rodent. Emily elevated her umbrella and poked him in the chest. "I would prefer that you keep your hands—and your thoughts—to yourself, my lord."

"Would you, indeed?" he asked softly. On the hearth, the wolf-dog stirred.

Emily took a firmer grip on her umbrella. She had no desire to skewer her host, but neither was she eager to make the intimate acquaintance of a vampire's fangs. Rather, she didn't think she was. At least, not yet. She did have a certain curiosity—

"What you don't know can't hurt you," murmured the Count. And then, without the slightest hint of fangs, he smiled. It was a roguish captivating smile that said 'you're the most delicious thing I've seen in a long time and I'm going to gobble you up slowly and savor every nibble' as clearly as if he'd spoken aloud.

Emily blinked. Ravensclaw must surely be the most irresistibly, wickedly beautiful being ever put on God's green earth.

In whatever century that had been.

And she was staring at him like a smitten schoolgirl.

Oh, bloody hell.

Chapter Two

Bees that have honey in their mouths have stings in their tails.

Emily glowered at her host. "I know what you are, Count Revay-Czobar."

"Ravensclaw," the Count reminded her, then added: "Isidore?" The old man popped around a corner, as if he had been eavesdropping just out of sight. "Have tea brought to the Lady's Chamber."

"Tea. The Lady's Chamber." Isidore twitched his nose.

The last thing Emily had anticipated was taking tea with an aberration. "We have no time for this!"

"We have ample time to become properly acquainted. Your driver left without you. The locals are a superstitious lot." Ravensclaw treated her, again, to that irresistible smile. "Wheesht, lassie, didna Kiuttlin' Kate lepit off the castle wall into the loch after cuddlin' with one lad too many and findin' herself biggend? Doesna Gawkit Gordy haunt the stables, or what were once the stables, where he was murthered by a manservant under circumstances best not thought aboot?"

The Count's Scots accent was uncannily accurate. Emily suspected he was again entertaining himself at her expense. In more normal tones, he added, "We also claim a woman in white who is most often seen on the stair, and the specter of a dog."

Emily glanced at the wolf, which rose and padded toward her. She backed away.

Ravensclaw snapped his fingers. The animal dropped to its haunches. "Drogo is no specter. Touch him and see for yourself."

Emily had no intention of doing anything so birdwitted as to pet a— A what?

Ravensclaw didn't *look* like a fiend from hell. Emily was less certain about the wolf.

"Moreover, there is always time for tea. If I may?" The Count held out his hand.

Against her better judgment, Emily surrendered her umbrella. Ravensclaw hung it on the candlestick beside her damp cloak, then indicated that she should precede him up the winding stone staircase.

The Lady's Chamber was a lofty, domed six-sided solar. Set into the walls were a fireplace, an arched cupboard and four windows, three of the latter wide with stone benches, the last a narrow slit with a stone sink in its sill. A carved screen partly hid a doorway leading off into a second, smaller room. False ribs, bearing faded red and black chevrons, sprang from corbelled colonnettes.

Here, decided Emily, was opulence enough to suit the most hedonistic Romanian boyar. Heavy oak furniture embellished with intricately carved animals and flowers; cabinets and bookcases inlaid with checkerboard parquetry and precious stones. She would have paid a pretty penny to possess that silver-embellished writing desk.

Multicolored woolen rugs were scattered on the stone floor. More medieval tapestries graced the walls, of a less morbid nature than those below. The chamber was illuminated by oil lamps suspended in metal rings.

A tea tray rested on an inlaid chest. "If you will do the honors?" asked the Count. With a sense of unreality, Emily set about the familiar, soothing ritual. Ravensclaw preferred his tea with a chunk of crystallized ginger, or so he informed her. Emily took hers with milk.

Ravensclaw settled back with his teacup, as at ease as if he sat in any London drawing room. Not that Emily knew many—if any— gentlemen who took tea. Nor had she any great experience with London drawing rooms. She stole a glance at her host, alert for signs of blood lust, an elongation of the teeth, a reddening or glowing of the eye. He lowered his gaze to the pulse point at the base of her throat.

Emily set down her teacup. "Permit me to explain my presence. I believe you are not unfamiliar with the Dinwiddie Society for the Exploration of Matters Abstruse and Supersensible."

Ravensclaw surveyed a plate of finger sandwiches, pastries and scones. "For my sins."

And what did *that* mean? "I am Emily Dinwiddie. My father was—"

"Professor Bartholomew Dinwiddie, creator of several strange inventions, most memorable among them a portable engine, in the way of a tobacco-tongs, by means of which a man may climb over a wall; an amphibious horse-drawn vehicle; and a gravestone sundial that celebrated the anniversary of the deceased's birth and death. Known to his detractors, unkindly, as Professor Dimwit." Ravensclaw reached for the teapot and refilled his cup.

Fortunately, her papa's critics hadn't learned of the little ladder that enabled spiders to climb out of a hipbath. The automaton that could play a flute. The mechanical quacking duck which appeared to digest and excrete its food. Emily said, "You are well informed, my lord."

"I suffer from insomnia." Ravensclaw gestured toward the bookshelves laden with reading material that ranged from early studies of anatomy, and treatises on fungi and pharmacology, to, unless Emily's eyes deceived her, *The Egyptian Book of the Dead.* "Perusing scholarly treatises such as those written by your father helps me fall asleep. Did you know that the ancient Egyptians were in the habit of annually burning alive an unfortunate individual whose only crime was to have hair the color of yours?"

Emily refused to be distracted. "Since you are so well-informed, you will also be aware that my father died in a laboratory mishap a little over a year past. I am now overseer of the Dinwiddie Society."

"Ah."

"Don't you *dare* point out that I'm a female."

The Count arched an eyebrow. "You malign me, Miss Dinwiddie. I was merely going to remark that you are very young to assume such responsibility."

"I am four-and-twenty. That is not so very young. Nor am I altogether ignorant, my lord. In addition to my extensive formal education, I worked with my papa, and consequently know about vampires and ghouls, shape-changers and werewolves." Emily glanced pointedly at Drogo, snoozing on the hearth.

Ravensclaw selected a cucumber sandwich. "I see."

For all her experiences with the Society—or the experiences she had read about in her role as her papa's amanuensis, he having been reluctant to let her *do* anything—Emily had never before met a supersensible being in the flesh. If 'flesh' was the proper term. She watched Ravensclaw bite into his sandwich with every evidence of enjoyment. A plump, black long-haired feline oozed through the doorway. At sight of Emily, it hissed.

"Machka," explained the Count, as he brushed crumbs off his breeches. "Romany for cat." The feline jumped, purring, into his lap.

Emily fingered her necklace and its assorted charms. According to the literature, animals fled in terror of the preterhuman, yet here Ravensclaw sat like any ordinary man, with a cat on his lap and a dog sprawled on his hearth.

No, she told herself; *this is more mind magic.* There was nothing ordinary about the Count, or the dog that could well be a lycanthrope, or the cat that was probably someone's familiar. "You will be wondering about the purpose of my visit. In short, I need your help."

Ravensclaw smoothed his hand along Machka's spine. "What has given you the impression that I'm a man who rescues damsels in distress?"

Emily hadn't the impression that he was a man at all. "How many times must I tell you that I know what you are? Need I remind you of Mercea the Wise, Vlad Tepes, Michael the Brave? You have lived in palaces and huts alike, foraged for food in the mountainous regions of Wallachia, Moldavia, and Transylvania; have seen Greeks fight Romans, Romanians fight Hungarians and Tatars, Turks fight Russians and Austrians, all because mankind must disagree with its neighbor's religion, covet its neighbor's land and goods. Some decades past, you withdrew to observe the human tragicomedy from a less volatile vantage point than Romania."

She paused, awaiting his reaction. Ravensclaw said merely, "You are well informed about my ancestors."

"I'm well informed about *you!*" Emily sprang up from her chair and began to pace. "I do not presume to judge you. The Society has a live-and-let-live-except-in-isolated-instances philosophy. Evil is in the eye of the beholder, and morality is a point of view."

"How remarkably open-minded," murmured the Count.

Emily eyed the fireplace, over which hung a thirteenth-century sword, a sharpened rod of triangular cross-section steel drawn to an acute point at one end and hilted at the other; and envisioned whacking her host over his aggravating, albeit handsome, head. "You may be interested to learn that the Society has, or had, in its possession a double-bladed athame with a cabochon ruby and a double ouroborus set into its hilt."

His blue gaze sharpened. "The d'Auvergne athame vanished centuries ago."

"Not vanished, was stolen. In 1544, to be precise, by Isobella Dinwiddie, and thereafter kept in a lead-lined chest locked in the Society's vault. A number of other items have also gone missing. You must help me get them back."

His expression was unreadable. "Must I?"

Emily counted to one hundred. Her first supersensible being was giving her heartburn. "Since the athame was originally stolen from you, you will know its powers."

"Stolen from my ancestor, you mean," the Count corrected. He had ceased petting Machka. The cat leapt down from his lap.

"Now you will try to convince me it's your ancestor whose name is on the Dinwiddie list! The Society has known about the Breaslă for some time, my lord. I doubt it would be in your best interest were the world to become aware of its existence as well. Papa told me that if ever I found myself in need of assistance, I should seek you out and remind you of the matter of St. Cuthbert's finger bone." He had also said she should proceed with caution, Emily belatedly recalled. "Don't just sit there looking inscrutable! We must retrieve the stolen items before the powers of darkness are unleashed."

"Such melodrama, Miss Dinwiddie." The Count reached for the teapot. "Tell me about your father's mishap."

The mishap that Emily was growing to suspect had been no mishap at all? "Papa was developing a pair of galvanic spectacles that applied electric current to the optic nerve by means of a small zinc and copper plate attached to the nosepiece. Instead of the nosepiece, the current was applied to himself." She adjusted her own spectacles, which had again slid halfway down her nose.

Ravensclaw said politely, "My condolences."

Emily reached into a pocket and pulled out a trinket of the sort that might have adorned a gentleman's watch fob, provided said gentleman was of an esoteric bent: a silver disc engraved with a serpent, its body in the form of an upright 'S', an apple in its mouth and an arrow piercing its breast . "After Papa's death, things were at sixes and sevens for a time. I only recently discovered that the athame had been removed from its chest. I found this on the floor."

Ravensclaw studied the disc. "Apollo's arrow piercing the green dragon of Hermetic philosophy. An image of the union between passive and active, spirit and life. Interesting, but your vrajă is far from an unusual piece."

Emily noted that the Count had called the charm by its proper name. And that he wisely hadn't touched the thing. "Not unusual, but not common either. I believe this particular talisman belongs to a man named Michael Ross. Mr. Ross is—or *was*—a favorite of my father's." She tucked the vrajă back into her pocket. "He left London for Edinburgh several months ago. I believe Michael took the athame with him. *You* have a home in Edinburgh. May we please leave now?"

Ravensclaw nudged the cat off his lap. "Humor me, Miss Dinwiddie. What do you expect to accomplish in Edinburgh?"

Count Revay-Czobar was not impressing Emily with his quickness of perception. "I expect to find a thief! Haven't you been listening?"

"And after you have found Mr. Ross, what then?"

Emily had not decided. Currently she was inclined to weigh him down with stones and toss him into the River Forth to drown. "Demand that he return the stolen items? Steal the dratted things from him? Maybe *you* can make him give them back. Naturally, you will prefer to travel under cover of darkness. Unless you can sprout wings and fly like a bat?"

Ravensclaw studied her as if she was some hitherto-unencountered species. "If I was what you think me, Miss Dinwiddie, should you not be afraid?"

Emily *was* afraid, more than a little bit, but would bite off her own tongue before she told him so. "You admit it, then?"

Gracefully, he rose. "I admit nothing. You will be my guest tonight."

His guest, or his dinner? Emily parted her lips to protest. Ravensclaw fixed his eyes on hers and the words died unspoken in her throat.

The Count moved toward her. Emily stepped back, hands raised to fend him off. Her fingers brushed his bare wrist.

A dizzying sense of mysterious dense forests, high craggy mountains, lush green upland pastures. A two-roomed cottage of solid well-hewn logs, roofed with laths. Wood floor covered with homemade woolen rugs. Similar rugs arranged neatly on the bed.

A woman with chestnut hair, wearing a sleeveless, richly embroidered jacket of fine white lambskin, a skirt woven in strips of light and dark red wool. Around her waist, an ornamental belt of different-colored wool interwoven with golden threads. Heavy wool stockings striped white and red and black.

"Trădător! Nelegiuit!" She backed away from him, making the sign against the evil eye.

Ravensclaw looked startled. Emily jerked her hand away.

Chapter Three

An ape's an ape, a varlet's a varlet,
though they be clad in silk and scarlet.

Thunder rumbled through the heavens. Raindrops rattled against the window glass. Emily slept fitfully.

Moonlight cast eerie silver shadows through the dense wild forest. She slipped out of the small cottage that nestled among the tall spruce trees. He was waiting in the mountaintop meadow where aromatic grasses and flowers grew.

"I hunger. Let me taste you." He spread out his dark cloak.

She steeled herself against him. "I know what you are."

He reached out his hand to her. "As I know what you are, iubită."

She moved closer to him, closer, unaware that she had moved at all. "You do?"

Cool fingers slid through her hair to the nape of her neck. "It is a matter of scent."

His eyes were blue as the ocean's depths. She whispered, "Scent?"

"You smell of garlic." He lowered his lips to her throat. His teeth found her pulse. Sensation flooded her senses, an intoxicating warmth—

Emily surfaced slowly from the depths of slumber, a heavy weight on her chest, the metallic taste of blood bitter in her mouth.

She had bitten her own lip. Emily touched it with her tongue. Found herself wondering, shockingly, if Ravensclaw would like the flavor of her blood.

Don't think of that, you pumpkin-brain! You must find the athame.

Warily, Emily opened one eye. She had read of incubi, that special class of demons who squatted on the breasts of sleeping women and made them long for things unimaginable in the practical light of day.

No incubus perched atop her chest, but Machka. They were almost nose to nose. The cat's whiskers tickled. After a moment's slit-eyed contemplation, Machka butted her head against Emily's chin and began to knead her neck.

Gingerly, Emily patted the creature. She hoped her necklace of talismans would prove effective against whatever Machka was. They weren't protecting her against the sharp claws that pricked her throat.

She turned her head on the pillow. The small cell-like stone room was simply furnished, her bed a straw-filled canvas mattress placed upon wooden slats. Easy to imagine an archer standing at the narrow vertical window, firing his arrows down on the enemy below.

The warped door creaked open. A maidservant bustled into the room. "Good morning, miss. I've brought your chocolate. Ah, the naughty *pisică!*" She scooted a hissing Machka off the bed.

Maidservant? The woman more closely resembled a tavern wench, brown-haired and buxom, with a fine color in her cheeks and plump pouting lips. Emily pulled herself into a sitting position. "What is your name? I didn't see you yesterday."

"Zizi, miss." The servant set down her tray, on which rested a pot of chocolate and a plate of biscuits. "There's three of us, not counting old Isidore."

Emily reached for the chocolate pot. Here a perfect opportunity to learn more about her enigmatic host. "Have you worked for the Count long?"

Zizi scooped up Machka, who was inching toward the biscuits. "As long as I can recall."

Glamour, Emily decided. Although Zizi, as opposed to being pale and wan as befit an undead's victim, was awesomely robust. Nor were there any fang marks on the startling amount of creamy neck and bosom that were on display. "Indeed?"

"As near as makes no difference." Cat tucked under one arm, Zizi began to tidy up the room. "Ravensclaw treats his people well. None of us would want to work elsewhere."

They wouldn't, would they, if Ravensclaw had bespelled them? It was only sensible of the Count to have servants do his bidding during the daylight hours when he couldn't be abroad. By means of the glamour, he blinded them to the knowledge that he was a bloodsucking fiend so foul no mortal could gaze upon his true form without being driven insane—

Insane with lust. Perdition! No incubus had sent that dream.

Zizi was still talking. "Himself says that as soon as you're ready, we'll leave for Edinburgh."

Emily glanced at the bright light streaming through the window. "Himself?"

"The master." Machka growled. Zizi set the cat ungently on the floor. "Will you need help dressing, miss?"

"Thank you," Emily said, "but no." Zizi closed the door behind her. Machka leapt on the bed, raised one back leg, and began to lick herself.

Leaving the cat to its ablutions, Emily swung her bare feet down to the cold floor. After a quick visit to the corner basin stand, she pulled off her nightrail, folded it neatly and placed it in the valise that Isidore had found abandoned at the bottom of the broken stone stair. She shook out her wrinkled gown, struggled into it, and set out in search of the Count. Machka jumped down from the bed to trail at her heels.

Ravensclaw was in the Lady's Chamber, Drogo dozing at his feet. The Count had dressed for traveling in fawn breeches that clung to his muscular thighs, snowy linen, a superbly cut brown coat, and glossy boots. His auburn hair was drawn back and tied at his nape.

He rose to greet her, a slender volume in one hand. "I am reading a formula for the manufacture and use of a magic carpet. A virgin is required."

Emily narrowed her eyes at him. Did not the undead, at the break of day, take refuge in their tombs? "*I* have read that one may vanish a nosferatu by stuffing his left sock with graveyard dirt and cemetery rocks, then tossing it into water flowing away from the area one seeks to protect. Supposedly, the demised may be controlled by the use of spiritwood and rum."

Ravensclaw awarded her his bewitching smile. "One needs to be naked during that particular ritual, I believe."

Wonderful. Now I'm thinking of him naked. "Alternately one might make a stake of ash, hawthorn, or maple and pound it into the corpse, put garlic in its mouth, and pound a nail in its head. Remove the heart and halve it. Incinerate the decapitated body and throw the ashes to the wind." Any of which, Emily admitted, would be a great pity in the present case. "You have a reflection. I saw it in the window yesterday."

"Why would I not have a reflection?" Ravensclaw replaced the book on its shelf. "I assure you that I am quite corporeal."

He was entirely too corporeal for her peace of mind. "I understand we are to go to Edinburgh."

"Is that not what you wanted?" Ravensclaw inquired politely. Drogo opened one yellow eye.

"What I *want*," retorted Emily, "is to be able to travel without the annoying restrictions placed on females." Curiosity got the best of her. "Tell me, does a sanguisurge discriminate between male and female blood?"

"The undead are amphierotic," Ravensclaw informed her. "Umbivalent, that is. I know this due to my vast reading, you understand."

Amphierotic? Umbivalent? "Are you mocking me?" Emily asked.

"No, Miss Dinwiddie, I am enjoying you. It is a very different thing." Ravensclaw scratched Drogo's head. The wolf parted his great jaws and yawned.

Enjoying her, was he? Emily wished she might say the same. "Speaking of Edinburgh, how do you plan to transport your, ah, resting place?"

"Has anyone ever told you that you are a very exasperating young woman? Come with me." Ravensclaw indicated a doorway in the far wall.

He stepped aside. Emily entered the adjacent, smaller room. She was no longer surprised to see antique furnishings and tapestries and colorful wool rugs. Never, however, had she seen anything like the canopied bed that dominated the chamber, its headboard and posts elaborately carved with figures in bas-relief. Behind her, Ravensclaw said, *"This* is where I sleep." His husky tones evoked erotic scenarios played out on the fur coverlet and linen sheets.

Cheeks burning, Emily bent to peer beneath the bed. She saw not a speck of dust or dirt. "I thought revenants couldn't go far from their native soil."

"I don't know about revenants, but I can go anywhere I please." The Count's amused voice came from the vicinity of her upthrust rump.

Hastily, Emily righted herself. "And can you cross running water, my lord?"

"I swim," he informed her. "I also bathe."

She wouldn't, she absolutely wouldn't, think of Ravensclaw bathing. Emily squinted at an ornate bedpost. Carved figures sat face to face, heels locked around each other's waists, their nether parts— *Oh, my.*

"Miss Dinwiddie?" inquired the Count. "I believe you are anxious to depart for Edinburgh?"

Miss Dinwiddie was anxious to depart Ravensclaw's bedchamber before she took leave of her remaining senses and dragged him down with her on that wicked bed, there to determine what was possible and what was not. Emily stalked out of the room with all the dignity at her command. In the Lady's Chamber, with the air of a magician, the Count produced her umbrella and cloak before he escorted her outside.

A closed carriage waited in the courtyard, on its doors emblazoned a coat of arms. Emily turned to watch Ravensclaw follow her out into the sunlight. He wore a pair of small, dark, round-lensed spectacles. Despite his assurances, she half expected him to burst into flames or crumble into dust.

He held out his hand to her. Ignoring his offer of assistance, Emily climbed unaided into the crimson-upholstered coach.

Drogo took up most of the floor space; Machka, one bench seat. Grumbling, the cat moved aside, then arranged herself on Emily's lap.

Closing the door behind him, Ravensclaw settled on the seat opposite. The coach dipped as Isidore climbed up onto the box. Emily hoped the old man had sufficient strength to control the team. Zizi and the other servants were to follow with the luggage in a less conspicuous vehicle. Emily wondered where all this equipment had been kept, and what else might be hidden in the castle ruins.

The carriage lurched forward, rattled under the rusted portcullis with its wicked-looking spikes, over an ancient drawbridge that looked incapable of bearing its weight. Emily threaded her fingers through Machka's soft fur. Among the carriage's amenities were locking shutters, a compass, silver-plated furnishings, and three lamps. Not for Ravensclaw, the indignities of traveling on a common stage alongside a matron with several squalling offspring, a parson, and several unhappily caged chickens. Emily had been happy to part company with her fellow passengers in Morpeth.

And now here she was. Emily had ridden in a closed carriage before, of course, but those previous excursions had in no way prepared her to share a small intimate space with Ravensclaw. The dead-alive were said to be of a seductive nature, and in this instance at least the literature was correct.

She was not alone with him, exactly. Drogo's weight was warm against her feet and Machka's claws pricked her thigh. And, unless Emily wanted to be remembered as the Dinwiddie who had let the genie out of its bottle, she must keep her wits about her and find that which was lost.

Stolen, rather. Emily thought of her intrepid ancestress Isobella. Isobella would have known what to say to the seductive stranger who lounged on the seat opposite. And what to do with him as well. The d'Auvergne athame wasn't the only thing that particular Dinwiddie had stolen during her adventurous career.

Emily was not like Isobella. She stole neither artifacts nor hearts, didn't dally with other women's husbands, and hopefully wouldn't drink poison at the end, which admittedly seemed an unlikely last act for a freckled, bespectacled spinster with frizzy masses of rebellious orange hair.

The silence was unbearable. Emily cleared her throat. "Is it true, my lord, that your kind can change shapes at will? Make yourselves invisible? Can you truly fly?"

He had been gazing out his window. Now the dark-lensed spectacles turned to her. "You remind me of a terrier with a rat,

Miss Dinwiddie. The dog sinks its teeth into its prey and refuses to let go until the rodent's neck is broken."

Emily, for some odd reason, found herself in the mood for a good quarrel. "Are you comparing yourself to a rat?"

"No, little one. Nor am I comparing you to a cur." Ravensclaw stretched out his long legs until one muscular calf rested against her skirts. "Loathe as I am to disappoint you, I'm not what you think. But I *am* something of an expert on supermundane matters, due to my extensive reading—I especially enjoyed *On the Masticating Dead in their Tomb* (1728), which puts forth the notion that having a virgin boy ride naked bareback on a virgin stallion will point the way to an inanimate's resting place—and consider it most unlikely that any being can crawl headfirst down a castle wall, or turn himself into a wisp of fog."

Maybe not, but he could turn her into a pudding. Emily found it difficult to gaze on the man—*the aberration!*—and retain possession of her wits. Proof, her papa would have pointed out, had he been privileged to be present, that the female constitution was unsuited to explorations of the extramundane.

She would prove him wrong. She *must* prove him wrong. "Tell me, why are you accompanying me to Edinburgh when you refuse to take me seriously, my lord?"

Ravensclaw reached over and plucked Machka from her lap. "Because you are a very reckless young woman, Miss Dinwiddie. And I possess a more chivalrous nature than I had previously understood."

Chapter Four

An arrow shot upright falls on the shooter's head.

Edinburgh perched perilously atop an extinct volcano. Stacked up like a great haphazard pile of rocks, the medieval Old Town's dark tenements glowered down at the New Town's neoclassical terraces and squares. Separating the two areas was a deep, broad bridge-spanned ravine planted with trees and shrubbery, once a lake where accused witches met their deaths, thereby being exonerated from all charges, for only the innocent drowned.

In the heyday of the Old Town, several prominent Elizabethans had chosen to live in the then less congested area of the Canongate, commuting to and from Edinburgh Castle along the Royal Mile. Count Revay-Czobar lived in the Old Town now, not far from the Castle, in a tall, five-story townhouse capped by two pointed gables of unequal size. The round-headed arches of the ground floor frontage were stained from centuries of billowing black smoke, fog, and rain. Curving forestairs jutted out onto the pavement. A lentil stone dated 1622 bore the words, FEARE THE LORD AND DEPART FROM EVILL.

The interior of the townhouse was furnished to suit its owner's taste, including tiled chimneypieces and fine tempera work. The master bedroom's beam and board ceilings were brightly painted with flowers and fruit. A deep arcaded frieze surmounted the tall, shuttered windows and adorned the stone wall above the fireplace and the curved wall that marked the turnpike stair.

Upholstered armchairs were scattered around the chamber. A coffer inlaid with holly and bog oak sat against one wall. Ravensclaw lay on another great carved bed—satyrs and satyresses, centaurs and centaurides, assorted gods and fauns and nymphs—his hands folded on his chest, as still as the mythological beings that guarded his rest. Or perhaps not precisely as still. One eyebrow twitched.

Abruptly, the Count wakened. If it could be called that. He lay motionless for a moment, orienting himself. Slumber now was not slumber as he had once known it, but a descent into a nothingness so absolute it might have been deeply disturbing if one dwelt on the matter, which he seldom did. Valentin Lupescu spent no more time regretting his inclusion in the Dinwiddie Society's annals of abnormalities than he did lamenting his own past. Truth be told, all in all, he thought himself damned fortunate.

Fortunate, if alone in his bed at the moment. He opened one eye. Isidore was hovering just inside the door. Val said, "Where are Zizi, Bela, Lilian?"

Isidore wrinkled his nose. "They say it isn't proper for them to be visiting your bedchamber with a young lady in the house."

Propriety, Val mused. What a novel concept. Especially in connection with Zizi, Bela, and Lilian.

Miss Dinwiddie was complicating his existence. With or without his cooperation, she would have made her way to Edinburgh, a curious lamb blundering into a lair of hungry wolves. He'd had no choice but to escort her. The matter of St. Cuthbert's knuckle bone aside, he had to destroy that blasted list.

In the interim, he would help the young woman retrieve her stolen items. If he took few things seriously, including himself, Val took the d'Auvergne athame very seriously indeed.

Isidore cleared his throat. Val threw back the covers. *"What?"*

"The chimneys needed sweeping. It turns out that Miss Dinwiddie has strong feelings about chimneysweeps. This particular chimneysweep was caught trying to steal a candlestick. By Drogo." Isidore's thin lips twisted. "Scared the *puşti* out of a good year's growth."

"What did you do with our young thief?"

"'He that may not do as he would, must do as he may'." Before Val could either comment or cuff him, the old man shuffled out the door.

Val pulled on fresh breeches. Though he had long been aware of the Dinwiddie Society's existence, he had *not* known that the d'Auvergne athame had come to rest in the Society's vaults. He wondered how far Miss Dinwiddie would go in her efforts to protect herself from him, and hoped she wouldn't drape herself about with bleached bones, or eat grave dirt.

Val was smiling as he tied his cravat. Of all things, he disliked being bored, which was why he kept around him an ancient manservant who spouted proverbs at him, and maidservants who were no better than they should be. Emily Dinwiddie promised to provide more amusement than he had enjoyed in a score of decades.

Contrary to custom, Count Revay-Czobar didn't let out each story of his townhouse as a separate flat: the ground floor occupied by a tradesman and his workshop; the lower floors provenance of aristocrats and prosperous merchants eager to escape the streets' dirt and stench and at the same time avoid the steep climb up the common turnpike stair; the highest floors home to servants and poorer workmen who reaped some benefit in that they were privileged to glimpse sunlight. Though the bottom floor of Val's house was indeed occupied by a small cloth merchant's booth, the MacCamishes were in his employ, and insured that during his absences the rest of the dwelling was kept secure and in good repair. The first floor housed his kitchen and dining area, the second his drawing room, the third his bedroom and adjacent study. Guest and servants' rooms were located above.

Val descended the winding turnpike stair to the drawing room, a cozy chamber with green-paneled walls and a simple fireplace, nail-studded leather furniture, faded rugs on the wood floor. Here, too, books littered every available surface, interspersed with maps of the world, a calculating board, and a perpetual almanac in a frame.

He paused unnoticed in the doorway. His house-guest was standing in a patch of sunlight that glinted off her spectacles, rendered her fair freckled skin almost translucent, and turned her fiery hair every shade from copper to gold. Val experienced a sudden urge to see the current head of the Dinwiddie Society wearing something other than unrelieved black. Or, even better, clad in nothing but clouds of frizzy ringlets and her fair freckled skin.

She was clutching a sooty urchin's elbow as she lectured him on the penalties for theft, which ranged from branding to transportation to simply being hanged. Drogo had taken up an alert position in front of the fireplace. Machka was engaged in an inspection of her nether bits.

Val strolled into the room. "Isidore informs me that we have a guest."

Miss Dinwiddie shoved the boy behind her. "I understand, my lord, that the chimneys of these old wooden buildings have to be swept lest the coal dust builds up and results in a house fire. I also understand that children, being small, are best suited to the task. I think *you* may not understand that a sweep's life expectancy is approximately six months. If he survives past his twelfth birthday, which is unlikely, his body will have been permanently deformed by the constant pushing of his limbs against the chimneys' brick walls. My papa was so appalled by this widespread barbarity that he invented a system of elongated hinged poles and a pulley apparatus to be used in our home." She paused for breath. Her captive muttered something uncomplimentary concerning contermashious sassenachs.

"Poles and pulleys," Val repeated. "I will be fascinated to learn the details. Your young friend has a somewhat noxious aroma about him." His houseguest, on the other hand, smelled like pasta tossed with sautéed garlic and olive oil. "Isidore. Take this noisome whelp away."

"I'm nae bastartin' whelp! Me name's Jamie." protested the sweep.

"*Neisprăvit,*" muttered Isidore, in the strangled tones of someone attempting not to breathe through his nose.

"No!" said Miss Dinwiddie in the same moment, and clutched the boy's filthy arm. "You shan't have him for your—er!"

For his breakfast, mayhap? "Isidore will speak with the lad's master. Zizi, Bela, and Lilian will give the brat a bath." Emily looked undecided. Jamie suggested that his captors awa' and bile their heids.

Much as Val disliked to impose his will on others, sometimes he had no choice. *Go with Isidore. Now.*

Jamie's jaw went slack. Isidore grasped the boy's ear and led him from the room.

Drogo padded after them. Machka rubbed against Miss Dinwiddie's ankles, for all the world as if she liked their guest. What Machka really liked was to be an annoyance. Val picked up the cat and set her on his shoulder. Machka licked his ear.

Emily removed her spectacles and gave them a brisk polish. "That was most impressive. However, you needn't try and bamboozle *me* into thinking I don't want Jamie as my page."

Val decided Miss Dinwiddie must be unfamiliar with the adage concerning fools and angels and the placement of their feet. "First you invade my castle and demand I bring you to Edinburgh. Now you introduce a thief into my household and insist on having him as your servant, although I doubt he has the faintest notion what a page boy does and will probably make off with all the silver plate. Don't put your back up; I'm not suggesting you should turn him out into the streets. Mrs. MacCamish could handle a regiment of Hussars. She'll brook no nonsense from a cheeky little scamp."

"Mrs. MacCamish?" Emily echoed suspiciously.

"My cook. Don't look so appalled. Contrary to what you seem to think, I do *not* have a taste for roasted guttersnipes."

She replaced her spectacles. "You're angry with me."

Yes, and wasn't that interesting? Anger wasn't an emotion with which Val often bothered. "I made some inquiries last night, after you went to sleep. Michael Ross is a familiar figure in Edinburgh society. Yes, I understand that you yearn to confront him, but matters will proceed more smoothly if his suspicions aren't aroused. In other words, you can't just march up to the door of his lodging house and demand he give back your belongings. If Ross *did* steal the things, you will have put him on his guard."

Emily tucked a rebellious orange ringlet back into her braid. "I'm sure that he stole it. Well, almost."

And therein lay a tale, thought Val. He wondered if he would enjoy discovering what it was.

"If one wishes to trap a thief, then one must go where the thief will be. Specifically—" One hand steadying the cat perched on his shoulder, he rifled through a stack of invitations. "Lady Cullane's musicale."

Emily sank into a chair. "You can't mean what I think you mean. I don't have time to attend any wretched musicale."

Val set aside the invitation. "One must make sacrifices, Miss Dinwiddie. In matters of this nature, a degree of discretion is required. Lady Cullane knows all there is to know about everyone in Edinburgh, and so Lady Cullane it shall be."

Emily drew in a breath and released it slowly. "You are the *most* annoying man."

Val didn't even try to resist temptation. "You no longer believe me a grotesquerie, then?"

"You are an exasperation! What am I to tell Michael when I see him, pray? He thinks I am still in London, mourning my papa. What possible reason could I have for being here?"

Val had asked himself that same question. "You have come to Edinburgh so that your family may provide you solace in your time of need."

Emily surveyed him over the rim of her spectacles. "I don't have family in Edinburgh."

Val stroked Machka. "You do now."

Chapter Five

Plant the crab-tree wherever you may, it will never bear pippins.

Cleaned up, young Jamie was revealed to be a gap-toothed freckled lad—'ferni-tickles,' he called them, observing that Miss Dinwiddie had her own goodly share—some ten years of age, with a sandy-colored 'coo lick' springing up from the crown of his head. Jamie confessed to having never had such good food, or clean clothes, or so warm a place to sleep as the wall bed near the kitchen hearth. He assured Emily he had no notion of running away; Isidore had warned him that if he was to scarper, that great wolf would track him down and gobble him alive. If Isidore was crabbit (grumpy), Mrs. MacCamish was couthie (kind); and Zizi, Bela, and Lilian were— Och. Words failed him. At least, words he could use in front of a young lady like herself. Jamie had been given strict instructions on how he was to behave.

Isidore hobbled into the kitchen, his expression suggesting a desire to give similar instructions to Emily, if not grill her over the fire on the brandiron. "The master has been waiting for you. As well as Madame Fanchon and Lady Alberta Tait."

"If he's waiting for them also," Emily shot back, "a few more moments will hardly count."

Isidore's nose twitched. "No, miss, *they're* all waiting. For you. In the drawing room."

Emily wrinkled her own nose. Ravensclaw had only to voice a wish to have it granted. It was most annoying in him.

Why must she bother with these women? There were missing things of power to be found.

If Ravensclaw didn't stop shilly-shallying, she would be about the business herself.

She *should* be about the business. It was due to her ineptitude that the thefts had taken place.

Tail straight up in the air like some sort of furry directional device, Machka led the way across the flagstone floor and up the stair. Emily managed, barely, to avoid tripping over the vexatious feline.

She hesitated in the doorway of the drawing room. Ravensclaw and two females were seated around a mahogany table on which had been set out a fine selection of delicacies, coffee, and tea. In front of the older woman rested a plate bearing the remnants of a smoked salmon omelet served with watercress cream. The younger had limited herself to a cup of tea. Ravensclaw appeared to have enjoyed a bowl of thick and wholesome porridge, which Emily considered queer in him indeed.

The younger woman was eyeing Drogo with trepidation. "Forgive me for asking, Count Revay-Czobar, but is that a *wolf?*"

"You have made a common error, Madame Fanchon," Ravensclaw replied. "Drogo is a rare Carpathian *copoi*, or sleuthhound."

"'Cabbage twice cooked is death'," muttered Isidore, as he gave Emily a none-too-gentle shove.

Three pair of eyes turned toward the doorway as Emily tripped over the threshold. Drogo swiveled an ear in her direction, then huffed out what she suspected was the lupine equivalent of a laugh.

The Count presented Emily to his guests. Lady Alberta Tait was a woman of a certain age, all wrinkles and powder and rouged sharp angles, her short curls blacker than nature had ever devised. Madame Fanchon was fair-haired and plump, impeccably dressed and coiffed. "We are in grave need of your assistance, Madame Fanchon," he continued. "Miss Dinwiddie requires dressing. There are a number of social events she is under obligation to attend."

Madame surveyed Emily and agreed that Mademoiselle was indeed in grave need of assistance. Emily, who had no interest whatsoever in such matters, felt like kicking them both.

Under obligation, was she? Emily supposed she was. But how *dare* Ravensclaw presume to dress her?

Undressing her was another matter. Emily curled her fingers into her palms.

Lady Alberta swallowed a last mouthful of omelet. "Her coloring! That hair. There is so much of it. She reminds me of a hedgehog. No offense, my dear. But it is such a vulgar shade."

"*Desordonnée*," agreed Madame Fanchon. "In a word: *vulgaire*."

And you're no more French than I'm a water kelpie! Emily was tempted to take herself and her vulgar curls right out of the room. Ravensclaw's voice stopped her. "Leave the hair alone. I like it," he said.

"Very well," Lady Alberta conceded. "Perhaps the spectacles... Remove them, my dear, and let us have a look at you."

What next? Would they inspect her teeth as if she was a horse put up for purchase? "I can't see without my spectacles."

Lady Alberta waved her fork. "You don't need to see, merely to be seen. Is there a dowry, Val?"

Val, was it? The informal nickname suited Ravensclaw. Since Emily could hardly hover in the doorway indefinitely, she settled into an upholstered chair. Machka jumped up and rearranged Emily's skirts to her satisfaction. Lady Alberta reached for a treacle scone.

Ravensclaw nudged the serving plate closer. "Miss Dinwiddie's financial situation is irrelevant. We're not trying to find her a husband, merely make her presentable."

Emily stiffened at the suggestion she wasn't 'presentable.' "Not that I don't consider Miss Dinwiddie to already be perfection," he quickly added. "However, it's not my interest she wishes to attract."

Emily swallowed a snort. Perfection. How absurd. As for attracting Ravensclaw's interest— Pigs would sooner fly. Today the Count's broad shoulders and muscular thighs were showcased by a well-cut blue coat and doeskin breeches. Scant wonder Madame Fanchon was staring slack-mouthed.

He turned his head. A lock of auburn hair tumbled forward on his cheek. The modiste almost dropped her teacup. Emily couldn't blame her. Shallow though it might be to judge on physical appearance alone, sometimes one couldn't help oneself.

Lady Alberta put down her fork. "I *do* enjoy a challenge! Forgive me for saying so, Miss Dinwiddie, but young ladies should not smell of garlic. Lavender is acceptable. Rosewater. Patchouli."

Lady Alberta should count herself grateful that Emily only smelled of garlic. The Japanese believed a raw fish would keep a decedent from the room.

"You look weary, Miss Dinwiddie," Ravensclaw remarked. "Did you not rest well last night?"

I hunger. Let me taste you. Again, Emily felt teeth, or rather fangs, nipping at her throat.

She bared her own teeth at him. "On the contrary, Count Revay-Czobar. I slept like the dead."

"Not pink, with her coloring." Madame Fanchon's tones suggested she was less enamored of a challenge than Lady Alberta. "Mademoiselle is too old for missish hues. She will excuse my plain speaking, for it is the truth."

Lest she indulge in some plain-speaking of her own, Emily pressed her lips together. Val said, "Green would suit her. Or azure. However, since she is newly out of mourning, we must restrain ourselves."

Emily pushed away a vision of the various ways in which Ravensclaw might restrain her. "Perhaps you should drape me in brown to match my freckles! This is absurd."

"Your freckles are hardly brown," he informed her. "Amber, perhaps. Sun-kissed gold."

Emily felt her cheeks redden. She didn't recall ever blushing before she met Ravensclaw, but now she couldn't seem to stop. Machka raised a lazy paw to bat at her assorted charms.

"What an ugly necklace!" tutted Lady Alberta. "It will have to go."

Emily extricated Machka's claws from the brass finger ring. "No."

Lady Alberta raised her eyebrows.

"The necklace is of great sentimental value," Ravensclaw explained. "It would be cruel to try and part Miss Dinwiddie from it. As well as pointless, I suspect."

Dubiously, Lady Alberta eyed the assorted talismans. "I suppose we might set a new style."

Emily had no desire to set a new style. All she wanted was to retrieve the items stolen from the Society's vaults. She sneaked another glance at her host. Well, maybe that wasn't all she wanted. Fatwit that she was.

"To set off Miss Dinwiddie's, er, striking looks," Madame Fanchon persisted, "Perhaps a *robe en caleçons*?"

The Count made several additional suggestions. Emily sat back and let the conversation swirl around her. Did Ravensclaw expect her to chair a meeting of the Dinwiddie Society wearing satin slippers and lavender gloves?

She wouldn't be chairing any meetings if she didn't find the d'Auvergne athame.

Ravensclaw certainly knew his way around a woman's wardrobe. Emily wondered how many females he had dressed, or undressed, during his long non-life. The conversation moved on to a discussion of stays: jean or buckram, long or short, whether the bosom should be pushed up or compressed to achieve an agreeable and graceful shape. The women's comments were not complimentary. Emily could happily have sunk right through the floor.

At last, to her relief, Madame Fanchon departed for her shop. Emily pushed Machka off her lap and rose. "You and Lady Alberta will wish to speak privately. I have some matters of my own—"

Ravensclaw caught her wrist in his strong fingers. "It would be unwise for you to venture out alone into the streets of Edinburgh."

Dangerous, he meant. But nothing could be more dangerous to Emily than Ravensclaw himself. No sensation of cool forests overcame her now, but tingles that began at the nape of her neck and tickled their way down to the tips of her toes. As if he'd brushed his fingertips against her bare skin. Or his wicked mouth. Those lips that could tease and tempt and tantalize could with her blessing nibble their way from her earlobes to her throat and from there downward to—

Botheration! There had been no warning in the literature that being in the presence of a gone-but-not-departed made one start behaving like a bubble-brain. While she stood here swooning over Ravensclaw, Michael could be engaging in heaven knew what manner of mischief with the athame.

"Most unwise," tsk'd Lady Alberta, who had been talking all this time. "You could easily get lost in these narrow alleys and wynds. Or worse! Most of the Edinburgh of early times still exists beneath the streets of the Old Town. Cold, dank dirt and stone-lined corridors. Underground chambers with rats and sewage seeping in from above. Not to mention the criminal fraternity. And then there are the ghosts. There must be hundreds of ghosts in the Royal Mile alone." She tilted her head to one side and studied Emily. "I am not acquainted with any Dinwiddies. Have you connections, my dear?"

Emily could only be grateful Lady Alberta hadn't heard of the Professor. "That depends on what you consider connections," Val interjected. "I am an old friend of Miss Dinwiddie's family."

Very old, thought Emily. There was mention of a Count Revay-Czobar in the Dinwiddie Chronicles as far back as the thirteenth century.

"Even so," said Lady Alberta. "The good ladies of Edinburgh would go off in a collective apoplexy were they to discover that you had a young unmarried woman of good family dwelling under your roof. I will be happy to provide whatever assistance you require."

"Excuse me!" interrupted Emily. "Is this necessary? I find it difficult to credit that you are not immune to the evils of gossip, my lord."

" 'What you don't view with your eyes don't witness with your mouth'," he told her. "As Isidore would say."

Emily bit her lip. She'd been so anxious to reach Edinburgh that she hadn't stopped to think what would happen after she arrived. "I never meant—"

"To put yourself under my protection? But that's exactly what you've done. Consequently, you must trust me to act in your best interests, in this instance recruiting Lady Alberta to your cause. I will leave the two of you to become better acquainted."

Nor had Emily any desire to become better acquainted with Lady Alberta. She didn't want Ravensclaw to leave off tracing lazy circles with his thumb on the inside of her wrist.

He smiled. She blinked. Lord, she *was* a fatwit. Emily turned her back on him and remained in that position until he left the room.

Drogo went with him, and Machka. The door closed behind them. Lady Alberta said, "I believe Val said you make your home in

London, Miss Dinwiddie. Is it true that poor Prinny has got so fat he's afraid to mount a horse?"

In point of fact, the headquarters of the Society was located some distance outside the City, but Emily saw no reason to acquaint Lady Alberta with that fact. She busied herself brushing cat hair off her skirt. "So I have heard."

"You have had a Season, waltzed at Almack's, been presented to the Queen? Forgive my impertinence, but one needs to know what one is working with."

"Yes to all your questions. I am also familiar with the British Museum and the Horticultural Society. I assure you, Lady Alberta, that I know how I am expected to behave." Knowing and doing were two different things, alas. Emily believed in her heart of hearts that her disastrous London debut had hastened her poor mama's death.

Lady Alberta propped her elbows on the table and with one finger trapped an errant biscuit morsel. "Frankly, Miss Dinwiddie, I don't care."

Emily blinked at her. "You don't?"

"I would prefer that you refrain from embarrassing me, but beyond that..." Lady Alberta popped the crumb into her mouth. "Ravensclaw will pay me handsomely to lend my aid to your endeavors, whatever they may be. To say the truth, my dear, I will be delighted to dwell under a roof that doesn't leak."

Emily quickly dismissed the suspicion that Lady Alberta was one of the supersensible. Nor was the older woman likely to possess so excellent a constitution that she could eat everything in sight and remain painfully slim. Her simple gown was so many years out of fashion that even Emily had noticed, and Emily was hardly *au courant* with such things. Ravensclaw was doing a kindness in offering employment to a gentlewoman fallen on hard times.

Ravensclaw was full of surprises. "If you don't mind me asking, how well do you know Count Revay-Czobar?"

"How well does anyone know Ravensclaw? We females all run mad for him. But you know how that is." Before Emily could ask further questions, Lady Alberta sat up straighter in her chair. "Am I to understand that this is your first visit to our fair city? Edinburgh is most progressive, for all we're considerably smaller than London.

We have the University, the acknowledged world leader in medical instruction, and the *Edinburgh Review;* John Dalton and his atomic chemistry, George Stephenson's steam locomotive that pulls a passenger car on wheels. Edinburgh leads the world in medicine and law, architecture and philosophy. Not for nothing are we called the Athens of the North."

Edinburgh also led the world in incidents of bodysnatching, reflected Emily, but didn't deem it prudent to state that fact.

"I like to read aloud of an evening," Lady Alberta continued. "Are you familiar with Mary Shelley's *Frankenstein?* A man destroyed by the monster he created. There are many lessons to be found in literature, don't you think?"

Dissertation on the Physical Traits of Bloodsucking Cadavers. Historical and Philosophical Dissertation on the Gnawing Dead. "Many lessons indeed, Lady Alberta. Are you familiar with Mr. Polidori's *The Vampyre?*"

Chapter Six

Fair is not fair, but that which pleases.

Edinburgh's Old Town was a bewildering wilderness of narrow streets and lofty irregular tenement houses known as 'lands,' some as many as eight stories high, built higgledy-piggledy like a child's city of playing cards, the rooftops an ocean of chimneys arranged at dizzying heights under an external pall of fog and smoke, many twisted and angled instead of standing straight up and down. Between the lands, which formed a continuous wall from one end of a street to the other, passages ran down the sides of the ridge on which the city was built and gave access to the properties behind, frequently small open areas with tall buildings peering down.

Night had settled on the Old Town. With it had come a thick mist that obscured vision, distorted sound. Fog wreathed the streetlamps, the picturesque shops, their exteriors painted with pictures of the merchants' wares. Each story from top to bottom was chequered with different forms and bright glaring colors—red, yellow and black on blue—until the whole resembled the stalls of a fair.

Those few honest wayfarers abroad at this late hour peered nervously over their shoulders and hastened their steps. Had that shuffling noise been caused by a stray dog rummaging through garbage, or a footpad creeping along behind a person, or worse? Impossible to anticipate what manner of apparition might burst forth from the murk.

A slender man walked along the High Street. None would dare accost him, not ghost, monster or footpad. Not so long as he was in possession of the d'Auvergne athame.

Marie d'Auvergne's athame.

He felt it, resting in its special sheathe, hidden underneath his shirt.

Light glimmered from the windows of a tall stone-faced building. A knock, a nod, and he was granted entrance. No door in Edinburgh was closed to him, not opera house or oyster bar, New Town mansion or Old Town gaming hell.

A suite of rooms on the first floor had been given over to various games of chance. Against one wall of the front room stood a buffet bearing food, liquor, and wine. In the middle of that same chamber was the *rouge et noir* table, on each side a croupier with a green shade over his eyes and a rake in his hand.

His entrance did not go unnoticed. A buxom brown-haired woman quickly made her way to his side. She murmured a welcome. He replied in kind.

He noted her drawn features, the shadows around her amber eyes. No more than eighteen, she was already weary of nights spent working these stifling rooms in a gown cut so low it showed a goodly portion of her plump breasts.

He felt no sympathy for her. This was the life she'd chosen, having abandoned a husband and babe to take up with a Captain Sharp, and so it was the life she was stuck with, and there was no use in crying over spilt milk.

"I'm for deep basset tonight," he said.

"*A bon chat, bon rat,*" she murmured, and beckoned a passing waiter, and took a glass of wine from his tray.

The slender man did not. He no longer had a taste for spirits of any kind.

"'To a good cat, a good rat'," she'd said. An appropriate remark, in view of the character of this establishment. Pigeons ripe for the plucking. Flats waiting to be fleeced. Elbow shakers playing with loaded dice.

None of the gamblers paid him any heed as he passed through the crowd.

Basset was a sort of lottery, said to have been invented by a noble Venetian, whose creativity led to his exile. The banker, or *talliere*, had the sole disposal of the first and last cards. He also had a much greater prospect of winning than those who merely played.

Nonetheless, the game was of so beguiling a nature, because of the several multiplications and advantages it seemed to offer an unwary player, that it was vastly popular despite the fact that the odds were hugely in favor of the bank.

The punters sat around a table, the *talliere* in their midst with the bank of gold before him. Each player held a book of thirteen cards and lay down the number that he pleased, with stakes. The *talliere* picked up the deck and turned up the bottom card or *fasse*, and paid half the value of the stakes wagered on any card of that sort.

The slender man took his seat, lay down his cards, placed his stakes. "King wins, ten loses." "Ace wins, five loses." "Knave wins, seven loses." He paid little attention to the game.

Across the table from him sat a fair-haired young gentleman. It took no preternatural abilities to read the panic in his pale eyes. The high points of his crisp shirt collar had wilted like lettuce during the excitement of the play.

The young gentleman was not destined to win tonight. The *talliere* had decided, and the *talliere* had the power to let a player have as many winnings as he found convenient, and no more.

It was one of the slender man's small vanities to influence such matters. He considered it in the nature of the cat giving the rat a sporting chance. As a result, when several shocking strokes of fortune brought the young gentleman's stake to *sois-sante-et-le-va*, thereby breaking the bank, the dealer was even more shocked than the young gentleman himself.

The slender man rose from the table a couple hundred pounds richer, it being impossible for him to sit down to play and lose.

The brown-haired woman was standing where he'd left her, empty wineglass in her hand. The gambling hell would be hard pressed to cover the losses suffered this eve. Later, when the hell had closed, her Captain Sharp would add new bruises to those already hidden by her gown.

It mattered not. The d'Auiergne athame was cool against his flesh. The slender man stepped out into the night.

Chapter Seven

Talk of the devil and he is bound to appear.

Emily studied herself in the looking-glass. Silvery grey merino crepe over black sarsenet, trimmed with lace and artificial roses around the hem— Ravensclaw must have paid Madame Fanchon a fortune to have the gown sewn up so quickly. It was the most beautiful garment Emily had ever owned.

She hated it. Almost as much as she hated what Zizi was doing with that hair brush. "You're hurting me!" Emily snapped.

Zizi tugged one last time on the brush, then stepped back to regard her handiwork. "Fine as fivepence, if I do say so myself."

Emily conceded that she had never appeared to better advantage. She didn't look the least bit like herself. Zizi's clever fingers had arranged her rebellious hair in an antique Roman style, the long braid wound up back and around, a few curls allowed to casually fall free. Emily was afraid to move her head for fear the whole thing would come tumbling down.

Zizi had not achieved this transformation without assistance. Crowded into Emily's bedroom were Lady Alberta and Ravensclaw's two other maidservants, Bela and Lilian, both of whom bore a marked resemblance to Zizi as regarded bosomly bounty. One was dark, the other fair.

Bela applied lavender water with a liberal hand while Lilian pinched some color into Emily's pale cheeks. "Edinburgh society is similar to that of London, albeit more limited," Lady Alberta informed her. "Theaters and assemblies and musical evenings, gentlemen's clubs that rival Watier's or White's." The older woman had also been gifted with a new evening gown, yellow with a draped tunic, which she wore with a turban headdress.

Finally, everyone left off their ministrations. Lady Alberta arranged a crepe scarf around Emily's shoulders and handed her a pair of black kid gloves. Emily snatched up her reticule, which contained her various protective charms, a small comb and mirror, and a pretty vinaigrette fashioned from bloodstone, its aromatic contents designed to 'correct the bad Quality of the Air.' One never knew what manner of creatures one might encounter when one ventured out into the world.

Ravensclaw was waiting at the foot of the staircase. He wore full evening dress: tight-fitting pantaloons and dark blue coat; white linen shirt and waistcoat; starched cravat with discreet sapphire stickpin in its folds; highly polished shoes. His long auburn hair was tied at the nape of his neck with a velvet cord. He looked mouth-wateringly handsome. *Glamour,* Emily reminded herself. *Vampire. Undead.*

They descended the outside staircase. A carriage waited in the street. With Ravensclaw's assistance, Lady Alberta climbed inside.

He turned back to Emily. " 'Fair as is the rose in May.' You are lovely, little one." His breath was warm on her cheek.

Breath? Did the insensate breathe? "I am 'presentable', then?"

Val touched the crucifix that she had refused to tuck away out of sight. "Did that rankle? I apologize. You are more than presentable." She shivered, and he frowned. "Are you nervous? Don't be. You are safe with me."

Emily barely refrained from snorting. She was safe with Ravensclaw like a hen was safe in company with a fox. "You don't seem to understand how urgent it is that we find Michael and retrieve the athame."

"I understand that nothing is served by cramming our fences. We'll find out if Mr. Ross has it in his possession soon enough." Ravensclaw's fingers lingered lightly on Emily's throat.

Pleasure prickled up her spine. "Um. Ah. How will we do that?"

"He will tell us. Have you not read of the persuasive abilities of my kind?"

Emily stared at him. "Then you admit—"

He laughed. "You are so serious, elfling. I could not help teasing you."

Val was smiling as he helped her into the carriage. Emily was not. She settled beside Lady Alberta, who immediately began talking. Ravensclaw took the opposite seat Emily stared out the window as the carriage jolted and swayed.

Mist wreathed the streetlamps. Easy enough to believe this place was haunted, especially when Lady Alberta was chattering about Johnny One-Arm and Cat Nick; the Mercat Cross, site of countless public tortures and hangings; Lady Glamis, burned alive on the Castle Hill. Ravensclaw remained silent. Emily wondered how much of Lady Alberta's ghoulish history he had witnessed firsthand.

The narrow, twisting streets of the Old Town by way of the North Bridge to the wider, and hopefully less haunted, neoclassical avenues of the New. Charlotte Square, Lady Alberta explained, had been designed by Robert Adams as a single unified scheme, the entire block fashioned as an urban palace with a grand central edifice and less imposing wings.

The carriage drew up in front of a residence with wide pilasters and balustered Venetian windows. Count Revay-Czobar's small party joined the people alighting from their carriages to ascend the outer steps where footmen waited, resplendent in white stockings and powdered wigs. Through the arched doorway, then, and into the lobby, a green-painted chamber with a glazed tile floor; past the tall hall clock to join the guests sweltering on the staircase that led to the second floor drawing room. It seemed everyone who was anyone in Edinburgh had come to Lady Cullane's townhouse tonight to hear 'A Highland Battle' played on the violin, and 'The Pic-Nic' on fiddle; 'Black Jock,' and 'The Sow's Tail.'

Emily's head began to ache in anticipation of another musical evening just like every other musical evening—save for the Scottish music— she had been forced to attend. The drawing room was furnished with the same classically inspired furniture and crystal chandeliers, exquisite paintings and marble fireplace; populated with the same pale-gowned young ladies whispering behind gloved hands and fans and simpering each time a gentleman younger than their papa came within spitting distance, the same gimlet-eyed matchmaking mamas busy sizing up their daughters' competition and calculating their matrimonial prospects. Only the windows were different, set deep in curtain boxes with drawn-up festoon drapes. That, and several of the gentlemen wore skirts.

Kilts, Emily corrected herself, and tried not to stare. Masculine knees certainly came in a great variety. Was that a dagger hilt she saw tucked into that gentleman's hose?

"It's a sgian dubh, or black knife," Val said, following her gaze. "A ceremonial weapon. That pouch worn around the waist is called a sporran. You're frowning, Miss Dinwiddie. Remember why we're here." Emily relaxed her forehead before Lady Alberta could remind her that proper young women didn't scowl.

They made their way deeper into the crowded chamber. The two women might as well have been invisible, because Ravensclaw drew every eye.

Glamour, thought Emily again. She watched closely, hoping to see how the thing was done.

Her papa hadn't believed in shielding children from knowledge of the supersensible. Emily clearly remembered her mama having hysterics at finding her playing with a shrunken head.

Admittedly, Ravensclaw's allure may have had a little bit to do with muscular thighs and broad shoulders, high cheekbones and ivory skin.

Emily endured another round of introductions. Between the two of them, Ravensclaw and Lady Alberta must have known everyone present in this place tonight. In the background, a young woman's harp rendition of "The Hen's March o'er the Midden" sounded less like a march than a limp. And then the crowd parted, rather like Moses and the Red Sea, and Emily found herself face-to-face with the most beautiful female she had ever seen. The woman's features were perfection, her skin the palest porcelain, her hair so dark it drank up all the candlelight. She wore a gown of crimson-colored gauze, the bodice cut low with corded edging, the sleeves shot with Spanish slashing, the scalloped skirt trimmed in twisted ribbon rolls. Her lush lips were painted crimson, her thick-lashed eyes were raven black. Escorting her was a tall, somberly-clad man as handsome as she was beautiful. His eyes were the color of violets, his hair a startling silver-grey. Had he worn lace at his throat and wrists, and jewels on his hands, he would have been the perfect image of a dissolute aristocrat of the *ancien regime*. Following behind them was a second man with chestnut hair and ice-green eyes and a harsh chiseled face marred by the scar that slashed one lean cheek.

The woman's gaze flicked over Emily. "Ah, Val, you are so surprised to see Lisbet that you forget to introduce your little friend."

The muscles of Val's arm tightened under Emily's fingers. "Lisbet, may I present Miss Emily Dinwiddie. Emily, meet Elisabeta Boroi. The gentleman accompanying her is Cezar Korzha." He nodded to the third man, who remained in the background. "Andrei Torok."

"*Mea amant,*" murmured Lisbet Boroi. "So civilized."

"We are paragons of propriety," agreed Lady Alberta. "You have been traveling, I believe, in some exotic clime. India, was it? Or the Orient?"

"I have concerns in Budapest," the silver-haired man said. "Val hasn't mentioned you, Miss Dinwiddie. I wonder, why is that?"

Emily didn't think for a moment that this was an idle question. Cezar Korzha was displeased by her presence. She wondered why that was. "Perhaps you should ask him that. Count Revay-Czobar is an old friend of my family."

"I myself have known Emily since she was a babe," said Lady Alberta. "Such a precious child she was."

"I'm sure," murmured Lisbet Boroi. "All those freckles. All that hair."

"In some cultures," Emily informed her, "freckles are greatly esteemed. The more freckles, the more beautiful a woman is said to be."

"And in other cultures, freckles are said to be an indication of a contentious nature," Val remarked.

Cezar Korzha smiled. His smile was not seductive like Ravensclaw's, Emily decided, but instead a little cruel, which was perhaps fortunate, since Ravensclaw's smile turned a person into a giddy goose. The violet eyes pulled at her. Deliberately, Emily looked away.

"It was a pleasure to make your acquaintance, Miss Dinwiddie," Cezar Korzha said. "And now, if you will excuse us—" Andrei Torok's watchful eyes scanned the room.

A frown marred the perfection of Lisbet Boroi's brow. "We will see you later, Val? Never fear, Miss Dinwiddie. I will return your 'old friend' to you safe and sound."

Emily watched them disappear into the crowd. She shouldn't be surprised to learn Val had a *petite amie*. Probably he had several of them. Mistresses who knew what he was like when he *wasn't* being civilized. Auburn hair tumbling down around his shoulders. Candlelight gleaming on his perfect pale skin.

All his perfect pale skin. Every glorious inch.

Maybe she should bind Ravensclaw in chains and toss *him* into the River Forth. She'd soon be a candidate for Bedlam at this rate.

She couldn't possibly be jealous, Emily assured herself. This queer feeling in her stomach was due to the miracle of engineering that made it appear she had a bosom, which was crushing her ribs. As soon as this matter of the d'Auvergne athame was satisfactorily resolved, Emily would return to the business of the Society, and Val would return to the business of being a supersensual—did ever a label fit so well?—and their paths would never again cross.

Drat.

Ravensclaw tucked his fingers under her chin and turned her face up to his. *Lisbet Boroi is of no consequence. You will not be disturbed by anything she may do or say.*

She would not— He dared to— Anger stained Emily's cheeks. *I will be disturbed by whoever I wish whenever I please! You will not tell me what to do.*

Val's fingers tightened. *Do that again. If you can.*

Lady Alberta pinched his arm. "Ravensclaw! Remember where you are."

Emily stared up into his startled face. "I don't know if I can or not."

An approaching figure caught her eye, and she drew back from him. "Michael Ross has just arrived.

Chapter Eight

A cat in gloves catches no mice.

Oh, perdition! Ravensclaw could hear her thoughts. Hopefully, not all of them, or he would know of the strong attraction that Emily felt for him. And of her equally strong desire to see Lisbet Boroi trip and fall on her oh-so-perfect face.

No time to wonder about that now. Emily turned away from her companions to watch Michael Ross tread his way through the crowd. The young man was no less handsome than she remembered, pale and poetically brooding in the fashion made popular by the unfortunate Lord Byron, a lock of dark hair draped artfully upon his forehead, a worldweary expression in his charcoal grey eyes. He was cropped and curled and clad in trousers that fitted without a wrinkle, a fashionable tailcoat with French riding sleeves and cuffs, and shoe buckles of polished cut steel.

His demeanor was not that of a gentleman unexpectedly glimpsing the object of his affections. Not that Emily supposed herself to be the object of his affections. Not any more.

The music changed to a lively tune played on hammered dulcimer with bombarde accompaniment. Ravensclaw and Lady Alberta withdrew to the refreshment table as Michael approached.

Be discreet, Emily told herself. *Remember what's important: the d'Auvergne athame.*

Thought of the athame in the wrong hands chilled her to her bones.

Although, truth be told, there were no *right* hands as regarded the d'Auvergne athame.

If only the thief had also taken the lead-lined chest.

The fact he had not argued an ignorance of the athame's power.

He, or she. Emily was trying to give Michael Ross the benefit of the doubt.

But Michael had been frequently at the house in the days following her father's death. Sticking his nose into everything. Preparing to take his place as head of the Society, as he had every reason to expect he would. Causing her to wish she might kick him in the arse.

He raised his voice to be heard above the music. "Hell mend it, Emily! What are you doing here? Has there been some new development?"

Really, the man needn't grimace like he'd bit into something sour. "Any number, since you ask. Portable gas cylinders have been introduced in London, at thirty atmospheres. The *Raith* from Leek was wrecked. Prinny has begun building the new Royal Apartments. Unless you were inquiring about something else?"

He frowned. "What the devil's wrong with you? I was referring to the circumstance that you are here instead of being closeted with your grief like any normal young woman should be."

Sitting on the shelf, he meant, like some trinket set aside until he decided it should be retrieved. Traditional rites of mourning lost much of their meaning when one was aware that the dearly departed didn't always remain snugly in their graves. "There is nothing 'wrong' with me, Michael. A year has passed since Papa's death."

He ran his hand through his hair, disarranging his carefully styled curls. "Has it been so long? I didn't mean to infer— Dash it, Emily, I didn't expect to find you in Edinburgh."

Obviously, he hadn't. The last time Emily had seen Michael he was promising he would return speedily to London, after which she'd heard not a word. "I daresay you didn't. Had we been in communication— I know! Your letters went astray."

A muscle clenched in his cheek. "I can explain."

And a pretty pack of lies *that* would be, she'd warrant. "You owe me no explanations. It's not as if we are betrothed."

Michael looked at her as if she were a loony. "I was called away on family business. Of course we are betrothed. The formal announcement was delayed due to your father's death." Belatedly, he smiled. "I am delighted that you have joined me here. You merely took me by surprise."

The wretched man was looking smug. He assumed she had pursued him to Edinburgh in hope of resuming their romance. Granted, he had reason. The Professor had been grooming Michael to be his replacement, and she had believed he knew best.

Well, he hadn't, had he, if she was correct in believing Michael was responsible for the thefts?

Michael hadn't even had the decency to wait until they were wed to start removing things from the vault.

Emily wondered what else her Papa might have been wrong about.

"I too am in Edinburgh on business." She smoothed her black kid gloves.

"Oh? And what business might that be?"

Had he always been so condescending and she too blind to see it? "Society business, of course. You do recall that the Society can only be overseen by a Dinwiddie?"

Michael crushed her gloved hands in his. "Blast it, Emily, don't go off on one of your queer starts now. Your father intended that we marry. I am to take the Dinwiddie name."

You may take your fine self to the nether regions. "Are you trying to break my fingers, sir?"

Michael did not relax his grip. "The Professor and I discussed the matter of our union at some length. Yours and mine, that is. I had meant to allow you sufficient time to recover from your loss, but since you've recuperated sufficiently to come to Edinburgh—" He squinted at her. "Something about you is different tonight."

If only she hadn't been persuaded to leave behind her umbrella. It would have been immensely satisfying to jab her suitor with its sharp tip. "So are you different, Michael." What had become of the courteous young man who courted her?

Again, Emily tried to free herself. Michael gripped her all the harder. "Tell me where you're staying. Clearly we must talk."

Here was a conundrum. *Don't put him on his guard.* "Since you make your home in Edinburgh, you may be acquainted with Lady Alberta Tait."

Michael glanced at that worthy, who was hovering near the punch bowl. "Everybody knows of Lady Alberta. What has she to do with you?"

Very little, truth be told. Emily thought quickly. "Lady Alberta is my aunt."

"Your *aunt?* The Professor never mentioned her." In his astonishment, Michael relaxed his grip.

Emily snatched her hands away from his. "Why should he have? They were estranged. Lady Alberta, um, doesn't approve of the supersensible." Before Michael could question her further, Emily pulled the vrajă from her reticule. "I believe this is yours."

He frowned at the talisman. "Where did you find that?"

"In the Society vaults. It has me in quite a puzzle, since Papa didn't permit anyone to enter the vaults other than myself."

Michael wrenched his eyes away from the talisman. "Following your father's death, there were countless people wandering through the house. I told you at the time that we should put more stringent security measures into effect. Perhaps the vrajă belonged to one of those people. Or even to the Professor. At any rate, it isn't mine."

"Oh? Where is *your* vrajă, then?"

Michael's hand moved to his waistcoat. "It didn't seem appropriate for an occasion such as this."

Since Emily had never seen Michael on an occasion such as this, she couldn't quibble with his statement. "You're certain that this vrajă isn't yours?"

Michael scowled. "Are you accusing me of something? I'll tell you what, Emily: grief must have unhinged your brain."

With difficulty, Emily kept rein on her temper. Silently she dropped the charm back into her reticule.

Michael's eyes moved from her reticule to her face. "I am anxious to speak with you at greater length. What is Lady Alberta's address?"

Be conciliatory, Emily told herself again. "At the moment, my aunt and I are guests of Lord Revay-Czobar."

Michael's mouth dropped open. "Ravensclaw? But why? Unless—" His gaze sharpened. "Is his name on the Dinwiddie list? What is he, werewolf, shapeshifter, the devil's spawn? You are not qualified for this work, Emily. You must leave his house at once."

What was it about her that made people try and tell her what to do? "Now who is unhinged, Michael? Ravensclaw is nothing of the sort. Ah, Lady Alberta is beckoning. You will excuse me." Michael pressed his lips together. Without further protest, he let her go.

At last the interminable evening ended, after a series of ballads sung in a sweet soprano voice, which— having progressed from *Loch Lomond* ("and me and my true love will never meet again") through *The Three Ravens* ("she was dead herself ere evensong time") to *Mary Hamilton* ("the land I was tae travel in, or the death I was tae dee")— left many of the revelers in a somewhat somber frame of mind.

Ravensclaw's carriage was waiting at the door. Lady Alberta climbed inside.

Val lifted Emily into the carriage as if she weighed no more than a feather. "I will speak with you tomorrow, little one."

"Tomorrow? But I must tell you what Michael said." Or *hadn't* said, but that was beside the point. Emily lowered her voice. "I think he may suspect what you are."

Val smiled. "If Mr. Ross's suspicions are on a par with yours, I'll not tremble in my boots just yet." He stepped back and closed the door.

Emily sank back on the carriage seat. Had Ravensclaw admitted what she thought he had? And if he *had* admitted it, then how dare he leave her here with a thousand unanswered questions buzzing about in her poor beleaguered brain?

"It may be unchristian of me to say so, but Lisbet Boroi is *not* a nice woman," remarked Lady Alberta. "And I have my doubts about Cezar Korzha as well. I don't mean to say that Korzha is a woman, because any fool can see he's not, which isn't always the case."

Counts who were Other, dogs that were werewolves—that sort of thing Emily could accept. But men who were women? Her companion must have imbibed more than was prudent of the champagne punch.

As, perhaps, had she.

She should be searching for the athame—but where to start? And so here she sat, twiddling her thumbs while Ravensclaw— Was where? Doing what? With whom?

Foolish questions. Ravensclaw was probably even then nuzzling and nibbling and sinking his teeth into Lisbet Boroi's throat. *Fangs!* Yes, and why had she been able to speak silently with him? *Did Michael have the d'Auvergne athame in his possession and, if so, what did he mean to do with it?* Emily leaned her head back against the carriage seat and closed her eyes.

Chapter Nine

Do not all you can; spend not all you have;
believe not all you hear; and tell not all you know.

Faint fingers of dawn crept across the somber sky. The early morning air was damp and chill and noxious, the sanitary arrangements in Edinburgh's Old Town being considerably inferior to the New, which made not a whit of difference to footpad or resurrectionist, randy young buck or supersensible creature or Lady Alberta's ghosts.

Ravensclaw wondered how Miss Dinwiddie felt about ghaisties. She would doubtless tell him in good time.

He climbed the exterior stair to his front door. His servants, accustomed to their master's nocturnal habits, were long abed. Val made his way up the inner stairway to his own chamber, where he found Drogo stretched out on the hearth, and Machka and Miss Dinwiddie stretched out on his bed. One of them was snoring. He doubted it was the cat.

Drogo rolled over on his back. Val paused to scratch the creature's belly before he walked closer to the bed. Machka opened one incurious eye and yawned.

Emily's spectacles lay abandoned atop a stack of correspondence. Society business, he gathered from what he could read upside down. A water kelpie had been sighted, in the form of a handsome man with seaweed in his hair instead of a bullish black beast with two horns.

Val wondered who had written the account. Water kelpies were prone to lure the unwary to watery graves.

Given the opportunity, Emily would more likely lure the kelpie to his.

She wore her necklace of charms, which was of no more practical use than the poppy seeds she scattered outside her bedroom door with the absurd notion that the undead had a compulsion to count everything in their path.

On the other hand, he wouldn't be at all surprised to discover she had hidden an axe in his pillows.

One bare foot peeped out from beneath the practical cotton wrapper that she wore over her voluminous night gown. A fragile little foot, with painful-looking blisters. Miss Dinwiddie's new slippers hadn't fit her any better than the role she'd played in Lady Cullane's elegant drawing room.

She turned her head on his pillow. Tendrils of hair had escaped from their braid to frizz around her face. Val slipped his hand under her foot, rubbed her sole with his thumb.

She lay on the woolen rug before the fireplace. He lowered his lips to her throat. Pleasure hummed through her veins. His teeth found her pulse, and nipped. A strange melting sensation, a growing warmth—

The young woman was preoccupied with throats. Val decided to advance her understanding a little bit.

His lips slid along her silken skin to the soft flesh of one breast. He teased her rosy nipple with his tongue until it pebbled, begging him for more. His mouth closed around her. She moaned.

Her scent surrounded him. Not garlic now, or lavender, but an erotic female perfume that made his nostrils flare. *Emily. Wake up.*

She opened her eyes, peered nearsightedly at him. *You said you weren't what I thought you were. You lied.*

Val traced the arch of her foot. *What did you expect? I am vampir.*

She considered this, and the hand that clasped her. *Are you lying now?*

No. Are you frightened, little one?

Maybe. Emily watched him trace a pattern on her ankle. *What are you doing to my foot?*

Caressing it. Do you mind?

Oh. She blinked at him. On the hearth, Drogo stirred. Machka opened one green eye and reached out a sharp-tipped paw.

Emily snatched back her foot and tucked it under her nightdress. "What are you doing here?"

Val shrugged off his jacket. "I sleep here, remember? Perhaps I should ask you the same thing. This is hardly so large a house that someone might get lost."

Emily fumbled for her spectacles and plopped them on her nose. "You said we would speak tomorrow. Well, now it *is* tomorrow, so don't try and put me off again. Have you found out anything about the athame?"

No, nor had he tried to, having had more urgent fires to douse. "Has anyone ever told you that you are as tenacious as a cockleburr?"

"Papa, when he was trying to keep things from me. Don't change the subject. I take it you did not."

Val did not feel inclined to explain himself. "You wanted to warn me about your Mr. Ross."

Emily looked away. "He's not my Mr. Ross."

Val shrugged out of his coat. "Nonetheless, you know him well."

"Not half as well as I once believed I did." Emily toyed with the edges of her sash. "Thanks to your insistence that I appear at Lady Cullen's dratted musicale, Michael thinks I followed him to Edinburgh."

"Why should he think you followed him? Unless you told him of your suspicions, and that you found his talisman. Did you return it to him, by the way?" Casually, Val removed his waistcoat and cravat.

Emily's cheeks reddened. "He claimed it wasn't his. Before my papa's death, Michael was, ah, courting me. He may think that we're betrothed."

Val pulled the velvet cord out of his hair. Scooted Machka out of the way and sat down on the bed. "Miss Dinwiddie, you are a *femme fatale.*"

Emily adjusted her spectacles. "Don't poke fun at me. I should have realized it was all moonshine. Michael wants to marry me and thereby gain control of the Society and my pocketbook. However, I have decided that I don't want to marry anyone. Papa managed matters so I wouldn't have to, despite the fact that the law doesn't find females fit to manage their own affairs. Do stop regarding me as if I were some raree show exhibit. You aren't taking this seriously enough."

If so, it was understandable: Val had during the countless years of his existence been hanged, shot, and staked, none of which had been particularly pleasant, but he had lived (so to speak) to tell the tale. "You are serious enough for us both. If Ross did steal the athame, he didn't have it with him last night."

Emily's expressive eyebrows climbed halfway up her forehead. "How do you know that?"

Val raised an eyebrow of his own.

She glared at him. "I fail to understand why your servants are so devoted to you. Unless you've swayed their minds."

"That would be unsporting of me."

"And you never take advantage?"

"We have strayed from the subject. Indulge my curiosity, Miss Dinwiddie. Most young women would settle for marriage at any price."

"Most young women are not as great an oddity as I am. Papa was almost pathetically grateful when Michael began to pay me court." Emily drew up her legs and wrapped her arms around her knees. "My parents had a marriage of convenience—her dowry and his convenience, that is. They rubbed on well enough together for the most part, except on such occasions as when his experiment with a reverse magnetosphere went awry, and we had rabbits in the drawing room, and Mama fainted into the teapot. I want more than that for myself."

"I see," said Val, and so he did. Miss Dinwiddie was an heiress. Every fortune hunter in Scotland would be hanging on her skirts. Or they would be if they knew about her situation, which wasn't likely, given the young lady's eccentricities. Thus, the field was left clear for Michael Ross.

Rather, the field *had* been left clear. Val had already arranged to introduce his ungrateful houseguest to what passed for Polite Society in Edinburgh, ostensibly to help her in her quest. She would hate every moment spent among her peers, and thereby amuse him even more. Maybe he would engage in an additional altruism, since she was clearly too impulsive to be left dashing about on her own, and make her financial status known. Val didn't imagine for a moment that Emily would thank him for it, which made the notion even more piquant.

Emily puffed up her cheeks and blew out an exasperated breath. "This is all far off the point! It is vitally important that we retrieve the athame. Why don't you just reach out and *find* the blasted thing?"

"Because I cannot."

"Oh. I assumed your extramundane senses— Isn't that unusual?"

"Yes. It may have been due to the bagpipes, or because I wasn't close enough, but I learned nothing from your Mr. Ross last night. Yes, I know he isn't yours, but I'm afraid you must act for a little while as though he is." It took no extramundane senses to hear the sound of grinding teeth. "If you will recall, it was our intention to flush out your fox."

"He's *not* my fox." She eyed him. "Why have you finally admitted what you are?"

It hadn't been solely for his entertainment, Val conceded to himself, although entertained he was. "I don't know that I did."

"I have never heard of a vampire with memory problems. Although, all things considered, I can see why it might be inconvenient to have encyclopedic recall." Val settled himself more comfortably. Emily cast a sideways glance at the strong thigh that pinned down her skirt. "I understand there is more than one traditional way to become a vampire. Were you set upon unawares and drained to the point of death?"

Val hoped Miss Dinwiddie's inquiring mind wouldn't be the death of her. Or him. "I'm sorry to disappoint you. It was nothing like that. I became what I am by choice."

Emily watched him stroke the cat. "Why would anyone become a vampire by choice? I do not mean to be insulting, but it is difficult to embrace the notion of drinking blood."

She had many more questions. He answered them as best he could. Val was not accustomed to being regarded as a scientific curiosity. He found himself equal parts annoyed and amused.

"Most females who find their way into my bed," he said, when his inquisitor paused for breath, "don't do so with interrogation in mind."

Emily sighed. "I'm being unforgivably *pushing,* aren't I? It's just that you are my first supersensible creature and there are so many things I'd like to ask. Are you afraid I can't keep a secret? I promise you I can. Is it true that the nonliving have remarkable regenerative powers? Hugely heightened senses? The ability to cloud people's minds?"

Val was going to have to cloud her mind. Eventually. He reached out and caught her hand.

She studied their intertwined fingers. *You're going to do that thing again. Where you read my mind.*

Eventually, but not yet. *I won't do this again unless you wish me to.*

Images flooded his mind. Images of the circumstances under which she might wish such a thing, which had to do with nibbles and kisses and nips.

And then he saw nothing, as if she'd slammed shut a door.

Val glanced at the window and the brightening sky outside. "I promise you will have your answers, and retrieve your stolen property. But now, you must return to your room, before the rest of the household begins to stir." She looked rebellious. *Go!* commanded Val.

She went. He lay back on his bed, imagining the so-curious Miss Dinwiddie's reaction were he to turn into a corpse before her eyes.

Chapter Ten

If an ass goes a-traveling, he'll not come home a horse.

Emily's foot still tingled where Ravenclaw had stroked it. Of course he would know how close he'd come to seducing her. Without even trying. For Ravensclaw to seduce females must be as natural as drawing breath.

Not that he drew breath.

She really must try to remember that.

All in all, she considered that she had exhibited remarkable self-possession for a young woman who had never before found herself sharing a bed with a half-clad gentleman.

Still, it might be prudent, in the future, to avoid champagne punch.

He hadn't seemed surprised to find her in his bed. No doubt Ravensclaw was accustomed to finding females in his bed. It was that ivory skin. Those sapphire eyes. Those oh-so-knowing lips. That glorious muscular chest with its furring of auburn hair. Emily reminded herself that the *strigoii* of Romania had two hearts. And that red-haired men who rose from the dead had the power to transform themselves into frogs. She tried but failed to convince herself that in his true form Ravensclaw was ugly as a toad.

Emily sighed, drawing the attention of the other occupants of the drawing room. Zizi, Bela, and Lilian paused in their attempts to instruct Jamie in the proper handling of a tea tray, it being customary for the first pot to be prepared in the kitchen and carried to the lady of the house. These being early efforts, Jamie carried a book—*A Greene Forest, or a Natural Historie,* divided into three sections, Animal, Vegetable and Mineral, an encyclopedic digest prepared by John Maplet in 1567—on the tray instead. Thus far he'd only spilled it thrice. Machka lent her efforts to the enterprise by winding around his feet. Sprawled in his usual spot on the hearth, Drogo surveyed the proceedings with an expression of lupine disbelief.

Lady Alberta put down the magazine from which she had been reading Mr. Polidori's account of Lord Ruthven, the fearless world-traveling aristocrat who lured innocent women to their deaths so he might feed on their blood. "Is something on your mind, my dear?"

Jamie did a nice turn with the tray. "Och, she's in a wee dwam."

"I'm no such thing," protested Emily. "Whatever it is."

Lady Alberta reached for an oatcake. "A dwam is a daydream."

Emily was in rather more than a daydream. She couldn't decide whether she should be pleased with her initiative at bearding the dragon in his lair, or appalled at herself. Bearding dragons was one thing, falling asleep in their beds something else.

She watched Jamie's contortions with the tea tray. Emily had brought the boy into a nightwalker's household, only to, preoccupied with her own problems, abandon him to his fate. Ravensclaw must surely dine on something more substantial than oatmeal and tea. "Jamie, has Count Revay-Czobar—" How best to phrase it? "Ah—"

Jamie stared blankly at her. As did Lady Alberta, Bela, Zizi, and Lilian. Emily cleared her throat. "Has he offered you advances that seem, um, unusual?"

Jamie hadn't survived ten years in the streets of Edinburgh by being slow on the uptake. "G'wa! Are ye thinkin' himself is a mop-molly?"

Emily wrinkled her brow. "A mop-molly? What is that?"

"A deviant, my dear," Lady Alberta said comfortably. "A gentleman who prefers relations with a member of the same sex. Or with an animal." She glanced at Drogo. The wolf growled. Lady Alberta picked up another oatcake. "But to each his own."

Jamie snorted. "Himsel's nae Jessie."

Perhaps instead of learning about matters supersensible, Emily should have devoted herself to the study of anatomy. *Umbivalent, actually.* Ravensclaw had said so himself.

Isidore carried a huge bouquet of roses into the room and plopped them on a table. "'One ass scrubs another.' And someone should have her mouth washed out with soap."

Someone regretted that she had ever opened her mouth. Emily said, "I didn't mean— Oh, never mind."

"She's in a fankle," explained Jamie. "Dinna fash yersel', Miss Emily. How wid ye ken such things, bein' unkenand lak ye are?"

"I'm no such thing!" Emily snapped, exasperated. All eyes turned on her. Zizi, Bela, and Lilian tittered. Lady Alberta paused with her oatcake halfway to her mouth. Emily demanded, "*What*?"

"Young Jamie said that you were unknowing," explained Lady Alberta. "You said that you were not. We were talking about gentlemen and their preferences. You understand our astonishment."

Bright-eyed Zizi added, "You admitted you weren't a virgin, miss."

"What's a virgin?" murmured Bela. Lilian giggled.

Emily ignored them, and Jamie's gap-toothed grin. "I *meant* I'm not in a fankle, whatever that is. At least I think I'm not. Where did the roses come from, Isidore?"

"You have a visitor." The old man squinted at the calling card he held between forefinger and thumb. "A Mr. Michael Ross. Shall I send him up?"

"You'll *bring* him up and announce him properly," Lady Alberta said sternly. "Pretend for a moment that this is a properly run household." She snatched the book off Jamie's tray. "We will need more tea."

Zizi hurried off to the kitchen. Bela and Lilian darted around the chamber, setting things to rights. The carpet was already in pristine condition, Drogo—exhibiting a fondness for oatcakes rivalling Lady Alberta's—having gobbled up all the crumbs.

"Jamie, wait." Emily followed the boy to the stair. "When Mr. Ross leaves, I want you to follow him. Don't let him see you. Then come back and tell me where he went."

Jamie shook his head. "I hae ma doots ye'll be unkenand long, miss, if ye keep on lak this."

Did the entire household know she'd fallen asleep in Ravensclaw's bed? "Mr. Ross may have something of mine in his possession. I mean to have it back."

Jamie brightened. "Shall I mak' the dive? Pick his pockets, miss?"

Emily was tempted. However, she had no great faith that Jamie was any more adept at picking pockets than filching candlesticks. "No. Just tell me where he goes."

She returned to the drawing room. Lady Alberta picked up her magazine and resumed where she'd left off. "'...the tale of the living vampire, who had passed years amidst his friends, and dearest ties, forced every year, by feeding upon the life of a lovely female to prolong his existence for the ensuing months...'"

Isidore reappeared in the doorway, announced: "Mr. Ross." Michael entered the room, a vision of sartorial splendor in a violet-colored coat, cream-colored breeches, and gleaming leather boots. In one hand he carried a tall beaver hat and leather gloves, items he tried to give to Isidore. Flapping his hands as if to fend off flies, the old man backed away.

Lady Alberta continued reading. "'...the dead grey eye, which, fixing upon the object's face, did not seem to penetrate, and at one glance to pierce through to the inward workings of the heart...'" Michael peered around the room, taking in every detail of his surroundings from the plaster ceiling to the perpetual almanac in its frame. Emily was not unhappy to see him so ill at ease.

Her wits *had* gone wandering. She had forgotten to warn Lady Alberta that they had suddenly become kin.

Hopefully, Lady Alberta's faculties were in better working order. Emily said, meaningfully, "Michael, I don't know if you have met my *aunt*, Lady Alberta Tait. Aunt, uh, Bertie, may I present Mr. Michael Ross."

"How do you do?" 'Aunt Bertie' shot Emily a speaking glance. "The roses are lovely, young man."

"A pleasure to make your acquaintance, Lady Alberta." On the hearth, Drogo stirred. "That's a wolf!"

"He's nothing of the sort. Drogo is a rare Carpathian sleuthhound." Emily gestured toward Machka, who was crouched to pounce, her attention fixed on the tassels attached to Michael's highly polished boots. "And that is a cat."

Michael hastily moved his foot away. Machka followed, a hunter stalking prey. "I dislike felines," he said. "Shoo. Go away."

Emily snatched up the cat and sank down in a chair. Machka hissed. "Stop that or I'll pull your tail. Pray be seated, Michael."

Lady Alberta gestured toward her magazine. "Are you familiar with Mr. Polidori's *The Vampyre,* Mr. Ross? '...his dead eyes sparkled with more fire than that of the cat whilst dallying with the half-dead mouse...'"

"I've no taste for popular fiction." Michael deposited his hat and gloves on a nearby table and arranged himself elegantly on an upholstered chair.

Zizi arrived with the tea tray. Lady Alberta put down her magazine. "Ah, black buns! I am especially fond of black buns." She picked up the plumpest, sweetest specimen and popped it in her mouth. Drogo edged closer to her chair.

Michael's vrajă—or one remarkably like it—dangled from his watch fob, Emily noted, and a sprig of hawthorn adorned his lapel. Hawthorn was useful in repelling the nonliving, according to the literature, which had thus far been proved wrong more often than right.

He was fidgeting about as if he expected Ravensclaw to pop out of the teapot and bite him in the neck. Emily murmured, "Compose yourself, Michael. The devil's spawn is out cavorting with his fellow fiends from hell. You've nothing to fear."

"You should not jest about such matters!" Michael drew in a deep breath. "Is there somewhere we may be private? I must speak with you."

Emily hadn't the least desire to be private with Michael. Unlike Ravensclaw. "You needn't mind Aunt Bertie, she's deaf as a post. What is it you want to talk about?"

Michael glanced dubiously at Lady Alberta, who had polished off her black bun and returned to her magazine. "I apologize for my behavior yestere'en. If I seemed a trifle high-handed, it is because I have your best interests at heart. Toward that end, I have made arrangements for your return home. I will join you there as soon as my business here is done."

And what about *her* business? Michael really did flatter himself that she would let him lead her around by the nose. "You may unmake your arrangements. I am perfectly comfortable where I am."

"What you are," hissed Michael, "is all about in the head. Someone must look after your concerns and Lady Alberta is clearly not up to the task. I see nothing for it but that you leave Society matters in my hands."

Emily saw a number of things. Michael's concern for her wellbeing was not among them. She watched Machka leap onto the table, settle down near his hat. "What you mean is that you consider me incapable of bearing responsibility for the Society."

Michael leaned closer. "You know bloody well you aren't. And then there is the matter of offspring."

"Offspring?"

"Children to carry on the Dinwiddie name. It was the Professor's dearest wish."

Emily tried, and failed, to imagine Michael touching her the way Ravensclaw had touched her in her dreams—and hadn't what he'd done to her bosom been interesting? Emily had not realized that bosoms could be the source of such intense sensations. She was curious to find out what else she didn't know.

But she didn't care to learn from Michael. And if Michael told her once more what her papa had wanted, she would box his ears. "Aunt Bertie! Did my papa ever tell you that his fondest wish was for me to bear offspring?"

Lady Alberta marked her place in her magazine with her fingertip. "Why no, I don't believe he did. Although perhaps he wouldn't have, because he knew that I was unable to bear offspring myself. Such a tragedy, I felt at the time. Although I have since changed my mind. Children are so unpredictable. You never know how they'll turn out. Why, I have a friend..."

"Why would he tell her anything?" muttered Michael. "You said they were estranged."

Emily decided she would box Lady Alberta's ears when she was done with Michael's. "They *were* estranged. Sometimes. And sometimes they weren't." Oh, to blazes with discretion. "Did the Professor ever show you a ceremonial knife with a cabochon ruby and a double ouroborus set into its hilt?"

He shook his head. "I'm certain he did not. Is it important?"

Important? Immensely. "The athame is missing. Did you steal it? Did you sell it? You have no idea how dangerous it is."

Michael looked astonished. "Are you accusing me of theft? How can you think such a thing?"

"You wouldn't like to know what I think of you in this particular moment," Emily informed him. "I must get the knife back."

"This is precisely why you need me! You shouldn't have lost the thing in the first place. Let us approach this in a logical manner. When is the last time you saw the athame?"

Emily did not choose to share any further information. "I cannot recall."

"So you don't know how long it's been missing. Or," Michael added shrewdly, "in fact, if it was ever in the vaults at all." He risked a glance at Lady Alberta, who appeared rapt in her reading. "Marry me, dammit, Emily. As soon as we're wed, I'll help you find your blasted knife."

Emily regarded him over the rim of her spectacles, which had again slid down her nose. "I don't believe I mentioned that the athame had been kept in the vaults."

He flushed. Lady Alberta read aloud: "'The dreadful shrieks of a woman mingled with the stifled, exultant mockery of a laugh...'"

Michael rose, brushing cat hair off his breeches. "You are determined to be difficult. We will speak of this another time." He snatched up his hat and gloves and stalked out of the room.

His voice drifted back from the stairwell. "My hat! That damned cat clawed my hat!"

Emily patted Machka. "Good kitty," she said.

In the silence came the distant slamming of a door.

Lady Alberta reached for another black bun. "I feel compelled to point out that one catches more flies with honey than vinegar. Yes, I know you don't care to catch Mr. Ross, but I think you want *him* to think you do. No, pray don't confide in me! I do not wish to know."

Chapter Eleven

Two sparrows on one ear of corn make an ill agreement.

Many legends surrounded Marie d'Auvergne's athame. Some said she had bargained with the Darkness, pledging her body and soul in exchange for twenty-four years' enjoyment of unlimited knowledge, power and wealth, but had never intended to repent before her time was up, believing that the Light would prove more potent than the Dark.

The time came for repayment. At midnight on the eve of the 395th day of the 24th year, a fearsome din was heard from Marie's rooms, and a woman's scream. When the servants dared investigate the next morn, they found no trace of Marie. The athame, which never left her possession, lay abandoned on the floor. Legend had it that the Darkness repaid Marie's treachery by imprisoning her in the knife itself, which is why the thing was sometimes called the Hand of the Undead.

It was pure foolishness, thought the slender man, as so many legends were, but there was no denying that the knife was a point of convergence for dark energy.

He savored its coolness against his flesh.

It was cold as the Thames in winter, and at the same time hot as sin.

Contained power that burned strong enough to melt flesh and bone.

His destination was before him. He closed one gloved hand around the knob of the shop door.

Madame Fanchon—*née* simple Franny Brown—was totting-up her monthly accounts. Astonishing, how one's expenditures could outpace one's income. She had closed the door to the workroom, so her employees couldn't catch her at her bookkeeping, and thereby be reminded that they also needed to be paid. When the shop door opened to admit an elegant visitor in a fashionable claret-colored coat, tightly fitting inexpressibles, gleaming Wellington boots, his cravat tied in the complicated Gordian knot, she shoved her post-obit bills into a drawer, pushed back her chair, and rose to greet her visitor with a smile.

That smile continued, broadened even, through an inspection of silks and muslins and cambrics, a perusal of hand-colored fashion-plates. So intense was her excitement that Franny almost forgot her accent, and had to fan herself.

The slender man leaned back in his chair. "I will give you the word with no bark on it," he said, interrupting the modiste's paean to jaconet and lutestring. "You may turn out my mistress in the first stare of fashion on one condition: tell me how it came about that you are dressing Emily Dinwiddie. Don't deny you *are* dressing her, I recognized your handiwork. And why you are costuming Lady Alberta Tait as well."

Franny's clients were not prone to appreciate their affairs being bandied about town. She murmured, *"Je m'excuse?"*

He raised one gloved hand in an impatient gesture. "Do not waste my time, madame. Answer my questions or not only will you not gain my patronage, you will lose your other customers as well."

Franny regretted, suddenly, that she had closed the workroom door. There was something about this client that unnerved her. A certain reptilian cast to his eye.

She was growing entirely too imaginative. One sometimes had to cut one's losses. "Ah, *that* Miss Dinwiddie. Now I recall. Ravensclaw summoned me to his house. The *demoiselle* required a refurbishment of her wardrobe. Ravensclaw said he meant to make her 'presentable.' Lady Alberta seemed to think Mademoiselle might set a new style."

Her visitor picked up a length of ribbon and ran it idly through his fingers. "And well she may. A style for freckle-faced little nobodies with portions of fifty thousand pounds."

Fifty thousand pounds? *Ma foi!* Franny wondered if Miss Dinwiddie might be interested in new fashion plates just arrived from Paris. A rose-colored shawl. Some lovely pearl embroidery.

"And your impression of Lady Alberta Tait?" the slender man persisted. "Had you any impression of a previous relationship between them?"

Franny goggled at him. "Between Lady Alberta and Ravensclaw? *C'est moui!*"

"No, you imbecile. Between Lady Alberta and Miss Dinwiddie."

Franny was not sufficiently an imbecile as to antagonize a potential customer, dislike him as she might. "I saw no indications of a previous acquaintance. Is one permitted to inquire why you ask?"

"One is not." He fixed his dead dark gaze on her. "Tell me everything that transpired, from the moment you arrived at Ravensclaw's house until you left."

Franny felt perspiration pop out on her brow. Not for the first time she wished she had been content to remain a simple seamstress instead of scheming to acquire her own shop, where people could walk in and abuse her at will. *"Comment?"*

"I'm waiting." The slender man rose from his chair.

Franny was tempted to tell this fine gentleman that he could wait until hell froze over. One look at that cold face caused her to change her mind. Franny recounted, as best she could, her dealings with Emily Dinwiddie, Lady Alberta, and Ravensclaw.

"Ah, so," he murmured. "It is as I had thought."

Franny thought she would happily forgo a commission, if only he would leave. Instead the slender man paused beside her chair.

She made as if to rise. He grasped her shoulder and held her in place. Franny stared at the flesh revealed between his gloves and the edge of his coat sleeve. Flesh that no longer looked entirely human. She tried to pull away.

Too late. She felt the ribbon slide around her throat. "Alas, Madame Fanchon," said the slender man, as she clawed futilely at his fingers, "I find that you shan't suit me, after all.".

Chapter Twelve

Who keeps company with the wolf will learn to howl.

Edinburgh's Royal Exchange, which boasted a fine piazza, was home to a custom-house and thirty-five shops, some with living-rooms above; ten other dwelling places; three coffee houses and now the Town Council, many of the merchants for whom the Exchange had been designed preferring to conduct their business elsewhere. The Exchange had been built on the steeply sloping site of several old closes and consequently stood four storeys high around the quadrangle which faced the High Street, while its north wall rose like a great grey cliff to the height of twelve.

Buried down around the Exchange cellars were remnants of streets that had been partially demolished during its construction, frozen in time since the seventeenth century. Derelict tenements and shops flanked the broken pavement. A tavern, a sawmaker's establishment. Warrens of interconnecting rooms where entire families had once lived. A stockroom, its ceiling still hung with gruesome hooks.

Deserted though the close might be, it was not forsaken. The secret meeting place of the Breaslă lay here, deep beneath the cobbled streets of the Royal Mile. One of the aftereffects of his condition being an ability to see cat-like in the dark, Val needed no lantern to light his way. He halted before a certain door, inserted a key.

Candles burned in ancient sconces set into the walls of the filthy cobwebbed room beyond, casting eerie light on the manacles hanging from the ceiling and the skeleton built upright into one of the stone walls, sights guaranteed to strike terror into the breast of any inebriate who ventured this far, as occasionally some sot did, after a night spent drinking Blue Ruin at one tavern or another, only to speedily return to the streets above with a garbled tale of unearthly screams and mysterious noises, ghostly specters of the plague victims who had been walled up here to die.

In the middle of the chamber stood a table of the sort more commonly found in an anatomist's chamber. Val wondered if Cezar would next acquire fragments of limbs, strew intestines about like discarded party streamers, artistically arrange a few gaping skulls.

By the table, Cezar waited, a dramatic figure clad in black, silver hair loose around his shoulders, beautiful features grim in the flickering candlelight, Ever-watchful Andrei stood a few paces to his left.

Val's nostrils flared. The cloying smell of decaying flesh hung heavy in the air.

He moved closer. Cezar stepped to one side. On the table lay a corpse, pale and pallid, slashed and stabbed. Female. Past her first youth, judging by her breasts. From the working classes, judging by the condition of her hands and feet. Her head had been lopped off below the chin, leaving a rough stump. "I found this on the back doorstep," Cezar said. "A pretty present, wouldn't you say?"

"Or a pointed statement. It would seem that someone wishes us ill."

"Not 'us', necessarily, although I am not aware of having made any new enemies of late." Cezar gestured. Andrei flung a blanket over the mutilated body. "The beheading suggests a vampire slayer. However, there remains the fact that she has been drained of blood."

"But not in the normal manner," Val pointed out. "No teeth marks."

"There wouldn't be, would there?" asked Cezar. "If the miscreant didn't want to be found out. But that doesn't explain the missing head."

"Or why it was left on our doorstep," agreed Val. "If this was meant to be a message, it could have been made more clear."

"'When opponents are at ease, agitate them'. Sun Tzu." Andrei's voice was hoarse, his throat damaged by the same weapon that had slashed his face.

"I suspect," mused Cezar, "that may be the point."

Val frowned. "You believe a *vampir* did this?" Though their kind were civilized on the surface only, and frequently fought among themselves, and jostled constantly for position in the hierarchy of the clan, only in case of extreme emergency did a member of the Edinburgh Breaslă kill. This was wholly due to Cezar, who had held dominance for a long time. *Use sense when indulging your nature; don't flaunt what you are in public places; never overindulge or get careless; appreciate the gift of life; never let the Darkness enslave your will.*

Cezar stepped away from the table. "I'm not sure what I believe." Andrei remained behind, standing guard. He was Cezar's Locotenent, a onetime member of the Order of the Dragon, soldiers who had protected the lands of Eastern Europe from the Turks. Andrei, Cezar and Val all three had fought alongside Constantin Brâncoveanu, and seen him beheaded at Mogosoaia. Had been present at the Walachian Vespers, when Michael the Brave summoned his creditors to his palace and had them massacred. Would never forget St. Bartholomew's Day 1459, when Vlad ordered thirty thousand of the merchants and *boyars* of Brasov impaled.

La dracu! Val hated politics.

Nevertheless, he owed Cezar his allegiance, and would do so even were Cezar not Stăpân. They had roamed the forests of their youth together in search of food and shelter, on guard against the malicious fairies that were said to dwell in the reeds of marshy streams, and the werewolves that supposedly haunted the narrow mountain valleys, and the witches that flew over upland pastures on moonlit nights.

Cezar raised an elegant hand. "It was unlucky to encounter a strange dog first thing in the morning. If someone passed a priest, or an elderly woman with an empty pail, he dared not speak to either of them or he'd have bad luck that day. What are you keeping from me, *camarad*?"

Val strolled around the room, paused to survey the skeletal wall decoration. "The d'Auvergne athame has resurfaced. I wonder if it may have something to do with your uninvited guest."

"That accursed athame. You said it had been lost."

"So I did. However, I admit to having been a trifle distracted at the time. It turns out the Dinwiddies have had the thing all along."

Cezar remained silent for a moment. He had an intimate acquaintance with the d'Auvergne athame. It had once been stuck in his back, which was how Val had come into possession of the thing. "Miss Dinwiddie intrigues me," he said, at length.

Val had expected that she might, which was why he hadn't mentioned the athame sooner. "Miss Dinwiddie knows about us. Not us, specifically, or at least not you, but that our kind exists."

"She knows what you are? How?"

"I admitted it." Val derived a perverse pleasure from seeing his old friend rendered speechless. "There was no reason not to; I'm on her blasted list. Too, Lisbet had upset her, you see."

Cezar looked as if perhaps he saw too much. Before he could comment, Val added, "Miss Dinwiddie then informed me that she would be upset by whoever she pleased whenever she pleased and I was not to tell her what to do."

"Val—"

"Emily would like to know how I became what I am. She doesn't think it is because I led a wicked life. She doesn't wish to infer that I *did* lead a wicked life, however. On the other hand, she doesn't imagine that I died a virgin. I particularly liked the suggestion that a dog jumped over my corpse."

Cezar's lips twitched. Even Andrei's harsh features grew momentarily less grim. "What did you tell her?"

"That I became what I am by choice."

"And then I hope you're going to tell me that you rearranged her memories. After she gasped and shrieked. Or sank into a dead faint."

"*Then* she asked if I could drink from other vampires, or from animals, or if I must confine myself to human blood. How often I had to hunt. Where I preferred to bite someone." Val smiled, remembering. "And if my eyes turned red. After which she apologized for being so *pushing*, but explained that I was her first supersensible creature and there were many things she wished to know."

Cezar's faint amusement faded. "Has it occurred to you that you may be mistaken in Miss Dinwiddie?"

"Constantly. To what do you refer?"

"Professor Dinwiddie not only invented an amphibious horse-drawn vehicle and an automaton that could play a flute, he duplicated the Everlasting Light of Trithemius, and had remarkable success in extracting metals from fruit. Lead from bladderwrack, as I recall. Mercury from Irish moss. Folly, to underestimate his daughter. She may be playing a deep game."

As might Cezar himself. Val glanced at the anatomical table. "Miss Dinwiddie is more interested in natural marvels than in alchemy. She hopes to meet a water kelpie while she's here in Edinburgh." He paused before he added, "There are other items missing from the Society's vaults."

"Miss Dinwiddie confided in you freely, knowing what you are."

"Emily is a very practical young woman. She needs my help."

The violet eyes narrowed. "Miss Dinwiddie claimed you are an old friend of the family. Does she know how truly she spoke?"

"No. And I don't intend to explain."

"What are you doing, Val?"

"Protecting our interests." Val met his Stăpân's gaze. "There is a possibility that she may be influencing my mind."

Cezar raised an eyebrow. "You are *vampir*. You should be influencing hers."

Val snorted. "Emily is not easily influenced. She can close her mind to me. If we're touching, unless I deliberately block her, she can read my memories. I should be able to hear her thoughts. She should *not* be able to hear mine."

"You like her," Andrei observed.

Val shrugged off the suggestion. "It is of little consequence whether I like her or no. Miss Dinwiddie is prone to rush in where angels dare not tread. Too, there is the matter of St. Cuthbert's knucklebone." He gestured toward the shrouded body. "What is to be done with this one? Who was she, do you know?"

Cezar approached the table. "I do. She is one Madame Fanchon, whom you had recently at your house. I believe I will invest in one of those patented spring-closure coffins outfitted with cast-iron straps. I would not care for the anatomists to get hold of this particular corpse."

Such an event was all-too-likely, in the normal course of things. Resurrectionists haunted the city's cemeteries, bent on providing surgeons and medical students fresh corpses to study and dissect by fair means and foul, thereby giving rise to public outrage, the Scots preferring their dear departed to arrive in heaven in an unkenand condition, as opposed to missing one or several body parts. Grieving families sometimes went so far as to pour vitriol and quicklime into the coffins of their loved ones to render the corpses unfit, which rather begged the question of arriving in heaven in one piece.

But, Franny? Why Franny? Had he brought her into this?

Whatever 'this' was?

Cezar interrupted Val's reflections. "One more thing."

"What's that?"

"If Miss Dinwiddie has the d'Auvergne athame in her possession, she can do a great deal more than push you from her mind."

Chapter Thirteen

A woman, a dog, and a walnut tree,
the more you beat them the better they be.

As structures in Edinburgh's Old Town climbed higher, their foundations sank deeper into the soft sandstone. The steep slopes on either side of the High Street had enabled builders to dig sideways into the ridge, building underground levels at depths not possible elsewhere. The foundations of the tenements resembled rabbit warrens, levels of cellars built one above the other, a cold, damp maze of tunnels and underground chambers teeming with beggars and criminals and other societal outcasts. Not to mention rats. Water for cooking and washing was carried by hand down the same winding tunnels into which the residents threw their household waste.

Jamie was familiar with the Old Town, having been left as a babe on the doorstep of the Orphan's Hospital in the shadow of Calton Hill. He didn't think it proper he was guiding Miss Emily through these crowded streets. Not that anything about Ravensclaw's household was proper. Jamie had squirmed down enough chimneys to realize that. "It's no' right," he repeated. "A young lady like yersef shoulna be daverin' aboot the Old Town alone."

Emily eyed him with exasperation. "So you have said, several times! Must I point out again that I am hardly alone? You are with me, and Drogo is with both of us, which is hardly a blessing, but he refused to be left behind. Moreover, we aren't davering. You are going to show me where Michael went."

Jamie kicked at a piece of broken cobblestone. Drogo, tongue lolling, leaned against her thigh. "Och, weil. Nae need t' be abstrakulous. I should hae gi'n him a cuddy lug."

Emily could only guess what a 'cuddy lug' might be. She caught her companion's shoulder and gave him a good shake. "No you should not! Listen to me, Jamie. I told you Mr. Ross may have something of mine. In truth, he may have stolen several somethings. He is not the gentleman he seems." She didn't bother to explain that the pilfered items weren't hers but belonged to the Society, and were meant in time to pass to her descendants, although Emily's papa may have been a trifle optimistic on that score.

Michael insisted they were betrothed. Did he justify his thefts as only taking what would eventually be his?

Well, they weren't betrothed, nor would they be, if Emily had anything to say about it, which she did and would.

Jamie pulled away from her. "I wadna be surprised if ye're no' a wee bit daft! Come awa' noo. 'Afore Isidore finds out where I brought ye and gie me a skelpit dowp."

"I'll give you a skelpit dowp, whatever that is, if you don't stop scolding. For the last time, show me where Mr. Ross went."

The air was damp with a grey mist, the "haar" Jamie called it, that was blowing in from the Firth of Forth. Emily brushed rebellious tendrils of hair away from her face.

Along the High Street Jamie led her, toward the Royal Exchange. Emily regretted she had no time to stop and warm herself in a coffee shop, listen to gossip and peruse the latest newspapers to learn what folly Prinny's Tory ministers had most recently committed and discover who of interest had lately gotten married, disgraced themselves, or died. She and Drogo followed Jamie down a flight of sloping stairs, worn from centuries of traffic, into another steep and winding street. They rounded a corner into a close— 'closes', he informed her, having once been private property, narrow canyon-like alleyways with buildings on each side that were gated to the public and often named after someone who had resided there, as opposed to 'wynds', open thoroughfares usually wide enough for a horse and cart to navigate.

Jamie pointed toward an archway. "He went in there." Drogo growled deep in his throat.

Emily hesitated. The entry looked ominous. But so had Corby Castle, and she'd marched right up to the front door. Emily didn't plan to accost Michael at his front door, of course, merely to pick the lock and have a quick look around. He shouldn't be home at this hour. But if he was—

She'd cross that bridge when she came to it. Emily had sat back and done nothing for far too long. If only she had taken inventory earlier, and opened that lead-lined chest, instead of seeking to soothe the warring factions of the Society while attempting at the same time to deal with her own feelings of inadequacy and loss—

But she had, and here she was. Resolutely, she took a forward step.

Or attempted to. Still growling, Drogo blocked her path. "I dinna think," protested Jamie, "that ye should go in there."

"Stop it, the both of you. Oh, do get out of my way!" Emily glared at Drogo, who didn't budge an inch. Then she scowled at Jamie. "Why are you staring at me as if I'd grown a second head?"

Jamie pointed. "Behind ye, miss!"

Emily spun around. Three hulking brutes loitered at the mouth of the close. No sooner had she spied them than they abandoned all pretense of idleness and advanced on her. Rather, two advanced. The third jerked like a puppet when he walked, his pale face twitching uncontrollably. In one hand he clutched a sack.

Emily might have run, but Drogo was tangled in her skirts. She raised her umbrella and prepared to defend herself.

The men were already upon them. Emily speared the instep of one assailant, whacked another in the shin, had picked up her skirts to flee when the twitching man yanked the umbrella from her hand and tossed a sack over her head.

Jamie, being of shorter stature and fewer inhibitions, had aimed directly for the nearest crotch. A moment of contact, an agonized bellow, and then he was batted into a towering pile of refuse. Drogo took to his heels.

'Twas a right bourach. Jamie flailed about in the slippery, stinking rubbish. Emily kicked and flung her arms about inside her prison, which smelled most unpleasantly of spoiled fish. "Bloody, blooming, blasted—"

Her captor punched the sack, hard. The blow knocked the breath out of her, and Emily went limp. She would have a sore belly tomorrow. Providing that she saw tomorrow. Why had these ruffians set on her? Were they resurrection men in search of a fresh body to steal and sell? An extremely fresh body, considering that she was still very much alive.

Why would they be interested in a little bit of nothing like herself? There was hardly enough meat on Emily's bones to exercise a surgeon's scalpel. Maybe her bones themselves were of more value. Maybe her skeleton would have a place of honor in some anatomist's dissecting room.

Emily didn't want to be dissected. *Concentrate!* she told herself. Her abductors were arguing. She heard the word 'feartie' mentioned, and more clearly, 'sweerbreeks.'

Oxter and Mowdiewarp, as they called each other, were the more vocal of the three. Emily was relieved to learn that these were not resurrection men, merely ruffians for hire; and it was just as well their employer didn't want the lass dead instead of tossed over Twitcher's shoulder like a sack of potatoes, because none of them had the stomach for such work.

Unnoticed by the others, Jamie squirmed out from beneath the pile of rubbish. He couldna lounge there lak a doolally, greetin' over the puir mawkit condition of his nice new clothes, now slechered in nasty substances he didna want to know the nature of. He must gather his wits about him so that he could follow when the bajins took Miss Emily away.

As it turned out, they took her nowhere. Drogo reappeared at the far end of the close. The wolf was not alone. Ravensclaw moved with startling speed to smash one man against the wall of a building. He flung another onto a rooftop. Twitcher took one look at the newcomer and promptly dropped his burden in the dirt. Ravensclaw caught him by the throat and lifted him off the ground.

Twitcher kicked and gurgled and struggled to escape that killing grip, those compelling eyes, those long, pointed, razor-sharp fangs.

His captor spoke in a deep compelling voice. "None of this happened. You and your companions spent the past two hours getting drunk as David's sow in that tavern on the corner. If you go near this young woman again, I will tear out your liver and wrap your intestines around your neck. Do you understand?"

Twitcher shuddered. "Aye." Ravensclaw let him drop to the ground. The man scrambled unsteadily to his feet and staggered down the narrow street.

Jamie emerged from the pile of rubble. "Och, those are some grand teeth ye hae! I expected ye wid bite that bajin's heid in twa. Be Miss Emily a'richt? Daft isna the half of it. She be a proper dare-the-de'il."

Miss Emily, sprawled on the cobblestones, withheld comment. Ravensclaw bent to lift her in his arms. "Heed me, Jamie. You saw no teeth. You were never here. Go home."

Jamie opened his mouth and closed it. A blank expression stole over his face. Without a word of protest, he left.

Emily opened her other eye. "Yes, he did. Teeth. Saw them. So did I." When Ravensclaw set her on her feet, she reached up and touched a curious finger to one fang. Winced as she sliced her finger on the sharp tooth. Said, "Oh, my."

Ravensclaw stepped back, turned away from her. Turned back, caught her hand, licked the blood oozing from her cut.

The feeling was indescribable. Emily drew in a sharp breath. Drogo growled.

Abruptly, Ravensclaw released her. *Go now. While you can.* Emily took a last look at his grim expression and obeyed.

Chapter Fourteen

He that would eat the fruit must first climb the tree.

Emily set down her book, an ancient grimoire which contained, among other fascinating information, a shape-shifting spell that involved sticking twelve knives in the ground at intervals and somersaulting over each one. She rested her head against the back of her chair. Her stomach was sore where the ruffian had hit her. Indeed, she felt like every muscle in her body ached.

Machka jumped into her lap. "It seemed like such a good idea at the time," Emily told the cat. Drogo, in his customary spot on the hearth, rolled one expressive eye.

Why had those men attacked her? Had it been a random act, or was it connected to the d'Auvergne athame? She had been almost on Michael's doorstep. Had he sent those men to frighten her off?

They had seemed less intent on scaring her than snatching her. Emily didn't care to dwell on what might have happened if the wolf—or rare Carpathian sleuth-hound—hadn't fetched Ravensclaw.

Yes, and how had Ravensclaw come to be so close at hand?

Ravensclaw. Emily's understanding of the ways of maids and men—or maids and the nonmortal—was increasing at an astonishing rate. First his touch, then the dreams, and now—

She regarded her wounded finger with awe. If a finger-lick could be so sensual, what must it be like to feel a vampire's teeth? To experience a full-fledged fanging, so to speak?

The drawing room was pleasant in the daylight, a chamber designed not for entertaining guests but for everyday use. Here, too, books were piled everywhere. The only discordant note was

Michael's roses, great luxuriant crimson blooms that hadn't yet begun to fade. Jamie and his clothing were being divested of their noxious stench by Zizi, Bela, and Lilian, a 'skelpit dowp' having turned out to be punishment delivered by Isidore to the boy's backside. Lady Alberta was absent, having gone to Princes Street in search of a corset designed to give her figure the graceful curves of youth.

Emily had ceased her stroking. Machka bit her hand.

Val walked into the room. "Isidore said—" He turned pale, clutched his throat. "Take those bloody roses away!"

Emily stood up so abruptly that Machka went sailing through the air to land atop Nostradamus's *Centuries*. She snatched up the roses and ran into the stairwell. "Isidore! *Isidore!*"

The old man was hobbling up the steps. She cried, "Ravensclaw is ill!"

Isidore took the vase from her. "The master is allergic to roses, miss."

Emily regarded him over the rim of her spectacles. "Then why in the name of heaven did you bring the blasted blossoms into the drawing room?"

"They were a gift. For you." Isidore dripped disapproval. "From your young man."

"He is *not*—" Emily stopped herself and drew in a calming breath. "What can we do?"

"There's nothing *to* do. The master will be right as rain." Isidore nodded to the roses. "As soon as I take these away."

"Then why don't you do that?" Emily bared her teeth at him. "*Now*, Isidore!"

" 'The butcher looked for the knife and it was in his mouth'." Having managed to get in the last word, the old man descended the stair.

Emily hurried back into the drawing room, flung open the windows, waved her hands to speed the scent of flowers from the room. "Roses? Not garlic or crucifixes or holy water, but *roses?*"

"Surely in all your reading you've come upon the superstition that a branch of the wild rose placed upon a corpse keeps a *vampir* trapped inside its grave." Val's voice was strained.

"I've also read that blood baths cure leprosy," Emily retorted, "and that the crowing of a rooster will scare away the undead. I presume this means you don't strew rose petals for your lady friends to lie upon?"

He loosened his cravat. "You know a great deal about strewing rose pedals, do you?"

"You can always substitute some other flower. Daisies. Lilies." *Forget-me-nots.*

Ravensclaw looked amused. Emily cleared her throat. "Thank you for rescuing us today. Jamie believes he accompanied me on an errand and had an unfortunate encounter with a rubbish cart. It was most impressive, the way you clouded his mind." *Drat it, stop babbling.* "You frightened me. Those wretched roses. I thought I was going to see you crumble to dust before my eyes."

Ravensclaw picked up Machka. The cat settled on his shoulder. "Would that distress you, little one?"

"How could it not distress me? I've grown, um, accustomed to you being around."

Val no longer looked amused. "Emily, we have to talk."

Emily *had* been talking. "About what?"

Val stroked the cat. "About what you're feeling. No, I haven't eavesdropped on your thoughts. It's what everyone feels after they've encountered one of us."

How serious he had become. How remote. In Emily's experience, when gentlemen became serious and remote, they were about to be even more annoying than usual.

She too could be annoying. "One of you? You refer to hemovores?"

Val ignored this provocation. "You liked it when I took your blood. Everyone enjoys it when one of us takes his—or her—blood." He paused reflectively. "Well, almost everyone."

Emily took off her spectacles and gave the lenses a brisk polish. "I daresay it isn't especially enjoyable to have one's throat torn out."

"Emily—"

She plopped her glasses on her nose. "I know all this. If you didn't make people think they were enjoying the experience, no one would ever let you feed. But I don't think you were *making* me feel what I felt, because to make me feel it, you would have had to overwhelm my senses, and I would have known." Emily paused, considering. "Not that the experience *wasn't* overwhelming, because it was. But it was my own overwhelming, not yours. At any rate, it's not as if you bit me. You only gave me a little lick."

Val still wore that closed expression. Emily folded her arms across her chest. "Are you acting so missish because blood-drinking is an adjunct of the amorous congress?"

"'Missish'?" Val ran a lazy finger over Machka's purring head.

Emily tilted her own head to one side. "Or perhaps vampires *don't*—"

"I can do everything a mortal man can." A twinkle lit Val's eye. "But better, of course. Are you asking if I am capable of amorous congress?"

No, because she didn't doubt it for a moment. Emily didn't care to dwell on what things Ravensclaw might do better than a mortal man. At least not until she was safely in the privacy of her bed. "You *did* say you were umbivalent," she allowed.

"I have said any number of absurd things to you. Since you bring out the worst in me, no doubt I will say more." Ravensclaw walked toward the doorway. "Isidore! I know you're lurking somewhere. Bring tea."

Emily felt her shoulders sag. For a horrid moment, she had feared he meant to leave the room.

She stiffened her spine. "You said you became what you are by choice, but how? Have you ever made someone? Brought them over? Whatever you call it?"

He turned back to her. "No."

"Why not?"

"It's not easily done." Ravensclaw plucked Machka from his shoulder and set her on the floor. Sulkily, the cat curled up in front of Drogo. The wolf began to bathe her head.

Lilian arrived, puffing, with the tea tray. Lady Alberta, she announced, had eaten all the black buns.

Emily waited impatiently until the maidservant left the room. Her hands shook slightly as she prepared Ravensclaw's tea. "If you were to drink from me, I wouldn't become like you are?"

Ravensclaw took the cup from her. "You would not."

Emily could see it now. Her first addition to the Dinwiddie Chronicles. *The Curious Episode of the Vampire Who Refused To Take Advantage.* "From whom *do* you feed?"

"I am a creature of sanguine nature. You must never forget that. As for my source of sustenance, that's a personal question, don't you think?" Ravensclaw set down his cup and rose from his chair.

Personal? Emily scowled at his back. *So is what you do in my dreams.*

He moved to a table, unlocked a drawer, extracted a small carved chest and brought it to her. "Permit me to offer you somewhat more potent protection than those charms of yours."

Emily ran her hands over the wood. The chest was very old. "Open it," Val said.

She did. Inside the chest, on a black velvet bed, lay a necklace wrought of intertwined gold. Emily touched a reverent finger to the pendant, a large blood-red ruby set against a double ouroborus. On the reverse was etched in tiny letters, 'Their swords shall enter into their own hearts, and their bows shall be broken.'

Psalm xxxvii, verse fifteen. "Marie d'Auvergne's amulet. Protection against witchcraft and sorcery and those who mean the wearer harm. She created the athame to draw dark power to her, and the amulet to repel that same power—and in so doing, the woman drove herself quite mad. You think I'm in danger, then?"

"You were in danger earlier today. That was no random encounter. Stand up."

Emily obeyed. "Those men were following me?"

Val fastened the pendant around her neck. "They had been following you for some time. Have you annoyed someone?"

Other than Michael Ross, who was determined she should bear his offspring?

She could have been kidnapped today. Snatched up and taken some unknown place for some unknown purpose. Might never have stood talking to this man again.

Vampire.

Whatever he was, Emily would have regretted her lost opportunities. She raised up on her tiptoes and brushed her lips against his. "Dinwiddies thrive on danger," she murmured. "Adventure. Exploring the unknown." Val raised his hand, ran one finger lightly over her skin, down the line of her jaw, coming at last to rest on the pulse beating wildly at the base of her throat. Emily took a deep breath and deliberately let down her guard.

Mind touched mind, a thousand times more erotic than skin brushing skin, for that contact was from outside, and this came from within. Emily felt Val's power, his hunger. His desire for her. Her legs grew weak, her mouth went dry. He caught her arms and drew her close.

Pleasure stole over her, and warmth. A sensual exhilaration. She was floating, flying, far above the ground. Soaring toward the heavens, on the wings of some hot unearthly bliss. Or, rather, very earthly. Fire flowed through her veins—

Emily.

Mm?

The d'Auvergne athame, Emily. Is it in your possession now? Do you know where it is?

The d'Auvergne athame? In this moment of intense intimacy, all he could do was ask about the d'Auvergne athame? Emily plummeted back down to earth. *If I had that blasted athame, I'd be safely at home instead of wasting my time with bloody obstinate stupid manipulative vampires!*

She felt his regret. *I'm sorry. I had to ask. We cannot be untruthful with one another when we are touching like this.* Val withdrew from her mind and dropped a chaste kiss on her forehead.

He could not lie to her? Emily grabbed his wrist and concentrated very hard.

Wind howled outside the cottage. A fire burned in the hearth, gleamed on the fair skin of the woman stretched out on a rug before the fireplace. Ana's lambskin jacket lay discarded on the floor beside her red woven skirt and gold-threaded belt. She wore only her embroidered blouse, and her striped stockings, and her long brown hair.

As if sensing an intruder, she sat up and drew the rug around her. "Valentin?"

Ravensclaw broke away. "What are you that you can do this to me?"

Emily felt equally unsettled. "Who was Ana?" she asked.

Val walked toward the window. "My wife."

Ravensclaw was hundreds of years old. Naturally he'd had a wife. Probably he'd had several wives. Only a goose would be jealous of the past.

Emily was a goose. "What happened to her?"

His voice was expressionless. "I presume she died."

She moved to join him at the window. "There's no mention of an Ana in the Dinwiddie Chronicles."

He glanced down at her. "Ana was before. I know this goes against your nature, but for your own well-being you must allow yourself to be guided by me."

First he kissed her on the forehead—the forehead!—and now he acted as if she were an ignorant miss. "You think my powers of intellect less acute than yours? Because you are a male?"

He winced. "That's not what I meant. You are not acquainted with the Darkness, for which you may be grateful. You don't want to become attuned to the Darkness, Emily."

"The Dark Ages, you mean?" Emily inquired icily. "We are no longer living in the Dark Ages, Ravensclaw. Females today do all sort of interesting and dangerous things."

His lips curved, just a little bit. "Such as?"

Emily thought of all the interesting and dangerous things she'd like to do with Ravensclaw himself. She sighed.

"Yet another sacrifice is required of you," Val told her. "We're engaged for the theater. Tonight."

Chapter Fifteen

It is idle to swallow the cow and choke on the tail.

Edinburgh's Theater Royal was located in Shakespeare Square, at the east end of Princes Street. Emily found little to criticize in the theater itself, which compared favorably with any outside London, due largely to the management of William Murray and his sister Harriet Siddons. Nor could she fault this evening's entertainment, which included the popular *Rob Roy MacGregor* or, *Auld Lang Syne,* a Musical Drama in three acts, based on the popular novel *Rob Roy;* and additionally *The Falls of Clyde,* a mélange of tragedy and comedy, action and pathos, dialogue and music all jumbled together in one grand mishmash. All her discontent was centered on the occupants of an opposite box.

Lady Alberta was in good spirits, currently discussing Sir Walter Scott, patron and outspoken friend of the drama, especially this drama, with a number of her friends: the poet was suffering a case of gallstones so severe that many people in Edinburgh feared he was on his deathbed. Her gown of purple-blue taffeta suited her, as did the turban she wore on her dyed hair. Emily felt rather fine herself in a gown of dark shot silk with a high waistline, short sleeves, and an ankle-length gored skirt. Rather, she *had* felt fine until she caught sight of Lisbet Boroi. Lisbet was seduction incarnate in sea-green crepe with a froth of flounces that reached to her knees. Her décolletage plunged almost that low, providing an admirable setting for her necklace, a series of large colored gemstones.

Had Ravensclaw given Lisbet that necklace? Did he give necklaces to every female he met?

Emily took herself to task. She was merely Val's houseguest, for all their odd communication of minds. It was his prerogative, were he so inclined, to ignore her all the blessed night. Thus far he had done precisely that, no sooner arriving at the theater than he had left Emily and Lady Alberta to hold court in his box while he withdrew to another, directly opposite, where he sat murmuring low in the lovely Lisbet's ear while Michael Ross attempted, thus far unsuccessfully, to strike up an intimate conversation of his own with Emily.

A steady stream of visitors had thronged to Ravensclaw's box immediately intermission began. It seemed every gentleman present tonight yearned to be made known to Count Revay-Czobar's houseguest, which Emily found more than a little odd, and gratifying only in that it put Michael's nose out of joint.

Michael leaned closer, half-suffocating her with the distinctive scent of Macassar Oil. "*What* Society business brought you to Edinburgh? Is Ravensclaw helping you search for your missing knife? You really should refrain from involving outsiders in such matters. Your father would not approve of you consorting with Ravensclaw."

"I'm not consorting with Ravensclaw," Emily retorted. *Alas.* "And, for your information, my father had a high opinion of the Count." *Or of the Count's abilities.* "In any event, my conduct, whether you approve of it or not, is nothing to do with you."

A muscle twitched in Michael's jaw, above the deep white neckcloth arranged so artistically around his neck, the crisp high collar that brushed his earlobes and framed his chin. Emily had time to admire his dark trousers and jacket, his black velvet vest with its thin cream satin stripe, before he controlled his temper sufficiently to speak again.

"It *is* my concern," Michael told her. "For all you may choose to ignore it, you are my affianced bride. And that is not all you are ignoring. Matters abstruse and supersensible, remember? Beings of such power that they can destroy you in less than a heartbeat and you will thank them for it, who can inspire so strong an amorous attraction that you will be willing to do anything for the sake of a mere smile?"

Rather more than a smile, thought Emily. She adjusted her spectacles, the better to regard her beau. "You are not equipped to deal with such matters," he added. "I wouldn't be at all surprised to discover you're bespelled."

"*I* wouldn't be at all surprised to discover that you've taken to eating opium! I can't imagine where else you might have got your fantastical ideas." Emily winced as Lady Alberta left off enthusing about Charles Mackay's performance to give her ankle a sharp kick. "That is, I appreciate your concern, Michael, unfounded as it is. Ravensclaw has been a perfect gentleman." Even when she'd prefer he wasn't. Except in her dreams.

Michael opened his mouth to argue. Emily turned away before she gave in to the impulse to clout him, which would hardly accord with Lady Alberta's advice on catching flies. The theater hummed with the conversations of the well-dressed ladies and gentlemen in the boxes, and the less prosperous citizens in the galleries and the pit; a hum that lessened only marginally once a performance was under way.

A barrister, a baronet, and the younger son of a marquess vied with one another to pay her fulsome compliments. Emily said all that was polite. Michael glared. After a few moments, Lady Alberta excused herself and, with her companions left the box.

Emily's admirers withdrew also, routed by Michael's glower. He immediately took possession of her hand. "I must insist that you return home," he said. "You are in danger here. A woman, unprotected and alone—"

Hardly alone, reflected Emily, even when she wanted most to be, as for instance now. She tried to pull her hand away. Michael refused to let it go. "I understand there was an incident just yesterday," he added. "You were set upon. Near the High Street. Not far from my lodgings, in fact."

And how did he know that? "Oh? I didn't realize you lived nearby. Ravensclaw came to my rescue. It doesn't signify."

He gripped her fingers harder. "On the contrary, it signifies a great deal. Has it occurred to you that Ravensclaw may have staged the assault himself, so that he could appear the hero in your eyes?"

"Nonsense." But that was just the sort of thing Michael might have done, Emily suspected, had he thought of it, which fortunately he had not.

He persisted, "Do you think this attempt on you has anything to do with your missing knife?"

"I don't know why it would. No one knows that the thing has disappeared but you and me. Unless *you* were responsible for the attack? Maybe you meant to force a marriage. Clandestine unions are legal and binding in Scotland."

"Hang it, Emily! You can't think that poorly of me." Michael snatched up her other hand as well. "You are maddened with grief for the Professor. That's why you're not acting like yourself."

What *was* herself? Emily was no longer sure. Mere months ago, she would have scoffed at the suggestion that she might lose track of priceless artifacts, be set upon by ruffians, develop a *tendre* for one of the walking undead.

Michael's gaze fixed on her pendant. "I haven't seen that necklace before. It looks very old."

"It is."

"What an unusual setting. I suppose the Society has many other treasures tucked away in the vaults."

He supposed that he might get his hands on them. Had her papa paid more attention to her admirer's character, he might have been enthusiastic about welcoming him into the fold.

"This necklace has nothing to do with the Society," she told him. "It was a gift."

"Who gave it to you? Ravensclaw? I do not approve."

"You do not approve of gifts in general? Or merely gifts given to me? I don't see that my necklace is any of your concern."

"Of course it's my concern! I'm about to be your husband." Michael rose so abruptly he almost overturned his seat. "Providing I don't strangle you first. Blast it, Emily, why won't you just go home?"

Because I don't want to. Because you're as jumpy as a cat on hot bricks. "Maybe because you want me to so badly. Why *are* you so determined that I leave Edinburgh?"

His face was white with temper. He opened his mouth, closed it, turned on his heel and stalked out of the box.

Emily leaned back in her seat, breathing in the familiar theatrical scents of oil lamps and candle wax. So much for the use of honey. Her nature was evidently less sweet than tart.

Even as she told herself she shouldn't look, her gaze strayed to the opposite box, where Lady Alberta was now chatting with Lisbet Boroi and Ravensclaw.

Lisbet looked annoyed. Perhaps Lady Alberta was enlightening them about Dugal Stewart's lecture on philosophy, which she had attended earlier this week. Mr. Stewart rejected metaphysics as a vain attempt to fathom the nature of the mind and in its place proposed inductive psychology, the patient and precise observation of mental processes without pretending to explain the mind itself.

Val glanced in her direction. Emily reflected that her own mental processes weren't working as effectively as once they had.

At least, she had thought they functioned well. Now she was less certain. Not only her papa was guilty of character misjudgment as concerned Michael Ross.

She recalled the day they had first spoken, during the unveiling of the Phantasmagoria Machine. Michael had been one of many young men who attended demonstrations at the Society. She next encountered him during her father's lecture on the Rule of Gradation. Michael had declared himself impressed by her comment that, though the variations seemed interminable, it remained uncertain whether they would delay rather than defy detection. Gradually, he eased his way into the professor's confidence, and her own as well. She had enjoyed his habit of asking her opinion of all manner of topics, and complimenting the quality of her mind.

The quality of her mind, indeed.

Emily shifted positions. Her bruised muscles protested with a particularly painful throb. She looked up to find Cezar Korzha seated beside her in the no-longer-vacant chair. Andrei Torok stood sentinel-like at the back of the box.

Mr. Korzha might not be mentioned on a certain list, but Emily suspected he should be. Bluntly she said, "What do you want?"

He contemplated the opposite box. "Are you feeling contentious this evening, Miss Dinwiddie? You are welcome to vent your spleen on me."

His voice was soft, spellbinding, seductive. Emily sniffed. "You and Ravensclaw have beguilement down to a fine art. The two of you go back a long way together. To Sarmizegetuza, perhaps?"

"You are a very bold young woman," Cezar said calmly. "Or a very foolish one."

"I'm fed up to the teeth with this 'young woman' nonsense," Emily retorted. "If I was a man, you wouldn't be having this conversation with me."

"You underestimate yourself." Cezar nodded toward her necklace. "Are you familiar with Sir John Mandeville, a French traveler in the fourteenth century? 'The owner of a remarkable ruby shall enjoy good relations with those around him and shall live his life in peace. He shall escape various disasters.' Providing that he wears his ruby as a ring, bracelet, or brooch, and on his right side."

"According to legend," Emily retorted, "the Greek god of war dwelled in rubies, and therefore the gems are full of energy. Rubies are additionally associated with blood, birth, and death. I repeat, what is it you want of me?"

"Merely a few moments' conversation. Concerning why you've come to Edinburgh. I know the d'Auvergne athame has been in your possession, Miss Dinwiddie. Mayhap it still is."

All Emily wanted was a few moment's conversation, if conversation she must have, with someone who wasn't under the impression she had more hair than wit. "And mayhap you can turn into a butterfly and waft about the theater. Has it occurred to you, Mr. Korzha, that if I had the athame, I would hardly need Ravensclaw?"

"If you had the athame, what better camouflage than to ensorcel one of us? I warn you, Miss Dinwiddie, I am less gullible than Val. Think before you answer. I could compel you to tell me the truth."

Emily didn't doubt he could. It was taking all her strength to maintain her defenses. Cezar Korzha must be very powerful, to affect her as he did. "I don't know which suggestion is the absurd, that Ravensclaw is gullible or that I might ensorcel someone. If you think I could ensorcel Ravensclaw, you must have windmills in your head." She grimaced. "That may have been a tad too blunt."

"Infinitely too blunt. You appear to be in some discomfort. Permit me to make it go away." Without waiting for permission,

Cezar placed his hand on her belly, directly above the bruise. Emily was too shocked to protest.

He had not overrated his abilities. The pain did go away.

Cezar withdrew his hand. "A word of warning, Miss Dinwiddie: you are in out of your depth. Val may be amusing himself with you, but at the end of the day, he will remain a predator and you, my pretty—" He flicked her cheek with his cool fingers. "Will still be prey."

Emily had endured quite enough male superiority for one evening. She stared straight into Cezar's handsome, soulless face. "As Mr. Shakespeare puts it, 'The world is grown so bad that wrens make prey where eagles dare not perch.' This conversation is at an end."

"For the moment, perhaps. You may be grateful that you also amuse me." Cezar rose and left the box. Andrei followed. Emily let out a shaken breath.

So much for her mental processes.

Unless she mistook the matter, she had just defied a master vampire.

Chapter Sixteen

As you make your bed, so you must lie on it.

If Val usually enjoyed the theater—having been privileged to observe its progression from *Gammer Gurton's Needle* to Edmund Kean's *Hamlet*—he had not done so tonight, although he *had* derived some satisfaction from the parade of visitors to his box, each determined to make the acquaintance of his houseguest, and the sight of Michael Ross's clenched jaw. Cezar's interest in Miss Dinwiddie, however, left him uneasy. Cezar would act always for the greater good.

So was Val acting for the greater good, stretched out like a sacrificial victim while Lisbet ran her skilled fingers over the contours of his chest, down his belly; scraped her teeth over his flesh.

"Lisbet." He wound his fingers in her hair, and tugged. "I must leave. It's almost dawn."

She raised her head. "You could rest here."

"You know better than that."

She rolled away from him. "You should have accompanied Cezar to Budapest. He was surprised to find me there."

"Had I known—" *I would have stayed a thousand miles away.* Val reached for his trousers. "I congratulate you. Cezar is not easily surprised."

Naked, Lisbet lounged back among her pillows. "They say absence makes the heart grow fonder. Is that true, *dragul meu*?"

Val shrugged into his jacket. "I am *vampir*, remember? We have no hearts. And now I truly must go."

She made no move to stop him. He was almost to the doorway when she spoke again. *"Iubiera ca moartea e de tare. Love is as strong as death. Remember that, baĭat."* Val stepped into the hallway and escaped into the night.

Or, rather, the morning. Edinburgh was already astir. By the time the bell of St. Giles had sounded seven times, shop shutters would be flung back on their hinges, the tradesmen leaning over half doors and exchanging gossip; and night soil men would be making their rounds.

The weather was damp and dreary. Fog wafted through the winding wynds and closes, wreathed the tall, forbidding tenements, crept down the cobbled streets. Easy enough to imagine Major Weir's spectral coach drawn by headless horses rounding the next corner, to hear a ghostly piper playing beneath the stones of the Royal Mile.

Instead, what Val heard was the sound of a footstep; and what he sensed was the presence of a drunken young buck intent on making mischief. He paused, waiting for the man to stumble into sight. A shock of wheaten hair, a pair of unfocussed red-rimmed eyes, the smell of fresh blood, as if the fool had recently cut himself, a strong impression of intended threat—

Val fed when he must, discreetly, and made it his habit to provide more pleasure than pain; even were he not already sated, he would have had no interest in such easy prey. He placed his would-be assailant under a compulsion to present himself naked at the Goblin Halls, caverns claimed by legend to exist beneath the Calton Hill, where every Thursday night the Fairy Boy of Leith and his companions joined goblins and elves, witches and ghosts, in feasting and revelry. Let the fool wear off his aggressions searching for something that didn't exist.

Val wondered if Miss Dinwiddie had heard of the Fairy Boy of Leith. It was the sort of tale that would appeal to her.

She'd actually asked if he was capable of sexual function. Val had come damned close to demonstrating that he was. He wondered if he'd survived all this time only for a curious, bespectacled spinster to drive him mad. A freckled, sharp-nosed spinster with a cloud of carroty curls that, unbound, must reach down past her hips. Val wanted to nibble on her neck, as well as other portions of her aggravating little person. To explore her with his lips, and fingers, and tongue. To kiss her until she was wild and then at last to drink her sweet rich blood. One tiny taste of her had left him ravenous with a hunger he hadn't felt in a very long time.

Val wouldn't slake that hunger. He wouldn't seduce Emily. Instead he let Lisbet believe she held him enraptured with her pale perfect body and her bedroom skills.

Had his performance been convincing? Because a performance it had been. Val had taken Emily to the theater and abandoned her, to demonstrate to Lisbet that she was of no consequence. Lisbet, and Cezar. Amusement had turned to affection, and Val found himself wishing to keep the exasperating Miss Dinwiddie locked safely away in his curiosity cabinet where she could come to no harm.

His home loomed before him. Isidore met him at the front door. In response to Val's quizzical look, he shook his head. "'Set a cow to catch a hare.' Young Jamie's guarding her door. Said if any bajins came around, he'd give them a right clout."

In other words, the night had been free of excursions and alarms. "Well done, Isidore. Get some rest." Val mounted the staircase. Jamie was indeed guarding Emily's doorway. He and Machka and Drogo were sleeping in a pile, alongside a Scottish claymore almost as big as Jamie himself. Drogo opened one yellow eye and blinked. Val left them to it and retired to his own bedchamber, on the floor below.

He locked the door behind him. With the draperies closed, the chamber was dark as a tomb. Val pulled off his boots, his jacket, his trousers, unwound his cravat and stretched out on the bed. With sunrise, he fell into a stupor, and though sleep didn't stay long with him, it truly was the sleep of the dead.

Usually he sank into peaceful darkness. Today the darkness was broken by a dream. A dream of a woman with gold-flecked eyes and a wild mass of flaming hair.

He lowered his face until his lips found hers, heard her quick intake of breath. Her hands clutched at his shoulders as he traced her mouth with his tongue, nibbled gently at her lower lip, teased her with feather touches until she opened for him.

His tongue slipped into her sweet, warm mouth. She caught her breath and stiffened, then relaxed against him. Her hands tangled in his hair.

He lowered his lips to the sensitive flesh of her throat, paused to taste her pulse. His lips slid along her silken skin to the soft flesh of one small breast. He tormented her rosy nipple with his tongue until she cried out for more. She shuddered and moaned as he covered every inch of her body with small close kisses; teased her slowly, mercilessly, with his tongue; laved her with long, slow strokes. She groaned. Her body pulsed beneath his hands.

His teeth scraped the inside of her thigh.

He smelled her excitement, felt her heartbeat.

His groin grew tight. He wanted her. The hunger made him burn.

She drew back. Not carroty hair now, but golden blonde. Amber eyes instead of brown. The d'Auvergne athame glowed in Isabella Dinwiddie's hand.

Val wakened with a start, relieved to find himself back in his own bed, in the dark bedroom, alone with the shattered fragments of his dream, and his concern about what it might portend.

Or *was* he alone? Val sensed a presence. Not Zizi or Bela or Lilian. Emily, Isidore, or Jamie. Machka or Drogo. None of whom could have got past his locked door.

Recognition was slow in coming. "Please let me still be dreaming," Val said.

"Is that any way to greet me after so long?" his visitor inquired.

Val screwed his eyelids shut. "Go away. You're dead."

"It's not kind of you to point that out." She sounded sulky. "I still have feelings, Valentin."

Val had feelings too, any number of conflicting ones. "What are you doing here?" he asked.

She sniffled. "You called me when you told that little *rosçat* my name. Names have power. You might pretend to be pleased to see me, you know."

He *hadn't* seen her, yet. "I didn't tell the redhead your name. She took it from my mind."

"You should be careful of that one. I'm amazed you've resisted the temptation to take her to your bed. I don't recall that you were used to withstand temptation at all. Maybe I should warn her that you will break her heart." A pause and another sniffle. "Like you broke mine."

Val knew he'd have to let Emily go. Eventually. "I'm not having this conversation." He pulled a pillow over his head.

And felt a swat upon his knee. "Oh, yes you are! It is the first of many conversations that we are going to have."

Not a dream, but another nightmare. Reluctantly, Val opened his eyes. Quickly, he closed them. Ana was as he remembered her, though unnervingly transparent. "I think I liked it better when you were calling me *tradato and neleguit.*"

"What did you expect? I had seen you die. And then you returned in the middle of the night and wanted to assert your husbandly rights." She sighed. "Not that I would be averse to a little tupping now."

Val looked at her more closely. Ana was displaying a great deal of bare flesh, draped about with wispy veils, sequins and beads. "A man can't tup a ghost."

"Tell me about it," she said gloomily. "Do you know what it's like to go eons without?" She eyed him appreciatively. "Of course you don't. Being *vampir* suits you, Valentin."

Being dead *didn't* suit her. "You can't stay here, Ana. Why haven't you moved on?"

"I don't want to move on," retorted Ana. "You can be sure there's no tupping *there!* You called me and now you're stuck with me until you give me what I want. It *is* your fault I'm dead."

Val regarded her with reluctant fascination. "How is it my fault that you took up with Teodor?"

Ana twirled a strand of ghostly hair around one ghostly finger. "Because you turned *vampir,* of course. I wouldn't have taken up with Teodor otherwise, or have wound up in the harem of Murcel the Magnificent, or have been tied up in a sack and dropped into the Bosporus to drown! And all because of a Nubian eunuch, may the snails devour his corpse. Don't dare tell me there is a moral to all this, because now I would give anything—not that I *have* anything, but you know what I mean!—to be tupped again. That's why I need your help."

"No!" Val said. "I will not—"

"Not you! No offense, but you *are* a vampire. However, I have seen your stacks of books. Books about sorcery and magic and I don't know what else. It should be simple enough to find a spell that will make me solid. Just for a brief time." She pursed her lips. "Or maybe not so brief. I learned a great deal in the harem. The Lovemaking of the Crow was my favorite. Followed by Splitting the Bamboo. The Sultan, curse his bones, especially liked the Churning of the Cream."

"Enough!" Ana incorporeal was every bit as provoking as she had been in the flesh. "I'm no sorcerer."

"Pfft! You raised *me*, didn't you?"

"From what you say, it was Emily who raised you." This was like trying to converse with a wisp of fog. "And I know of no such spell."

"Then I'll wait until you find one!" Ana settled against the bedpost. "Since you're dead, and I'm dead— Are we still married, do you think?"

It wasn't enough that Val must contend with missing athames and inquisitive virgins, now he must placate the ghost of his dead wife. He groaned and pulled the pillow back over his face.

Chapter Seventeen

It is a dangerous fire that begins in the bed straw.

Emily paused on the threshold of Val's small study. A chandelier with iron branches hung from the painted ceiling. Old oak bookcases were set against the walls. Faded rugs were scattered on the wood floor. A piece of seventeenth-century crewel work in the tree of life design hung near a fine long-case clock.

Opposite the fireplace, in front of half-glass shutter windows, stood a large oak table with elaborately turned bulbous legs and square blocked feet. On the table an untidy stack of ancient books—she recognized Albert Magnus's *The Alchemist*, the *Grimoire of Honorius*, Frances Barret's *Celestial Intelligence*—perched beside a tray bearing an empty teapot and the remnants of cheese scones, a leather portfolio, an inkstand, and Machka, dozing on her back in a feeble splash of sun. Behind the table, Ravensclaw sprawled in a low-backed armchair. He wore leather breeches, and a shirt open at the neck. His auburn hair was mussed as if he'd repeatedly raked his fingers through the thick strands.

If only she might run *her* fingers through it. Hands clenched firmly at her sides, Emily walked further into the room. She recognized the arcane symbols on the pages of the book Val had been reading. "Don't tell me you're trying to raise the dead."

"I am trying *not* to," Val retorted. "But the sole banishing spell I've found requires powdered dragon's blood. Why aren't you wearing your pendant?"

An odd moment, surely, to recall that a phallus made of amber was considered the ultimate protection against the evil eye? Emily raised her fingers to the modest neckline of her muslin gown. "You said the pendant would warn me if I was in the presence of evil intent. It didn't react to Cezar Korzha. Perhaps it has lost its power."

"The pendant *will* warn you, by growing dark." Val leaned back in his chair. "Has it occurred to you that Cezar might not wish you harm?"

"It occurs to me that you may have good reason to want me to think so. How many of your kind *are* there in Edinburgh? Beside yourself and Cezar Korzha and, I assume, Andrei Torok?"

Val rubbed his temples. "Tell me you didn't accuse Cezar of being *vampir.*"

"I didn't. Not exactly." Emily contemplated *Egyptian Secrets, White and Black Art for Man and Beast.* "Mr. Korzha said I was either very bold or very foolish. He seems to think I may be running some sort of rig with that dratted athame."

"You astonish me," Val murmured. "What else?"

Ravensclaw didn't look astonished. Appalled might be a better word. "I believe I told him that he had windmills in his head. Don't look at me like that! He told *me* that you're a predator and I'm likely your next meal."

Val pushed the books aside. "I would never harm you, Emily."

She moved closer to the desk. "I don't mind if you do. Or just a little bit. Unless— Is Lisbet Boroi your mistress?"

"The less you have to do with Lisbet the better for us all." Val reached out and stroked Machka's furry belly. The cat curled herself around his hand.

Emily slapped her own hand down on the table. "Answer the question, Ravensclaw."

He shifted in his chair, moving slightly away from her. "Let's just say your life would be more pleasant if Lisbet didn't take you in dislike."

"Why? I already dislike *her.* Lady Alberta says I should agree to marry Michael. Just for a little while. Not marry him for a little while, but pretend that I will."

Ravensclaw frowned. "Is that wise?"

"Probably not. Once Michael has control of the Society within his grasp he'll not willingly let it go. On the other hand, he's hardly confiding in me now."

"Perhaps you might adapt a more conciliatory attitude."

"Perhaps you might show me how. I'll pretend to be Michael, you pretend to be me. 'Blast it, Emily, don't go off on one of your queer starts now. Be reasonable. You must marry me. It's what your father wanted. I will take your name.'"

"'Blast it'? Truly? I'm surprised you didn't box his ears. Very well, try this." Fluttering his lashes, Val clasped his hands to his chest. "You do me great honor, sir. I am flattered that you hold me in such esteem. Pray forgive me if I do not give you my answer right away. We helpless females require some time to focus our vapid little minds."

Emily bit her lip to keep from laughing. "But your eyelashes are longer than mine. And he *doesn't* hold me in esteem. Ah. I'm presumed to be such a nitwit that I think he does."

"Precisely. Go on."

Emily paced the room, trying to remember what other idiocies Michael had uttered. "'I had sought to give you sufficient time to recover from your loss, but since you have followed me to Edinburgh'—that's not what he said exactly, but what he meant— 'Marry me, dammit, and I'll help you get back your blasted knife.' And then he lost his temper because Machka had sharpened her claws on his nice beaver hat."

Val smiled. "I see your problem, little one."

Was there ever a smile so devilish, so bewitching, so wickedly seductive as Ravensclaw's? Emily pushed aside the tea tray and perched on the edge of his desk. "Last night, he said he wished to strangle me. For some reason, he is very anxious that I leave Edinburgh."

Val studied her face for a moment, then clasped her ankle, pulled off her sandal and propped her heel on his strong thigh. Sensation flooded her. He pressed his thumb into the arch of her foot.

Emily closed her eyes. Val's touch was heaven. "Cezar Korzha doesn't trust me. Do you?"

Val worked his thumb in a circular motion all the way from her heel to the base of her toes. "Trust you?"

Emily changed her mind. Heaven could not feel so good as this. "Mean me harm."

He caught her largest toe and tugged it. "What are you talking about, Emily?"

She opened her eyes. "I had the strangest dream. You were doing all sorts of interesting things to me. And then I had the athame and you were in my power."

That certainly had caught his attention. Val was frowning as he took Emily's ankle in his hand. "Did you like it? Me being in your power?"

If he had shared her dream, he already knew the answer. Emily curled her toes. "I expect I might have liked it, but I woke up too soon. I think I would very much like to do to you the things you did to me in my dream."

His gaze darkened. "I didn't send you that dream."

"Fustian. I've been dreaming every night since I first met you." An odd expression crossed his face. "Are you brooding? I don't think I've seen you brood before."

Val smoothed his hand over her calf. "Before I met you, I didn't have anything to brood about."

Her skin quivered where he touched it. Emily experienced a shocking impulse to yank her skirt further up, and her stockings down. "I thought it was in the nature of your sort to brood."

"What sort is that?"

"Vampire. *Kudlak. Striga.*"

He kneaded her calf with his strong fingers. "Why should my sort brood?"

"Why shouldn't they?" Emily picked up the leather portfolio and began to fan herself. "A nonmortal by his very nature outlives his family and friends. He must deal with the pain of loss over and over again, all the while foreseeing an endless future of lost loves."

"Not so lost as one might wish," Val murmured, as he released her and leaned back in his chair. "You paint a grim picture, little one."

"Oh, that's but the beginning." Since he appeared to be done with her right foot, Emily presented him with the left. "Your self-healing abilities can become a curse, for your body is capable of withstanding torture far longer than your mind. You could be eternally trapped inside a prison that wouldn't let you escape into death. Then there is the fact that if you are deprived of, um, sustenance for a prolonged period, you will rapidly revert to your true age."

Val pulled off her other slipper. "A pretty thought indeed."

Emily exhaled blissfully as his hand cupped her foot. "There you have it. Vampire angst. Were you to discover how to animate a corpse, we could ask Papa what happened that day in the laboratory, and who took the athame." Which might not be such a good idea, because once her mysteries were solved, Emily would have no more reason to stay in Edinburgh, and she wasn't ready to leave. Not the city, but Ravensclaw. Hardly appropriate behavior for the overseer of the Dinwiddie Society, but there it was. Mercy, Ravensclaw knew his way around a lady's foot. Doubtless Ravensclaw knew his way around a lady's everything.

Val interrupted her reflections. "You still haven't told me why you aren't wearing the pendant."

Because she didn't care to be protected, specifically from him. "I'm not wearing any charms at all. Surely I don't need them in your house. Unless *you* mean me harm?"

Exasperation tinged his voice. "I don't, but others might. You're not immortal, Emily. Even I am not immortal, as you so recently pointed out."

She didn't care to think of that. "You already died. What was it like?"

Val grimaced. "Painful. I'll spare you the details. I assume you interrupted my studies for a reason. What did you want?"

To rib her hands and lips and body against his body, as she had done in last night's dream. Unfortunately, Val didn't seem to be in a similar frame of mind.

Emily knew he wanted her. She'd felt his desire. *Why* he wanted her she couldn't imagine, but Emily wasn't one to look a gift horse in the mouth.

Or a gift vampire.

At least, he'd wanted her *then*. In this particular moment, Ravensclaw gave no indication of being in the throes of lust.

Appearances could be deceiving. This foot rubbing was pleasant, but it did not satisfy her. Emily slipped off her spectacles and dropped into his lap.

Val went rigid as a statue. *What are you doing, Emily?*

She wriggled into a more comfortable position. *Sitting on your lap.*

So I see. But why?

So I might more easily do this. She reached up and kissed the hollow of his throat. Nuzzled the underside of his jaw. *Because I dreamed of you. Because I am tired of your acting so infernally coy.*

"Not coy, but prudent. One of us must be."

He was holding her away from him. Emily scowled. "I don't see why."

"Permit me to show you." Val's voice had roughened. He cupped her face between his hands. She flattened her hands on his broad chest and stared straight into his eyes.

His emotions swept over her, hungry and dark. Her blood went thick with longing as he gently loosened her braid and ran his fingers through her hair.

"Emily," he murmured. She blinked at him, bemused. Val bent his head and took her mouth in a kiss so deep, so carnal, that she forgot to breathe. The feel, the scent, the taste of him burst over her senses. Chin to cheek to brow. He paused to explore her earlobe with his tongue.

Her skin felt hot. Her heart thudded wildly in her chest.

He set her away from him. Emily touched her tingling lips. That kiss had been even better than her dreams. Now if he would just get on with whatever happened next.

He didn't *look* like he intended to get on with anything. Emily retrieved her spectacles, the better to study his face. Perhaps Val had not shared the intensity of her experience. Hadn't felt the earth move, seen showers of shooting stars.

She thrummed with excitement. Anticipation. Impatience. *"Well?"*

"Well?"

"You said you'd let me *do* things."

"I have. I let you have your first kiss."

Emily glowered. "What makes you so sure it was my first?"

Val quirked an amused eyebrow.

Odious annoying vampire! Emily kicked him in the shin.

Chapter Eighteen

Three may keep council if two be away.

The Twitcher was confused. He didn't know what his companions were havering about, nor why they were both so sunk in gloom. Here the three of them sat, in their favorite oyster cellar, which had stone floors and tallow candles and wooden tables placed in front of a warm fire. If the air was far from fresh, it hardly signified, because here a lad could get minced collops, rizared haddock or tripe, a roasted skate and onion, and wash it down with pints of beer.

Oxter and Mowdiewarp—so called because one resembled a mole and the other smelled like an armpit—were regarding each other gloomily. Oxter muttered, "'Tis a fashious lass."

Mowdiewarp looked fair to weep into his beer. "Aye."

Oxter poked his haddock with a fork. "An' she has a wulf."

Mowdiewarp picked up his mug. "Aye."

"An' t' other un."

Mowdiewarp took a great gulp of his beer.

Mention of a wolf gave Twitcher goosebumps. "What wulf?" he inquired.

"*Thon* wulf, ye pure mad dafty!" Oxter snarled. Ever the peacemaker, Mowdiewarp added, "The wulf what wis wi' t' fashious lass." Her that was responsible for Oxter's sore foot, and Mowdiewarp's bruised shin, and the fact that one had been flung onto a rooftop and the other into a wall.

Twitcher studied his own pint doubtfully. Maybe he'd drunk more than he thought.

And maybe his companions were having one over on him. It wouldn't be the first time. He squinted at Oxter. "An' then yer arse fell aff."

"Get off *yer* arse, ye auld weegie bampit!" Impatiently, Oxter reminded Twitcher of the bit of bother they'd encountered while trying to carry out a simple chore, to wit snatching up a certain bit of merchandise and delivering it as arranged, and if one of them wasn't such a gamaleerie, the plan wouldna hae gone agley.

"It wisnae me. I dinna!" Twitcher protested. "I wis in t' tavern, drunk as David's sow."

Mowdiewarp wrinkled his brow. "Who wis David, then?" Twitcher had to confess that he didn't know.

Oxter thumped his fist upon the table. "Ye're goin' doolally. Mayhap it'll all come back if I gie ye a chaup on the heid."

Maybe someone had given Oxter a chaup, causing him to spin tall tales. Twitcher turned to Mowdiewarp, who shook his head. "I wisnae in the tavern, then?"

Mowdiewarp looked as sympathetic as was possible for a man who resembled a mole. "Nay. Ye had the lass tossed o'er yon shoulder like a potato sack." He swallowed. "An' then—"

He'd had a lass tossed over his shoulder? Twitcher was black affronted. True, not many lasses cast their eyes in his direction, but if one had done so, he hoped he would have better manners than to treat her like a sack of potatoes. "I ne'er!" he said.

Oxter grimaced. "He's aff 'is heid."

"I'm no'!"

Mowdiewarp patted Twitcher's arm. "Ye *are* looking a bit peely-wally, son. Let's call each other no more names. Like it or no', we've a bit o' work to do."

Twitcher might be a little slow of understanding, but he wasn't altogether a numptie. He squinted at Mowdiewarp. "The lass?"

"The lass wi' the wulf," explained Oxter. "An' the bogey."

Twitcher was getting a headache. It had something to do with livers being cut out and intestines wrapped around necks. "Hing aff us. There's nae sich thing."

"Hah!" retorted Oxter, and reached for his pint.

"Saw it mesel'," interrupted Mowdiewarp, in an attempt to prevent hostilities from deteriorating into a right rowdy-do. "'Twas tall as a building—had to be, did it no', t'throw me atop one? Eyes as red as fire. And thon teeth—" He shuddered.

Twitcher shuddered also, at a faint memory of sharp fangs. "Wha' aboot t' lass w' her wulf and her bogey? No' that I believe a word o' it!"

"Believe it." Oxter gestured for another pint. "We're to snatch 'er up agin. An' if we fail this time—" He made a slashing gesture across his throat. "Tha'll be the lot o' us. Unco' deid."

Silence fell, if not in the oyster cellar, where some of the diners had taken it in their heads to attempt to dance, then at the table that was graced by the three associates in crime, at least one of whom was in favor of abandoning the noble ideals that had thus far prevented him from stooping so low as to rob a cemetery or transport body parts. Scruples were all well and good until one was confronted with building-tall bogeys with wicked sharp teeth.

Mowdiewarp ordered yet another pint. Twitcher muttered, "It'll be the worse for ye," for reasons he couldn't have explained. Several pints, and more argie-bargies later, the trio was encouraged to depart the premises. They stumbled out into the street. Twitcher muttered, "Drunk as David's sow."

"Am no'!" protested Oxter, who was. "A wee bit blootered, perchance."

"Och, ye're right buckled!" said Mowdiewarp, whose own legs weren't functioning exactly as they should. Now that he thought on it, he couldn't feel his knees. Twitcher, meanwhile, began to sing:

As I went by the Luckenbooths
I saw a lady fair.
She had long pendles in her ears
And jewels in her hair.

"Shoosh!" Mowdiewarp might not be able to feel his knees, but he knew better than to be singing about ghaisties in the haunted streets of Edinburgh. Or bogeys. Or wulves. Twitcher subsided into sulks.

The night was dark and cold and damp, not fit for man nor beast nor ghaistie. Twitcher might have asked where they were going, were he not so capernoited, and were not Oxter such a carnaptious old de'il. Still, he was uneasy, and finally whispered that very question in Mowdiewarp's ear.

Mowdiewarp shook his head. "I dinna ken." Oxter turned and glared and hissed that nobody with a grain of sense would choose such a moment to be bumping their gums.

"Sich a moment as wha'?" asked Twitcher. Oxter scowled. Before he could start to scold again, there came the sound of a kerfuffle up ahead.

The noises grew louder as they drew closer. Unpleasant noises, thumps and gurgles. They looked at one another, then inched forward to peer around the corner of an ancient building, one above the other, like a tipsy totem pole.

The lane ended in a cul-de-sac, illuminated by a strange red glow that emanated from a bloody knife held in the hand of a figure cloaked in black. Impossible to see his face in the shadows of his hood. Impossible not to see what he was doing. Another swish, a thud—

"Bogey," said Twitcher, with considerable assurance.

The hooded figure turned toward the watchers.

As one, they fled.

Chapter Nineteen

Dogs bark but the caravan goes on.

Val made his way along the broken cobbles of Mary King's Close, past the ancient shops and tavern to a certain doorway, inserted his key in the lock. Red eyes glowed at him from a dark corner. He thought the rat a nice touch.

No candles burned in the ancient sconces, not that Val's keen eyes had need of their light. The chamber was as he had last seen it, save that the anatomist's table, and its unfortunate occupant, no longer stood in the middle of the floor. Val avoided a dangling manacle, walked up to the skeleton built in the stone wall, and twisted a femur. A section of the wall swung open. Val stepped into a room as different from the one he'd left as chalk was from cheese. Behind him, the wall swung shut.

Here was no filth, no cobwebs, no crimson-eyed rodent. The large chamber was lit with oil lamps and furnished in a Spartan style. An ancient oval shield ornamented with a floral device hung on one wall, beside a few pieces of ornamented pottery and a wooden Byzantine cross. Simple benches were placed about the room, and plain long-backed chairs. The room had been designed for meeting, not for lounging. Members of the Brotherhood were, for the most part, indolent and fond of luxury. Made comfortable enough, they would never leave.

A pathway had been cleared down the center of the chamber. At its termination, Cezar stood poised with a long stick and a small leather ball. At the bottom of the stick was fastened a piece of wood, flat on one side. The aim of the undertaking, Val had been informed, consisted of propelling the tiny ball through innumerable obstacles to eventually drop it, hopefully with a smaller number of strokes than one's adversary, into a tiny hole in the ground.

Cezar claimed to like the game. Val didn't understand why. From what he could see, Cezar was no better at it than anybody else, despite his superior coordination and strength, and the fact that he'd been a member of the Honourable Company of Edinburgh Golfers (though they didn't realize it) since their inception in 1744.

Cezar positioned himself, his feet spread at shoulder width, his knees relaxed, bending slightly from the top of his hips. He narrowed his eyes at the target, then gently stroked the ball, which rolled into a little tin cup. "You've been practicing," Val observed.

Cezar replaced his putting cleek in a bag with other clubs: longnoses, grassed drivers, spoons, and niblets, their shafts fashioned of ash and hazel, the heads from tough wood or hand-forged iron. He bent and picked up the little ball, which was made from tightly compressed feathers stitched into a horsehide sphere. Due to Cezar's enthusiasm, Val knew a great deal more about the game of gowf, or golf, than he had ever wanted, including the fact that King Charles I had been on the course at Leith when given news of the Irish rebellion in 1642.

Cezar dropped the ball into his golf bag. "Lisbet doesn't come here, so I do. She's not the easiest of houseguests. Andrei is entertaining her today."

Val picked up one of the clubs and swung it. "I sympathize, having houseguests of my own. One of whom you informed that she was to be my next meal."

Cezar looked contemplative. "I don't think I said that, precisely. Your Miss Dinwiddie is astute."

Val dropped the club back into the bag. "If you meant to frighten her, you didn't succeed. Now she would like to know what it's like to be bitten by one of us. And she doesn't mind if it hurts a little bit."

"No maiden's gift will make you mortal, *camarad.*" Cezar moved the golf bag out of Val's reach.

"Next you'll tell me witches don't turn their husbands into horses after sunset and ride them at night." Val eyed a Hucul *tshaken,* a beautifully carved stick with an axe-shaped handle, once handed by a bridegroom to his betrothed's brother on her wedding day; and wondered why Cezar had kept the thing.

Cezar added, "You know her lifetime will pass by you in the blinking of an eye."

Val did know that, all too well. He remembered Ana sitting at her spinning wheel, her hair hanging down her back in plaits woven with strands of brightly colored wool. Ana stirring the cooking pot. She'd been a terrible cook, but he hadn't cared. Ana wearing nothing but her striped stockings and sandals with turned up toes.

How much time had passed since he'd last remembered Ana? Val felt very old. "No answer is also an answer," Cezar pointed out.

"Miss Dinwiddie informs me that our kind fall prey to angst because we outlive everyone we care about. Not, of course, that we are exactly alive." And not that the past was altogether behind them, though Val wouldn't acquaint Cezar with this news just yet.

Cezar watched him move around the chamber. "Did you explain that 'our kind' care about little but ourselves?"

"I had no wish to disillusion her."

"Disillusionment is one thing. Do you trust her, Val?"

Did he trust Emily? Not entirely. Did it matter? No. "You are determined to see Miss Dinwiddie as a villainess no matter how many times I tell you she is no such thing. I'd know if she was."

"Since I am your friend, I won't remind you that you also claimed you knew Iso—"

"No names," Val interrupted, having recently discovered the folly of bringing the not-so-dearly departed into the conversation.

Cezar looked mildly curious. "Does *this* Miss Dinwiddie know the history of the athame?"

"The Dinwiddie Society knows all sorts of things."

"Including what you are. Because of she-whom-we-won't-name."

Rather, she-whom-Cezar-wouldn't-let-him-forget. "I have it on good authority that you have windmills in your head."

"Did Miss Dinwiddie tell you also that she quoted Shakespeare at me?" Cezar's violet eyes were cold. "You realize that if you don't deal with her, I must."

Val tensed. "Even think of 'dealing' with her and I'll forget you are my Stăpân."

Cezar's gaze grew icier still. "You would defy me for this girl? Remember you are *vampir*, Val."

Whatever he was, Val had given Emily her first kiss, and felt as if he had received his own. Which, combined with the reappearance of Ana—which he sincerely hoped had been a nasty dream and very much feared was not—gave him much to think about.

A pity the golf clubs were out of reach. Val would have derived considerable satisfaction from breaking one of them.

"I have put it about that Miss Dinwiddie is almost as rich as Croesus," he said. "Every bachelor in Edinburgh will soon be vying for her hand." It had given him no little pleasure to interfere with Michael Ross's carefully laid plans. "As for her motivations, why should either of us care what they might be?"

Cezar raised one hand to touch the ancient oval shield. "I dislike repeating myself. However, if Miss Dinwiddie has the d'Auvergne athame in her possession, she could do you irreparable harm. And if she *doesn't* have it, have you thought what harm you may be doing her while you entertain yourself?"

Val was silent. Much as he disliked Cezar's accusation, he had to admit its truth. He had already influenced Emily more than was wise.

Cezar put on a pair of dark glasses similar to Val's own. "Come. There's something I would have you see." They exited the chamber through a portal supposedly known only to the two of them and Andrei, and made their way out into the streets.

Edinburgh's Royal Mile had a long and varied history. The main thoroughfare of the medieval city, it had witnessed a steady parade of thieves and street entertainers, beggars and soldiers and merchants, regal processions and street fairs. The nobility had made their homes here, close by the law courts.

Today was market day. Stalls lined the whole length of the High Street. All manner of iron and copper wares were offered for sale, woolen stuffs and hardware, leather goods and children's toys. They strolled by grocers and shoemakers and milliners. Val paused by a shop and, with a smile and a wink, relieved the baker's lass of a beef pie.

Cezar regarded the pie with revulsion. "I don't understand why you eat that offal when you don't need sustenance."

Minced beef, suet, and a sprinkling of finely chopped onion wrapped in pastry, brushed with milk and cooked until golden brown— "I don't understand what pleasure *you* get from playing golf. You enjoy that; I enjoy this. It is much the same thing."

Cezar was unconvinced that a beef pastry could compare with golf. Val insisted that the pastry easily won. This disagreement occupied them until they arrived at their destination, a dwelling in Fames Court: the home of Ian Cameron, an anatomist said to be one of the finest surgeons in Europe, who could amputate a leg in twenty-eight seconds, and on one occasion had amputated two of his assistant's fingers and the patient's left testicle as well.

Cezar led the way around the side of the building. "In public Ian denounces the resurrectionists. In private he encourages them not only to unearth his own patients to see how his handiwork has held up, but also to retrieve any of his colleagues' clients who had interesting anatomical peculiarities." He unlocked a basement entrance. "The good doctor found himself compelled to be elsewhere or he would be pleased to show us around."

"I assume he owes you a favor." In company with at least half the city's more influential inhabitants.

"He does. Come."

Val followed. He held no high opinion of anatomists. Ian Cameron was no different from other members of his profession, back to and including Herophilus, the so-called father of anatomy, the first physician to dissect human bodies, whose enthusiasm had led him to cut up live criminals, six hundred by one account, which gave some credence to Hippocratus's theory that the human brain was a mucous-secreting gland.

This private dissecting room was not so gruesome as others Val had seen. No skulls bobbed in a boiling pot, no fragments of limbs crunched underfoot, although a nice selection of body parts was preserved in buckets of brine.

Cezar gestured toward the corpse laid out on a dissecting table. "Do you notice anything strange?"

Val pulled off his dark lenses and stepped closer. The body was male, middle-aged, shabbily dressed. "Other than that it has no head?"

Cezar pointed. Val looked closer. "A *nefinistat.*"

The *nefinistat,* the unfinished, were those who failed to make a successful conversion to *vampir* and were impaired. The more violent among them were discreetly disposed of, the others allowed to exist unmolested so long as they didn't draw attention to themselves.

They did not tend to live long. Most drank animal blood, because they couldn't bear to feed off humans, but animal blood lacked sufficient life force to enable them to remain entirely sane.

Cezar approached the corpse. "This one was found in Greyfriars Kirkyard, laid out with his arms folded on his chest as neat and tidy as can be. As if he was in his coffin, except for the missing head. Do you notice anything else?"

Val looked at the marks left by a several-bladed scarifactor applied by a none-too-skilled hand. "Why would someone drain his blood?"

"To drink it, what else?"

"What sort of fool would drink the blood of a *nefinistat?*"

"A desperate one," said Cezar. "Or someone so ignorant as to hope that by drinking a vampire's blood he would gain vampiric powers." He met Val's gaze. "Or, perhaps, someone who wishes it to seem I can't manage matters in Edinburgh."

"You think this has to do with the athame?"

Cezar shrugged. "Whoever did this was interrupted. The body hasn't been staked. I will dispose of it, of course."

"Of course." The Brotherhood dealt with their own, unfinished or whole. If they did not, they were like to find themselves facing an inquisition by the High Council, the Consiliu.

Politics, damnable politics. Apprehension stole over Val. And with it, resignation. Emily and her bloody angst.

As he thought of her, an image formed in his mind. "Damnation!"

Cezar frowned. "What now?"

Val was already halfway toward the doorway. "Emily has left the house. Alone."

"You remain convinced of her innocence?"

Val hesitated. Emily wasn't so innocent as she once had been, before he started meddling with her dreams. That hadn't been well done of him. But it *had* been most enjoyable. And he'd probably do it again unless he managed to put her safely out of reach. Which led him back to that last strange dream, when Emily had turned into Isobella, and held the athame over his head.

Val shook away his untimely thoughts. "Innocent. Yes."

Cezar studied him. "You're the one who brought her to Edinburgh, and you're the one who lost the athame to her ancestor. If you are mistaken in her, the price will be heavy, Val."

"I'll stake my existence on it." Val glanced at the *nefinistat*. The price was already high.

Cezar inclined his head. "Done. Now go. I will deal with this."

Chapter Twenty

Who spits against the wind, it falls in his face.

Although it had been her intention, Emily was hardly unescorted. She scowled at Drogo. "You shouldn't be wandering the streets. People don't like wolves, in case you didn't know." He sat in front of her, tongue lolling, looking as innocent as it was possible for a wolf to be.

Emily sighed. "I'm stuck with you, aren't I?" In truth—not, of course, that she was frightened—Emily was grateful for the company. If wearing a wolf's tooth protected her from evil, she must surely be triply blessed by the presence of the entire beast.

Emily wasn't deaf to all the warnings she'd been given about venturing out in the Old Town without adequate protection. However, an adequate protector would have gravely interfered with what she had set out to do. Which, first of all, involved finding out the truth of Michael's mysteriously disappearing and reappearing vrajă. She hefted her umbrella. "Very well, then. *En avant!*"

The Lawnmarket was cramped and crowded with a confusion of vendors and shoppers and market stalls. Well-dressed citizens bustled about their business in the midst of squalor and poverty. Tall, gloomy houses towered high overhead, many with pillared piazzas on the ground floor, under which were open booths where merchants displayed their wares. Edinburgh Castle constantly appeared and reappeared above the gabled roofs.

Beyond High Street and the Lawnmarket— Emily glanced at the slip of paper in her hand. Through that archway, into a dark alleyway— Drogo whined.

"You're the one that wished to come with me!" snapped Emily, who was feeling none too confident herself. The noise of the street was deadened here by the buildings rising on all sides. Unfriendly-looking buildings, but Emily wouldn't permit herself to turn craven now. Umbrella at the ready, she followed the passage between the houses until she arrived in a courtyard. One more glance at her directions, then she descended a short flight of stone steps, knocked briskly on the left-hand door.

There was no response. She twisted the knob. The door swung open. Emily stepped inside.

It took a moment for her eyes to become accustomed to the gloom and clutter. Books and bottles and a jumble of merchandise spilled out of countless cabinets and shelves. Emily touched her pendant. Drogo bristled and growled. A harsh squawk made them both jump. Emily stared up at the raven on its perch. "Pretty bird," she said.

A white-haired man bustled out of a back room and murmured soothingly to the bird, referring to it as 'Styx'.

A raven named after the chief river of the underworld? She had come to the right place. To make doubly certain, Emily said, "Mr. Abercrombie?"

He nodded and bobbed and came closer, revealing himself to be of stout middle age, little taller than Emily, with an unnerving wandering eye. His smile faded when his gaze fell on Drogo. "That's a wolf. We don't allow wolves on the premises." Drogo padded toward him, baring his teeth.

Mr. Abercrombie fell back a step. "In this case, perhaps an exception can be made! What can I do for you, miss? Angelica and rosemary for a domination spell? Caraway seed to discourage your poultry from straying? Sage for cleansing, myrrh or sandalwood?"

Emily thought of Val and his arcane studies. "Have you any dragon's blood?"

Alas, Mr. Abercrombie did not. Perhaps he might interest the young lady in Thor's nettles or Job's tears instead. A Love Drawing Oil made with sweet almonds and an infusion of fresh basil leaves. A recipe for Raven's Feather Ink.

The raven muttered into its wing.

Emily shook her head, briefly distracted by the notion of a lust-spell. "I might be of more assistance," said Mr. Abercrombie, "if I knew what it is you need."

Emily drew the vrajă from her reticule. "Do you carry items like this?"

Mr. Abercrombie did. He would have happily showed Emily his entire stock had she not interrupted him mid-speech. "I don't wish to purchase such a talisman. I *do* wish to know who has recently bought one."

Mr. Abercrombie shook his head. "I can't tell you that. All transactions are private. I must protect the interests of my clients. Confidentiality is my stock in trade."

Judging from the dust and cobwebs all around, Mr. Abercrombie's clients were few. "I am prepared to reimburse you handsomely for any services you might provide me, sir."

Mr. Abercrombie's gaze moved from the reticule Emily was dangling in front of him to Drogo's sharp teeth. "I suppose I might make an exception this once."

"The transaction would have taken place during the past few days. A man of perhaps nine-and-twenty. Dark-haired. Pale. Well dressed. Michael Ross by name."

"Hsst!" Mr. Abercrombie held up a chubby hand. "No names. What a body doesn't know can't hurt him, I always say." He also said that a gentleman of that description had indeed recently purchased a vrajă, in addition to some yarrow, mastic pearls, and bloodstone.

Emily's spirits plummeted, foolishly, because the shopkeeper had only confirmed her suspicions. She opened her reticule. Mr. Abercrombie's face lit up at the sight of her assorted charms. He especially admired the tiger's eye and the seal of St. Benedict. The young lady was well-protected. His eyes moved to the pendant. Well-protected, indeed. Perhaps she might be interested in a spot of trade.

And perhaps the shopkeeper thought he might snatch the ruby off her neck. Emily raised her umbrella. Drogo growled. The raven croaked.

Mr. Abercrombie dropped his hand. "No offense intended, miss."

"None taken." Emily placed a gold coin on the counter. "Should the gentleman return, you won't tell him I was here."

"Mum as an oyster, miss." The shopkeeper radiated sincerity.

Came those flying pigs again. Given sufficient monetary motivation, Mr. Abercrombie's oysters would flap tongues hinged on both ends. Emily hoped Michael wouldn't soon return to the shop. And what did Ravensclaw mean to do with dragon's blood, which despite its intriguing name, was nothing but an herb? Emily climbed the steps back up to the street. She was thinking of the odd theory that sleeping with a wolf's head under one's pillow protected against nightmares when she bumped up against a solid and very aromatic bulk.

"Och, now we have ye!" said the bulk, and grabbed her by the arms.

He was overly optimistic. Emily kicked him in the knee; then as he bent over, brought her umbrella down smartly on his head. Drogo leapt out from behind her to sink sharp teeth into the most convenient chunk of flesh.

"Ow! Ow! Ow!" wailed Oxter. "Get 'im aff me arse!" The shopkeeper stuck his head out the door to see what the commotion was about and as quickly retreated, a convenient deafness also being required of a person in his line of work.

Emily pulled her little pistol from her pocket. "Well met, gentlemen. I had hoped to speak with the three of you. Drogo, release your captive and make sure none of them escape." Flight was clearly on the mind of at least the twitching man, who was pale as a ghost. "Let us introduce ourselves. As you may or may not know, I am Emily Dinwiddie." She gestured with the pistol. "And you are—?"

"Oxter," groaned Oxter.

"Mowdiewarp."

"Dinna— Cannae—" muttered the third.

Oxter gave him a clout on the head. "Tha's Twitcher. 'E's a dunderhead."

"Nae need t' be fashious, lass," soothed Mowdiewarp. "We meant ye nae harm."

"Nay." Oxter clutched his bleeding rump and nodded. "We dinna, but somebody else might."

"Awa', ye glaibit bastid!" snapped Mowdiewarp, whose peacemaking tendencies went only so far. " 'Tis but a misunderstanding. We've 'ad a wee drappie. I widna wonder if we was no' richt smeekit. No hard feelings. We'll just be on our way."

"No, you won't." Emily aimed the pistol at Oxter. "Not without telling me why the three of you are making a habit of accosting me."

Twitcher moaned. "It wis no' me, I dinna."

Oxter smacked him again. "The de'il will get ye for tellin' lies."

"Tha's enow clishmaclaver!" Mowdiewarp interrupted sternly, one eye fixed on Drogo, and the other on Emily's gun. "Twitcher's in a richt pelter, lass. Not t' mention he's a windae-licker. Pay nae mind t' anything he says. Noo aboot this wee stooshie—"

Twitcher might be embarrassed at having tossed the lass over his shoulder like a sack of potatoes, and also terrified by the vague notion that it would go the worse for him if he lay a hand on her; but there was a limit to the abuse a lad could take. "Wha ye callin' a windae-licker, ye eejit?" he demanded, and popped Mowdiewarp in the nose. Caught off guard, Mowdiewarp fell on his own arse, blood streaming down his face.

"Haud on, ye sumph!" snarled Oxter, and grabbed Twitcher by the arm. Twitcher took offense at being grabbed. Mowdiewarp climbed to his feet. A proper stremach ensued. Emily and Drogo watched. Emily concluded that Jamie's bajins were fools.

Fools with a mission. She raised her voice. "Stop that at once or I will shoot one of you!"

Twitcher pointed at Oxter. Before he could voice the suggestion that danced on the tip of his tongue, a tall figure appeared at the end of the close. Tall as a building, eyes as red as fire. A reluctant closer inspection, and Twitcher conceded that the eyes weren't red as fire. Yet.

The face was unnervingly familiar. Twitcher had a terrifying memory of being held far above the ground. Threats involving livers and intestines. Monstrous sharp teeth. "Ah dinna ken ocht aboot it," he moaned, and sank into a swoon.

Emily was more interested in the newcomer than in her accostors, the other two of whom were cowering in the shadows of a building. She glowered at Drogo. "Traitor," she said.

Val clamped a strong hand on her shoulder, and squeezed. Emily dropped both pistol and umbrella. "I told you to pretend to be a nitwit, not to act like one," he snapped.

There was some justification for his comment. Not that Emily would admit it. She jerked her chin at the pendant. "I wasn't in any real danger. Look, it hasn't turned dark."

Twitcher stirred. Drogo, who was sitting guard, licked his face. Twitcher opened one eye, moaned, and scuttled off to join his comrades by the wall.

All three were babbling at once. Emily snapped, "Now see what you've done!"

"What I've done is nothing like what I'd like to do to you." Ungently, Val tucked her under his arm.

A second figure appeared at the opening of the close. In the blink of an eye he was beside them. Oxter goggled and gasped as Cezar grasped him by the throat. "Wrens making prey, Miss Dinwiddie? Shall I pinch off this one's head?"

"Um." Emily was distracted. Val's body was solid against hers. Almost as solid as when she'd sat on his lap and nuzzled his neck.

When he'd given her her first real kiss. For good measure, she kicked him again. "Why is it males must meddle? I wished to find out who sent these men after me. Clearly someone sent them because they haven't a brain to share among all three! There was no need for you to interfere."

Val released her to rub his shin. "How inconsiderate of us. And just when things were going so well."

Cezar surveyed the gibbering Oxter. "You believed they would confide in you?"

Emily bent to pick up her umbrella and her pistol. "Don't bother pointing out that I can only shoot one of them."

"Oxter!" suggested Mowdiewarp. Twitcher agreed. Oxter struggled all the harder in Cezar's grasp.

Cezar tightened his fingers until the man's eyes bulged. "Perhaps you will allow us to assist you."

"*You* assist her," Val said coolly. "I'm still sulking. She called me a meddling male."

Emily glared at him. "You're enjoying this far too much."

"On the contrary, Miss Dinwiddie." Ravensclaw's smile was feral. "I'm not enjoying this at all."

He was truly angry with her. Emily felt like she'd been frozen by a blast of frigid arctic air. "Then go to the devil! I didn't invite you here." She turned to Cezar. "Yes, assist me, please."

Cezar loosened his grip so that Oxter could gulp in breath, then fixed the man with his stern gaze. Oxter's face went slack. His eyes rolled back in his head. After a moment passed, Cezar released him. Twitcher moaned as Oxter flopped to the ground.

Emily surveyed the fallen man. "Will he be all right?"

"No, but he'll be no worse than we found him," Cesar told her. "This one knows nothing, not even how his instructions were received. He experienced them as a compulsion in his mind."

Val looked at the other men. "They know even less."

"Don't hurt them," Emily said quickly. "As you say, they're merely dupes, and they did me no real harm." She turned to Cezar. "Perhaps a strong suggestion that they find another line of work?"

"It's hardly that simple. Their employer won't be pleased when he learns his plans were foiled." Oxter had wakened, and Cezar contemplated the quivering trio. "I suggest we implant some suggestions of our own."

"Such as that this never happened?" Val frowned at Twitcher. "I already tried that."

Twitcher clasped the top of his head. "Ye'll no' chop it off!"

Emily pushed up her spectacles. "No one's going to chop off your head. Why would you think that?"

"Bogeys!" wailed Twitcher, and buried his face in Mowdiewarp's coat.

Mowdiewarp patted him. " 'Twas no' these lads. Look ye, Twitcher, they're tae tall." His eyes narrowed. "Lest they can shrink themselves. Than bogey wis shorter, smaller. We couldnae see his face, bein' as he wis wrapt in a dark cloak. An he glowed. Something in his hand."

"The d'Auvergne athame," murmured Emily. Val and Cezar exchanged a glance. She opened her mouth, but Val turned his frown on her, and she closed it with a snap. Clearly he was in no mood to tuck her up against him again. A pity. She was feeling unaccountably cold.

Cezar made further inquiries. The trio knew only that they had interrupted what they called a bogey at his work not far from that spot. Cezar sent them on their way with the understanding that they had neither seen Emily nor had this encounter, that they weren't going to see Emily again even if they fell smack on top of her. The three of them shambled down the street.

Cezar turned to Emily. "Perhaps you will explain how is that *you* can close your mind to us, Miss Dinwiddie."

Emily was feeling ill-used. "Perhaps I won't."

Two pairs of cold eyes rested on her. Drogo bumped against her knee. "Oh, very well! My papa taught me from the cradle how to block my emotions." She glared at Val. "So that no selfish supersensible creature could make me his dupe."

"Enough." Val moved, and somehow the pistol was no longer in her hand, and her arm was in his grasp. Emily tried to jerk away from him. His fingers were like iron. "We are going home now, Miss Dinwiddie. I am going to lock you in the dungeon until I cease to be annoyed."

Emily paused in her struggles to peer up into his face. Val looked as if he might well carry out his threat. "I've never explored a real dungeon," she confessed. "Does yours have a torture chamber? A scavenger's daughter? Thumbscrews?"

Val clamped his teeth together. Cezar murmured, " 'Where eagles dare not perch'. "

Chapter Twenty-One

Better some of a pudding than none of a pie.

Lady Alberta frowned at Val over the top of her teacup. "Tsk!" she said.

Val closed his eyes against the pain of the first headache he'd experienced in decades. "Tsk?"

Lady Alberta selected another piece of shortbread. "It was not well done of you to make Emily cry."

Granted, Val had lost his temper, also for the first time in decades. Granted, he had said things better left unsaid. Even so, surely the most critical of observers must admit he'd had sufficient provocation to test the patience of a saint.

Apparently not. The various members of his household were treating him as if he'd brought home the plague. Zizi, Bela, and Lilian had turned a collective cold shoulder, while Isidore informed him sternly that no garden was without its weeds. Jamie had damn near dumped the tea tray in his lap. All this despite the fact they had all been so caught up in helping—or in the case of Lady Alberta, hindering—Mrs. MacCamish create a hotchpotch that Emily had been able to slip away unnoticed from the house.

Lady Alberta was still glowering. Val bowed to the inevitable. "Where is she?"

"In your study." Lady Alberta pushed the tea tray toward him. "A peace offering might be in order. I know for a certainty Emily has had nothing to eat today."

Val picked up the tray. Clearly, Lady Alberta considered Emily's refusal to take sustenance his responsibility. He supposed he would also be blamed for whatever folly she might next commit.

He couldn't fairly fault her for impatience. She must feel that he'd done little, despite her request for his help. Life—or his existence—had been simple once, before Miss Dinwiddie came knocking at his castle gate. Val climbed the stair and pushed open the study door.

Emily sat at the oak table, the *Orimorium Verum* open in front of her. Sunlight struggling through the ancient windows made a fiery halo of her untidy hair. Machka was curled up by her elbow. Drogo sprawled at her feet.

Even the animals regarded him with disfavor. Val set down the tea tray. "Out," he said. Drogo padded toward the doorway, giving him a wide berth.

"You, too." Val picked up Machka and deposited her in the stairway. Emily rose from her chair. "Not you," he said.

She sat back down. He closed and locked the door. "Lady Alberta suggested you might like some tea." Emily shook her head, her gaze fixed firmly on the grimoire.

He moved toward her. Emily glanced up with a combination of defiance and dread. Val plucked her up out of the chair and sat down, holding her on his lap. She was stiff as several fence posts. He set aside her glasses and pulled her against his chest.

Gradually, she relaxed against him. He waited patiently. At last a gruff little voice muttered, "You don't have a dungeon. You lied to me again."

"I do have a dungeon. It just isn't here." He experienced a sudden urge to take her back to Corby Castle, lock himself with her in the dungeon, and let the rest of the world go and be damned.

Emily's feelings were firmly closed to him. Still, she moved one hand to rest against Val's chest. "I suppose you expect me to apologize."

"For what?"

"You said I was a nitwit. Among other things."

"I said you *acted* like a nitwit. As for those other things—" Val rested his chin on the top of her head. "I was frightened for you."

A pause while Emily mulled over this. "Were you, really?"

"Yes."

Emily hesitated. Val felt her reach out to touch his mind. He lowered his guard and let her in. She was cautious, like a babe taking its first steps, exploring the parameters of this new world. It was both endearing and almost unbearably sensual. Val tamped down his emotions, and let her poke around.

She withdrew, shifted in his lap so that she might see his face. "I shouldn't be able to do that, should I?"

"No." Her soft little bottom was snuggled against him in a most distracting manner. Val stroked one hand along her spine.

She lowered her gaze to his chin. "I have learned from my reading that for each *vampir* there is an *ailaltă*, one destined other, who must be proven worthy by meeting a challenge, a *provocare*. Rather like a knight of old slaying a dragon for his ladylove. Since you and I have a special affinity, I wonder if perhaps I am your *ailaltă*." She blushed.

The idea of Emily slaying dragons for him chilled Val to his toes. "I suspect this 'affinity' you mention is more likely because your ancestress and I— Well."

She stared at him. "You and Iso—"

"Don't say that name! I'm afraid we did. Curiosity seems to run rampant in the female members of your family."

"I suppose it does." Tentatively, Emily reached out and touched his lower lip; ran the tips of her fingers over his cheeks, his jaw, his throat.

Val held very still, and contemplated thwarted lust. If she didn't soon stop stroking him, Miss Dinwiddie would find out for herself if vampires wept tears of blood.

Before he realized what she was about, Emily snatched up his letter opener and slashed her arm. A red ribbon flowed over her freckled skin. "I have come to the conclusion that if one desires something, one shouldn't sit about waiting for it to fall into one's lap. Taste me," she said.

He truly didn't wish to. Rather, he wished to—Val hadn't experienced this ravening a thirst in all his countless years—but he tried very hard to refrain. And then Emily raised her bleeding arm to his lips, and the barriers between them came crashing down.

Val groaned and surrendered to his nature. Emily watched wide-eyed as he licked away the blood, then pressed his mouth against her flesh.

Her pleasure curled through him, her heat. Her heart sped up as his hunger shot through her, shocking and intense.

He bent to kiss her. Emily's mouth was soft beneath his, eager, warm. Val bit gently at her lip. Her neck. His teeth found her pulse—

I am willing. Drink from me.

Those simple words stopped him. Val drew back, appalled at what he'd almost done.

Emily's disappointment washed over him. She looked bereft. Val ran his thumb over her soft lower lip. "You can't want this."

Emily caught his hand. "Don't tell me what I want! I know from my reading that for you to drink the blood of another is the ultimate intimacy. *Dissertation on the Bloodsucking Dead.*"

Val was stunned. She trusted him. He couldn't remember when he had last been given someone's trust.

Not something he'd missed, trust, and the responsibility that accompanied it. Val clamped his teeth together and his sharp fangs nicked his lip. Emily caught the trickling liquid on her fingers and raised them to her mouth.

Val *was* a blood-drinker, albeit a regretful (at least in this moment) one, and it was beyond his power to stop Emily from this highly erotic act. It was barely within his power to stop himself from leaping on her and sinking his fangs into her tender throat. "You don't understand what you're asking," he growled.

"Fustian!" said Emily. "You're being noble again. I wish you wouldn't do that."

Val looked at his blood smeared on her lips. Watched her pink little tongue lick it away. Gazed into her gold-flecked eyes. Lovely eyes without her glasses. She blinked owlishly at him and he felt himself falling into those warm, gold-flecked depths.

Had she indeed ensorcelled him?

He had long ago learned 'twas folly to underestimate a Dinwiddie.

Emily was a Dinwiddie, when all was said and done.

The devil with it. Val touched his fingers to the pulse beating so rapidly, so richly, at the base of her throat. Emily clasped his shoulders, arched her neck. Val leaned closer, and—

A throat cleared: "Ahem!" Emily's eyes jerked open. She gaped at the specter that hovered just above Val's desk. He bit back a curse.

Emily fumbled for her spectacles. "You didn't tell me that this house was haunted. Whyever not?"

She sounded irritated, as if he'd withheld some great treat. "Because it wasn't," Val replied. "Until recently."

Emily peered at the apparition. "Did one of the castle ghosts follow you here? It doesn't look like a Gowkit Gordie or a Kiuttlin' Kate."

Val's headache had returned, threefold. "Meet Ana," he said.

Emily's eyes widened. "Your wife?"

Ana jiggled one faint foot. "Where are your manners, girl? Don't you know it's rude to talk about me as if I weren't here? Not to mention sitting on my husband's lap."

Emily was exactly where he wanted her. Val tightened his grip. She squirmed. He winced.

Emily paid him no attention. She said, to Ana, "You poor thing! Doomed to wander through eternity until your death is avenged."

"Avenged?" Ana attempted, unsuccessfully, to pick up a piece of shortbread. "Oh, I dealt with *that*! Oko was set upon by wild dogs on his way to the *souk*, may he fester in his grave."

Emily looked fascinated. "Then why are you still here?"

"Everyone is trying to get rid of me! Well, you shan't. Not until I've been properly tupped." Ana considered. "And maybe not even then."

"Tupped?"

"You know. Tup. Swive. Dance at the buttock ball. Must I spell it out? A man has a manroot. Like a maid has—"

"Don't say it!" Emily's cheeks were rosy. "I think I understand."

Ana tilted her head. "It appears to me, Valentin, that you've lost your touch. Mayhap vampires don't —"

"I assure you that vampires *do*," he snapped. "Unless uninvited guests take it into their heads to interfere." For which Val should probably be grateful, but frustration had him in its claws.

Emily pushed up her spectacles. "You *are* referring to the amorous congress, ma'am?"

"Call it whatever you like! You're welcome to him, miss whoever-you-are, as soon as he gives me what I want. And until he *does*—" Ana shook a ghostly finger. "There'll be no tupping hereabouts."

Emily turned to Val. *This is why you were in need of dragon's blood.*

It is.

But we can learn so much from her!

"Bloody hell!" sighed Val.

Chapter Twenty-Two

A crow is never whiter for washing herself often.

Emily was eager to have further conversation with her first ghost. She had many questions to ask. For instance, where had Ana been between the time of her demise and her reappearance in Ravensclaw's study? What had she been doing, and with whom? Not that—the hereafter being doubtless an immensely large place—Emily imagined Ana had encountered her papa. Were that not enough to occupy her mind, there was the additional revelation that Ravensclaw and Isobella Dinwiddie had had intimate relations of some sort.

Isobella had had intimate relations with any number of gentlemen, from all accounts. Emily supposed she should have guessed that Ravensclaw might have been among them. However, she hadn't, and the discovery made her cross.

Gaining Ravensclaw's cooperation had been her original reason for seeking him out. Cooperation concerning the matter of the vanished athame. But then she had become distracted by neck-nibbling, and couldn't seem to put it from her mind. Emily retitled this episode of the Dinwiddie Chronicles: *The Perplexing Problem of the Prudent Fiend.*

What in heaven was she thinking? Ravensclaw was a vampire. A vampire who in this particular moment was waltzing gracefully with Lisbet Boroi. Lisbet wore a gown made from a cashmere scarf, with a scalloped bottom and split oversleeves, and a broad, low neckline which left most of her shoulders bare. Maybe it was Lisbet who was Val's *ailaltă*, in which case Emily had made a cake of herself. Cezar and his shadow, Andrei, were nowhere in sight. She hoped they were searching for the d'Auvergne athame. Lady Alberta rapped Emily's wrist with her fan. "You're staring, dear."

So she was, and why shouldn't she? Every other female in the Assembly Rooms was doing the same thing. Val's dark coat was molded to his broad shoulders, and his breeches to his thighs. His auburn hair, tied back with a velvet thong, gleamed in the candlelight. He looked handsome as Adonis, and wicked as sin.

She watched him smile at Lisbet in an annoyingly intimate manner. "Tell me, Lady Alberta, what do you see when you look at Ravensclaw?"

Lady Alberta glanced at the dancers. "An extraordinarily handsome gentleman who has every female in the vicinity panting after him. We can hardly fault him for enjoying it. My dear, do you feel unwell?"

So much for the *glamour*. Ravensclaw was as he was without the use of artifice, unless he knew how to alter perception on a monumental scale, and the overseer of the Dinwiddie Society was no different from any other female: she had offered herself up like a plump piglet on a platter, and he had turned her down. Although perhaps he might not have, save for the interference of his dead wife.

Tupping, indeed. Emily's education was proceeding in leaps and bounds. She knew she wasn't the sort of female to attract a gentleman's attention in the normal way of things, and since the man, if not gentle—and, for that matter, not a man—was the most gloriously masculine creature she'd ever set eyes upon, and since he could cause her to practically dissolve in pleasure by merely looking at her—

Lady Alberta nudged her. "Emily?"

"I am quite well, thank you. Merely a little overwhelmed. There are so many people here." Emily gestured vaguely at the glittering throng. Lady Alberta glittered a bit herself tonight in a gown with gold banding on her neckline, the scooped edges of her overskirt, and the ends of her short sleeves. Once assured that Emily wasn't going to swoon amid the crush of bodies, Lady Alberta resumed her lecture on Edinburgh, which had been founded nine hundred and ninety years before the birth of Christ, or alternately in 330 B.C., and had definitely been given a Royal Charter in 1329.

Mirrors at each end of the long chamber reflected a sea of dancers dipping and swaying to the music of the orchestra. An astonishing number of young men had asked Emily to dance, or if they might escort her to dinner, or call on her tomorrow, or at the very least fetch her a glass of lemonade, all of whom she'd sent away with the excuse that she was but recently out of mourning, and therefore it wouldn't be fitting for her to engage in such frivolity.

"Gracious!" murmured Lady Alberta, as yet another suitor was sent to the rightabout. "You are all the crack. How strange. I mean—"

"I know exactly what you mean," retorted Emily. "And it is."

"Unless they have all heard a certain rumor." Lady Alberta watched the dejected suitor disappear into the crowd.

"What rumor?"

"Fifty thousand pounds. Was it supposed to be a secret, dear? Val seemed to think not."

"Damn and blast!" said Emily, then lowered her voice, though she need not have: what in a mere miss would have been considered uncommonly rude was in a wealthy heiress thought refreshingly frank. "So that is why everyone is emptying the butter dish over my head. How *dare* Ravensclaw interfere in my affairs?"

"Did you not ask him to?" Lady Alberta turned her head, causing the plume in her turban to quiver as if wafting in a gentle breeze. Emily frowned so ferociously at a hopeful young gentleman that he changed direction and headed for the refreshment table, where he sought solace for his failure to recite a poem he'd composed in honor of the heiress's exquisite eyebrows. "Forgive my presumption, but you *are* wealthy, are you not?"

She was less wealthy than before Ravensclaw had started buying her clothing, Emily reflected. Of course she would repay him for this extensive wardrobe of which she had no need. Tonight she wore another of Val's selections, a dark gown with a draped bodice and underskirt. "The Society—that is, my family has done well on the Exchange. We invested in a company that financed Sir Francis Drake's piratical attacks on Spanish commerce. Even more important, we were fortunate enough to avoid the South Sea Bubble. We also made a nice profit from tulip stocks."

"Ah," said Lady Alberta, her expression glazed. Emily didn't expound upon her own fascination with Interest, Discounts and Transfers; Tables and Debentures and Shares. Her feet in their pretty slippers ached.

The waltz gave way to Scottish country dances, and still Val remained on the dance floor. Set to and turn corners— Emily wished she might see Lisbet strike her hands and give three jumps. Even more, she wished she might see Lisbet jump off the Castle Rock.

Lady Alberta broke off complaining about a gasworks in the Canongate that had a chimney more than three hundred feet high. "Here comes Mr. Ross at last. I believe I shall visit the supper room." She whisked herself away.

Michael made a stiff little bow. "Emily. You are but newly out of mourning, so I won't ask if you care to dance."

The dancers were now attempting to bump elbows together, first the right and then the left. Lisbet and Val had vanished from sight. Had they too withdrawn to the supper room, or discreetly retired for a different sort of snack? Emily returned her gaze to Michael. He was a veritable tulip of fashion. She wondered if his tailor had been paid.

Was *he* in need of a fortune? If so, scant wonder he wanted her to leave. One thing to have a wealthy fiancée safely tucked away in London, another altogether when said fiancée suddenly arrived on the scene and showed him no more affection than a gnat.

"'Family' matters brought you to Edinburgh, I believe you said. Should you not introduce me to your family, Michael? They will be curious about the female you seek to marry. You should give them an opportunity to welcome me into the fold."

"All in good time," he said vaguely. "We are attracting undue attention. Pray lower your voice."

The man grew more and more annoying. Emily wished she might punch him, like Twitcher had punched Mowdiewarp, right in the nose. "I have made some interesting acquaintances. They are known as Oxter, Twitcher, and Mowdiewarp. You may know of them, perhaps?"

Michael's brows drew together. "I have not. What maggot have you taken into your head now?"

He might have been telling the truth. Difficult to tell. Most women averted their gaze when lying, whereas men could stare a person right in the eye. "Never mind. You seem out of sorts, Michael. Have you been burning the candle at both ends?"

"What would you care if I did?" he retorted, then forced an apologetic smile. "In truth, I haven't been sleeping well. Maybe you do have feelings for me, if you're concerned about my welfare."

Emily was also concerned about the welfare of the three corkbrains who were so determined to abduct her. She didn't point this out. When her companion failed to broach the matter of their union, she said, "Do you still wish to marry me, Michael?"

He gaped at her. "Have you finally come to your senses, then?"

Emily pinched him. "That was hardly romantic."

"I'm not—" Michael grimaced as if a headache gripped him now. "Emily, be my wife."

Emily knew she was not the sort of female to inspire ardent declarations. Why, then, was she suddenly depressed?

"You do me great honor, Michael. I hadn't realized you held me in such esteem. Pray forgive me if I don't give you my answer right away. We helpless— Ah! I will require some time to make up my mind." He appeared unconvinced. Emily offered up an eyelash flutter and a coy glance.

He looked bewildered. "You've never required any time to make up your mind before. Why are you blinking like that? Is there something in your eye?"

So much for lash-fluttering. "I know you purchased a vrajă from Mr. Abercrombie, Michael. Perhaps you might like to explain?"

"Why should I? Unless— You can't believe I had something to do with that attack on you!"

Emily studied his flushed face. "Actually, I don't."

He shook his head, as if to clear it. "Have you found your missing knife? If indeed it *is* missing. I'm not convinced of that."

Emily for her part was convinced of nothing. She was relieved when Lady Alberta returned and drew Michael into conversation about Arthur's Seat and the old Tolbooth, the Luckenbooths and the Krames. Emily clutched Michael's arm all the harder when she saw Lisbet and Val making their way toward them.

Michael turned irritably on her. "Why are you clutching at me?" His eyes narrowed. "Your pendant has turned dark."

Emily lowered her head and squinted down her nose. The pendant had also grown warm. Neither of which were particularly helpful since she was in the middle of a large crowd. "Gracious!" said Lady Alberta. "Does that signify something, dear?"

It signified that she was beyond foolish for being without both her pistol and her umbrella. Emily would have to rely on her wits. What was left of them.

Lisbet's voice grated on her ears. "You have been neglecting me. Leaving me too much to my own devices. You know how much I dislike that, Val."

Val smiled down at her. "I haven't entirely neglected you. Must I remind you of the other night? As for abandoning you to your own devices, some bothersome details have taken up my time."

She was a bothersome detail? Emily's cheeks burned. When she recalled her behavior— She reminded herself that Val had been the one to set her in his lap.

Emily imagined he had done a great deal more than set Lisbet in his lap. There was little question of what 'haven't entirely' meant. Val's glance flickered indifferently over her and away.

He might as well have plunged a knife into her heart.

Peawit! Cabbagehead! Beetbrain!

Michael frowned at her. "Emily?"

"I have made my decision. I will marry you, Michael."

Emily had spoken loudly enough that everyone in the vicinity heard her. Lisbet appeared mildly interested. Val looked distinctly annoyed. Michael recovered from his astonishment to raise her hands to his lips.

Oh, heavens, what had she done? Lady Alberta whispered, "Smile!"

Chapter Twenty-Three

When you are an anvil, hold you still;
When you are a hammer, strike your fill.

The skirt of Emily's voluminous dressing gown swished along the bedroom carpet. Late though the hour was—or early—she was unable to sleep. She had tried to pass the time in reading, had discovered that to protect herself from danger she should carry the tip of a calf's tongue; that safety in battle was achieved by rubbing oneself all over with leeks; that one's home might be protected from witches by hanging the diseased leg of a calf near the hearth, or keeping a bull's heart stuck with pins in the chimneypiece; had finally flung the book into the fireplace and with some satisfaction watched it burn. That would show Val. *What* it would show him was uncertain, unless it was that Emily could behave as badly as anybody else.

The rest of the household had long since retired. Only Machka remained, less to share her vigil, Emily suspected, than because the cat was loath to give up her warm spot in the center of the bed.

She walked to the window. Dawn would soon break. Emily didn't want to dwell on Ravensclaw and what he might have been doing in the hours since they'd left the Assembly Rooms.

Didn't want to dwell on it, but couldn't help herself. Emily indulged in a string of oaths that would have distracted even her papa from his studies. Machka pricked one ear and buried her nose beneath her tail.

Men! What blessed use were they? *Vampir* or not, in that regard Ravensclaw was very much a man. Emily no sooner suggested she was his *ailaltă* than he decided to marry her off to someone else, because what other reason could he have had to noise her fortune about? And where had he come up with the figure of fifty thousand pounds? Emily picked up a pillow and threw it at the wall, then plopped down in a chair and glared at her open door. She was determined to waylay Val the moment he set foot upon the stair.

Unaware of the freckled fury awaiting him—although he surely would have been, had he opened his mind to her, which he had no intention of doing, because he was very cross—Val walked through the late-night streets. First Emily had suggested she might be his *ailaltă*, then she announced she meant to marry Michael Ross. Val didn't know which displeased him more.

Yes, he'd thought that she should marry. He'd even meant to provide her with a choice of suitors, not realizing, until he surveyed the prospects, that the field of eligibles was so thin. One of Emily's new admirers was a close-fisted clunch, another a corny-faced cod's head, a third a lascivious old goat. The unmarried gentlemen of Edinburgh might have been astonished to discover that Ravensclaw considered them all twiddle-poops, beau nastys, and jaw-me-deads. Val might have been amused to discover himself so high a stickler, had not his sense of humor abandoned him.

The air was chill, not that the weather much concerned him. Val was largely impervious to extremes of heat and cold, the latter most common to this city, which lay a scant mile from the sea. On a rainy night like this, Edinburgh seemed a strange piling up of rocks, with roads rushing downhill like rivers, and buildings soaring up to the sky as if spit out by the old volcano on which the city had been built. He remembered when Heriot's Hospital had been erected, the first stone laid for the North Bridge. When the Old Town had been a fashionable address, instead of the dangerous and overcrowded slum it was becoming. When the narrow passages between the tall medieval houses had doubled as sewers and cesspits, and it had been forbidden to empty waste into the street until the curfew bell rang at ten o'clock.

Sometimes change was for the better. Val was unlikely to forget how Edinburgh had smelled. Auld Reekie the city had been, and to Val always would be. "The Athens of the North," they called it now.

As for progress, he conceded that gangs of apprentices, the youngest of them as little as twelve years old, no longer roamed the streets at night, to bludgeon and rob anyone unlucky enough to cross their path. Instead, factory boys had their earlobes nailed to a board if too many of the spikes they produced were bent, while in the Lothian mines young women hauled coal carts through the suffocating darkness using harnesses that twisted them into hunchbacks. Val hadn't needed Emily to tell him of the plight of chimneysweeps. He could hardly be unaware of the vast injustices in the world, having had more than ample time to observe them all. However, he didn't know what he might do about such things. It had not previously occurred to him that he *should* do something, his kind generally being exempt from any civic responsibility other than not draining away the life of one of mankind's benefactors.

He doubted Emily would agree. Which, since Val was at the moment in huge disagreement with Emily, suited him very well.

What the devil had she been thinking, to betroth herself to Michael Ross? Oh, he knew *what* she'd been thinking, because he'd heard it clearly, and only remained uncertain whether 'peawit', 'cabbagehead', and 'beetle-brain' applied to her or to himself.

Val opened his front door. Why was no one standing guard? His temper soured further when Emily popped up in the stairwell like a ghost. These days, Val was somewhat sensitive on the subject of ghosts. Surely he hadn't spent good money on that shroud of a night-rail.

She got in the first blow. "Pray tell me why in *Hades* you put it out that I'm an heiress, you— You toad!"

Val found his own mood perversely improving: Emily was fit to murder him. He scooped her up and carried her, protesting, into her room; dropped her without ceremony into the middle of the bed. Machka opened one eye, blinked, and went back to sleep.

Emily struggled upright among her pillows. "I passed *such* a charming evening, thanks to you. Have you any idea what it's like to be besieged by lovesick swains—sick of love for my pocketbook, that is! I am extremely angry with you. Perhaps I shall scream until I am purple in the face."

"I beg you will not." Val seated himself on the bed's edge, a prudent distance from her. "Think what Isidore would say."

Emily pushed up her glasses. "Isidore informed me earlier that those who eat cherries with great persons must expect to have their eyes squirted out with the stones. *Why* did you do it, Val?"

He wasn't certain. What had seemed a splendid notion at the time seemed remarkably wrong-headed now. "Perhaps I sought to see you comfortably bestowed?"

"Perhaps you wished to entertain yourself." Emily pointed an accusing finger at him. "I understand you, Ravensclaw."

Val wasn't so lackwitted as to respond to that accusation. "Speaking of cork-brained behavior, you're the one who's on the verge of being leg-shackled to Michael Ross."

"That was because—" Emily broke off.

"I know what it was because of," retorted Val. "And it makes me fit to murder *you*. I told you already that Lisbet is of no consequence."

"Of no consequence, is she? So where *did* you spend the evening? Forget I asked you that, it's none of my affair. I'm not going to marry Michael. But I wanted him to think I was. He is more likely to confide in me if he believes I'm to be his wife."

Cezar believed Emily was using Michael Ross as a diversionary tactic, a smoke screen of sorts. Val did not. If Emily couldn't draw out the young man, Val would take steps of his own.

She was regarding him suspiciously. "Did you flutter your lashes?" Val asked.

"And simper like a ninny? He asked if I had something in my eye." Ruefully, she smiled. "When I said I'd marry him, poor Michael was shocked."

Poor Michael, indeed. Within grasp of a tidy fortune, only to see it snatched away. And it *would* be snatched away. If Emily didn't break off the betrothal, Val would do it for her.

He marveled at himself. From whence had come this dog-in-the-manger attitude? This feeling of protective possessiveness? Val could not remember when he'd last felt this way. Not for Ana, certainly; and sometime during the countless years since then, he had ceased to care. One willing body had been much like another. While he had enjoyed them all, he had also known that any interaction must be temporary, because of what he was.

Emily was broadening his horizons. Pillowy breasts and quivering thighs were all fine in their place, but eventually a man grew hungry for something different. Specifically, a stubborn, brown-eyed, redheaded termagent whom he couldn't have. Whom he would have taken anyway, and the consequences be damned, if not for the interference of a certain ghost.

Val supposed he should be grateful to Ana. He rose and moved toward the door.

Emily looked very small perched in the middle of the bed. The sight of her would have tugged at his heartstrings, had he any, which he didn't. At least, he wasn't supposed to. "I apologize for my high-handedness. In the future, I promise not to act in your best interests without consulting you first."

Emily flushed. "I daresay I should apologize also, for calling you a toad."

"Toad is the least of the things I have been called, elfling. Now I will bid you a good night." He walked out of the room and softly closed the door.

Emily lay back beside Machka on the bed. She had been behaving badly, and enjoying every moment of it. Interesting, how it was so much more gratifying to misbehave than the opposite.

Ravensclaw had been in her bedchamber. They had shared a bed. At least, they had both sat upon it. Sharing a bed with Ravensclaw had put her in a much better frame of mine.

A toad, she'd called him. How ironic it all was. Aberrations had been lurking in the shadows ever since Adam's first wife coupled with fallen angels near the Red Sea, yet humans refused to concede that supersensible beings might exist outside the pages of sensational fiction. Mankind was very good at believing what it wished.

Herself, Emily chose to believe that Ravensclaw would in time come to realize that she was his *ailaltă*. She was smiling as she fell asleep.

Chapter Twenty-Four

Don't play with the bear if you don't want to be bit.

Princes Street—named for the sons of King George III after His Majesty objected to christening it after the patron saint of the city, on the grounds that St. Giles was not only patron saint of lepers but also the name of a notorious London slum—divided the Old Town from the New. Wealthy residents lived here, on the one side of the street where building was permitted: they could afford to insure nothing spoiled their panoramic view. Cezar Korzha was among those residents, his home a surprisingly plain house of three stories and a basement with a small garden behind—plain, that was, save for the conservation where he experimented with exotic plants. Stables and a coach-house were entered from a mews lane at the rear, Rose Lane to be precise, the haunt of prostitutes, and what better place for blood-drinkers to quench their thirst?

Cezar Korzha, whose current enthusiasm was cycads, an ancient group of plants that were growing when dinosaurs ruled the planet. He also had a curiosity about Gesneriaceae and Zingiberaceae. Even now he sat with his nose deep in *The Botanical Register: or, Ornamental flower-garden and shrubbery, consisting of coloured figures of plants and shrubs, cultivated in British gardens; accompanied by their history, best method of treatment in cultivation, propagation, etc.*, a golf club propped against his chair.

As always, Andrei Torok was with him. Andrei's company was hardly more stimulating, his main interest being warfare, specifically the battle strategies of ancient China: 'Hide the Dagger Behind a Smile', 'Lure Your Enemy Onto the Roof, Then Take Away the Ladder', and 'Tie Silk Blossoms to the Dead Tree.'

And then there was Ravensclaw, whose passion was for pleasure, and who—

What? He didn't know.

The slender man knew none of these things, these people, and yet he did.

He stared at Cezar Korzha's house.

Headless bodies. Corpses drained of blood.

The first had been a warning, the second a promise of things to come.

The third would test even the Stăpân's power.

How long had he lingered in the shadows? The slender man had no recollection of his arrival here.

He had forgotten many things. Others, he wished he might. The stink of blood. The impact of axe against bone.

Beyond the filled-in Nor' Loch towered the tenements of the Old Town. On the west, Castle Hill sloped down toward Holyrood on the east.

As long ago as 850 B.C., a hill-fort settlement had stood where Edinburgh Castle rose now.

His vision blurred. He blinked. He feared to close his eyes for long lest he'd not be able to open them again.

Unbidden words and images beat at his brain.

Edinburgh. Castles and ghosts.

He inhaled. Smells seemed sharper to him. Edinburgh stank of the smoke and soot of countless coal fires.

Another scent flooded his nostrils, mysterious and dark. Bergamot, sandalwood, musk. A hint of burning amber.

The athame in its sheathe stirred.

In some dim recess of his mind he was aware of the need for food and water. The things that sustained mortal man.

He no longer knew if he was mortal. If, indeed, he was a man.

Sometimes, though there was no one present, he heard a woman's screams.

Sometimes he felt like screaming himself.

They might scream until hell froze over, and it would make no difference.

He dug his fingernails into his rotting flesh.

Chapter Twenty-Five

A word and a stone let go cannot be called back.

When it came to bridge-building Edinburgh had no equal, which was perhaps not surprising since there was a mountain in the middle of the city, causing unexpected alternations of heights and depths.

Bridges blended into existing streets. The gaps they spanned had been filled in, developed, and built up, buildings constructed above and on either side until the mighty structures were almost concealed. The arched, bricked-in vaults were a warren of nooks, crannies, and tunnels used for wine storage, leather works, and a multitude of small businesses; and used as well as living quarters for the city's unwanted and unseen poor. Also stored there were cadavers resurrected from fresh graves or plucked from the streets and sold to Edinburgh's Medical School.

Drogo whined, sensing his master's mood. Val touched the wolf's sleek head. *Dog*, he reminded himself. *Rare Carpathian copoi. Believe that and I'll sell you a fine barren moor.* It was due to the ungrateful Miss Dinwiddie that they were out so early, Val's dark spectacles set firmly on his nose. If sunlight posed his flesh no danger after so long a time, it still caused discomfort to his eyes. After several hundred more years had passed, provided he survived them, he might be able to put the spectacles aside.

Several hundred more years. Val felt like crushing the spectacles in his bare hands. Several hundred years ago he had married Ana, in a ceremony that began when his spokesman, Cezar, had gone to her family's home to woo her with the tale of a young emperor and a flower which couldn't bear fruit until it was planted in the proper soil. Then Val had been obliged to solve a series of riddles to prove his cleverness. Following that were three days of ceremonies, ending with a dance of masks. Ana had worn a traditional costume and flowers in her hair.

Val wondered how Andrei would react to the discovery that Ana had returned to them, and why, and what use Cezar might make of a ghost. Val had delayed telling them, perhaps in an attempt to protect Ana, and more likely himself.

Time had passed more quickly than he could have imagined. Several hundred years from now, when he could venture into the sunlight without dark glasses, Emily would have long since shuffled off this mortal coil. Would have gone the way of all flesh. Would be dead as mutton, and Val very much feared he would still be missing her. Would Emily haunt him then, as Ana was doing now? Demand he make her corporeal so she could tup someone, but not him, because he was *vampir?*

Vampir. Condemned to lifetimes of loneliness. Yearning to live and love like an ordinary man. Feeling bloody mortal. How damnably trite of him.

Had any of Ravensclaw's acquaintance been out and about so early (which was unlikely), and had they encountered him in this particular part of the Old Town (which was even more unlikely), they would have deduced from his expression that he was appalled to find himself so far from his bed. Drogo knew better. He pressed closer, and whined again.

"You're right." Val rubbed the wolf's ears. "I'm as addle-brained as those three oafs we sent to the docks." Because Emily had been worried about her inept assailants, he'd volunteered them for a sealing expedition sailing from the Port of Leith, thereby hopefully removing them from underfoot without doing lasting harm. Val didn't delude himself that Emily would be grateful. She would probably demand he rescue the seals.

The addition of a sticky-fingered chimneysweep to his retinue had been sufficient. Val refused to introduce any marine life with webbed flippers into his household.

These ruminations took him past the Lawnmarket, along a passage between two houses, into a dark courtyard surrounded by ancient high buildings, down a short flight of stone steps that ended at two doors. Drogo leaned his weight against the left. The door swung open. Val stepped inside. It occurred to him that he was acting in Emily's best interests without consulting her, again.

This place was not unfamiliar to him, though he did not know the little man who bustled out of a back room. "Mr. Abercrombie, I presume. I see you have not changed the decor. Hello, Styx." The raven flew down from its perch to alight on his shoulder and mutter in his ear. Mr. Abercrombie's wandering eye moved from Val to the raven and then to Drogo, who had padded forward to rest his damp nose against the little man's thigh. Mr. Abercrombie squeaked, "And may I know who you are, sir?"

Val took off his dark glasses. "I am Ravensclaw."

Mr. Abercrombie smoothed a hand over his balding pate and professed his desire to be of service. Would the gentleman be interested in a crescent-shaped charm made from a boar's tusk, or a chicken's wishing bone? A cure for the ague? He had recently acquired an especially fine batch of bull's-horn plantain. Maybe, some alchemical supplies?

"Thank you, no," Val interrupted. "A young woman came here recently. Red-haired. Freckled. Inquisitive."

"Aye. I recognize her, er, companion." The shopkeeper looked startled, as if he'd meant to say something else.

"You will tell me what you told her."

Looking even more bewildered, Mr. Abercrombie obeyed. Val was briefly distracted by the notion of Emily in conjunction with a Love Drawing Oil. "The young woman was well protected," the shopkeeper added. "Might you know where she found that pendant, sir?"

"What pendant is that?"

"Ah. Yes, indeed. As you say. Perhaps I might interest you in a recipe for Raven's Feather Ink?"

"You may not." Val lifted the indignant raven back up on its perch; moved around the cluttered shop, inspecting the jumble of books and bottles, the muddle of merchandise in the cabinets and on the shelves. "Tell me what you know about Michael Ross."

Mr. Abercrombie hesitated. Drogo nudged him. The shopkeeper looked down at the wolf, whose jaws were uncomfortably close to his most vulnerable parts. "Like I told the young lady, he bought a vrajă, in addition to some mastic pearls, yarrow, and bloodstone. That's all I know. I swear."

The shopkeeper appeared as innocent as a babe newborn. Ravensclaw wasn't deceived. Things of power rested in this room, amid the cobwebs and clutter.*Tell me everything you know of Michael Ross. Now. Do not waste my time.*

In the end, Mr. Abercrombie did not know much. Michael Ross had sold the shopkeeper a number of books—an English translation of the *Rosarium Philosophorum; Geber's Discovery of Secrets; An Hundred Aphorisms Containing the Whole Body of Magic, 1321;* though Mr. Abercrombie had passed on a tattered copy of *The Hermaphrodite Child of the Sun and Moon*—and had in turn been most anxious to procure a copy of *The Book of Thoth.* The Egyptian god Thoth had been credited with the invention of both magic and writing. To possess a copy of his book was to command and control destiny itself.

Were Mr. Abercrombie in possession of the secrets of the universe, he tittered, he would hardly be tending this dusty little shop. He had sent the young man off with *The Book of Raziel* instead.

So. Michael Ross had sold a number of volumes concerning the manipulation of natural forces and powers to achieve a predetermined end. Sorcery, in a word. The sort of volumes that might have once resided in the Dinwiddie Society's vaults.

Val had a sense that time was running short. But, since he was here— "What would you recommend as the best way to rid oneself of a ghost?"

Mr. Abercrombie ruminated. Had the gentleman tried stuffing his keyholes full of fennel? Burning powdered bistort? Throwing beans at the apparition? Alternately, one could place three peeled cloves of garlic in a bowl with a handful of sea salt and fresh rosemary leaves, grind and mash them together, and sprinkle the result to create a boundary.

Val doubted anything so mundane would inspire Ana to depart. He put on his spectacles and climbed the stair.

The Book of Raziel had been written by a sympathetic angel and given to Adam to compensate for his exile from Eden. Val was familiar with the tome. For that matter, he also had in his possession *The Book of Thoth,* although he had no sense of controlling destiny, not even his own. Miss Dinwiddie had seen to that.

Even as he thought of her, Val felt Emily's presence, some distance away.

She was frightened. Val reached out with his senses and found her, backed into a dark dead-end alleyway by an amorphous blob that sometimes seemed to be a snake and sometimes to have wings. She was holding the pendant out in front of her and chanting. The gem was black as coal.

Jamie and Lady Alberta had been tasked with guarding Miss Dinwiddie. Yet even with the added efforts of Zizi and Bela, Lilian and Isidore, they had apparently been unable to keep her safely within doors.

Chapter Twenty-Six

Believe nothing of what you hear,
and only half of what you see.

Emily was draped about with all her various items of protection. Unfortunately, her assorted charms were proving no more useful in this moment than her sharp-pointed umbrella, or her little gun. Only Marie d'Auvergne's pendant kept the thing before her from gobbling her down like a tasty snack.

No question that it had been foolish to come out alone. But the note slipped to Emily had demanded secrecy and stealth, and promised her questions would be answered if she complied. *Not only foolish, but gullible!* She clutched the pendant so tightly that her fingers burned.

The thing, whatever it was—most likely a demon—continually changed shape. In one instant it was snake-like, then winged with cloven hooves; a manlike figure with an unnatural number of fingers and something monstrous about its mouth and teeth; a pillar of smoke; wavering lights. In all its configurations, piercing dark eyes nailed her to the ground. The thing advanced, retreated, circled, writhed.

Emily struggled to free herself from paralysis. She wasn't so foolish as to wish to do battle with an otherworldly creature; she wanted to run away. At least, that's what she thought she wanted. Difficult to concentrate her mind when reality was shifting all about. She even thought she heard the howling of a wolf. The monster must have shared her auditory hallucination; it turned away. In that instant, as its attention wavered, Emily saw through the illusion. Her assailant was a winged manlike being of terrible beauty. She had but a brief glimpse before he changed again, into a great scaled fire-breathing dragon with vicious curved talons like those of a bird of prey.

Demons, Emily told herself. To name a demon was to lessen its power. But there were 4,601,200 demons, according to the *Egyptian Book of the Dead.* Or 7,409,127 commanded by seventy-nine princes, if one preferred the sixteenth-century physician Jean Weir. According to legend, King Solomon of Israel shut up seventy-two rebellious kings into a brass vessel and threw it into a deep lake. In an attempt to locate great treasure, the Babylonians had broken open the vessel, allowing the demons to escape into the world.

Focus, you ninny! "Glasyalabolas," she muttered. "Raum. Flauros. Seere, Andromalius, Balaam." Now that the demon's attention was no longer fixed on her, Emily found that she could move.

A scuffle behind her, the sound of struggle, a snarl and yelp. Emily spun around. Drogo sprawled on the filthy pavement, blood streaming from a deep gash in his flank. She dropped to her knees beside the wolf, pulling at his thick fur as if she could hold the edges of the wound together and staunch the flow of blood. Drogo whined. *Emily!* came Val's voice in her mind. *Leave this place, at once.*

Ravensclaw? Emily raised her head. Her thoughts moved slowly as molasses in wintertime.

This was not Val as she knew him. His face was leaner, harsher, his fangs fully extended; he seemed taller, broader in build. Viciously sharp claws extended from his fingertips. His eyes bled black fire. *Go!* he said again.

I won't! Emily took a firmer grip on Drogo's sodden fur, gasped as the demon slashed at Val and drew blood. Emily was no stranger (though she should have been) to the gentlemanly art of fisticuffs, but in a struggle between vampire and demon, the ordinary rules did not apply. Here was no boxing in Mendoza's scientific style, no cross-and-jostle work or application of Jack Broughton's favorite hard right to the abdomen. This was a struggle to the death with talons and fangs. Val caught the demon and flung it against the side of a building with such force that, had the thing hit, the ancient structure might have tumbled down. Instead the demon dissolved into mist, and reformed itself as a huge apelike creature with powerful arms and huge hands and a coat of silver-yellow hair. Val slammed the beast to the ground. It was erect in an instant, and delivered a rib-breaking blow. Val grunted. The demon raked him with its claws, severing tendon and sinew.

Emily's mind was clearing. This wasn't going well. "Cimeries, Sytyr, Vassago—" Drogo whined. Emily glanced down at him and glimpsed her reticule, its chain still wrapped around her wrist. The demon knelt on Val's back with an arm around his neck, prepared to twist.

The literature claimed a vampire would die if its spine was snapped. Emily fumbled her fingers into her reticule, brought out a pinch of salt and flung it. The demon burst into flames.

The ape-thing disappeared. Before Emily stood the beautiful manlike being with his vast wings and red hair. He appeared annoyed. He also looked a trifle singed.

Red hair. A great serpent with twelve wings who flew like a bird. She said, "Samael."

The demon released Val and turned its eyes on her. Before that terrible gaze could again ensnare her, Emily held up her little mirror and captured its reflection. "Samael, angel of death, prince of the fifth heaven, genii of fire. Samael, accuser, seducer, destroyer. Who interfered with Abraham, wrestled with Jacob, took part in the affair of Tamar—"

The demon unfurled a sooty wing and examined it. "You needn't belabor the point."

"Samael, angel of death, prince of air, demon who tempted Eve," Emily continued. "Samael, lord of demons, leader of the angels who married the daughters of men. Tremble, O Demon, enemy of mankind, source of avarice, seducer of man, root of evil, discord and envy—"

"You do me too much credit." Samael plucked out a singed feather and eyed Emily. "And that should be seducer of womankind."

She gripped the mirror tighter. "In the name of Yod, Cados, Eloym, Saboath, and Yeshua the Anointed One, I command you to return from whence you came."

"If you insist." The demon spread his great wings and disappeared.

Emily exhaled in relief. One could never be certain of the outcome when dealing with a demon of such strength.

Cezar spoke from behind her. "Well done, Miss Dinwiddie. I wouldn't have expected banishing demons to be one of your skills."

Emily twisted around to frown at him. "I don't know why you should be surprised. Papa *did* teach me things, even if he was reluctant to let me practice them. How long have you been here?"

"Long enough." Cezar moved closer. "Our friend doesn't look well."

If Val's spine remained unsnapped, the pavement around his body was dark with his blood. Emily's hands tightened in Drogo's fur. "I thought your kind could heal yourselves. And don't insult me by saying you don't know what I'm talking about."

"I won't insult you, Miss Dinwiddie. We do have remarkable regenerative powers. However, that was a demon. And we cannot replenish our own blood."

Val lay unnervingly motionless. Emily experienced a cold chill. "How can you just stand there? Why *did* you just stand there when you might have helped?"

"It wasn't my battle. I couldn't influence the outcome." Cezar knelt and touched elegant fingers to Drogo's wound. The wolf whined.

Emily watched. "I thought werewolves—"

"Could heal themselves? It would appear, Miss Dinwiddie, that there is no end to the nonsense you believe."

Emily sniffed. "If not for my beliefs, you'd still be standing there watching a demon destroy Ravensclaw. And speaking of Val—"

"That was no ordinary demon." Cezar pressed the edges of Drogo's wound together. "It couldn't have been called up by ordinary means. Which returns us to the matter of the d'Auvergne athame."

Emily fumbled for her spectacles. Was it a trick of the shadows that made her think the wolf's wound had begun to mend? "Oh, bugger the blasted athame! You're healing Drogo. Can you heal Val?"

"Drogo is a dumb animal." The wolf growled. "Apologies, my old friend. Val can heal himself, Miss Dinwiddie, as you have already guessed. But he won't survive without blood."

Emily stared at Cezar in growing horror. "Then give him some!"

"Our kind cannot derive sustenance from one another."

"Then bugger you too!" Emily looked frantically around her for something sharp.

Nothing came to hand. She rose and crossed the pavement to kneel by Val. He opened his eyes. They were merely sapphire now, but his face retained its feral cast.

Gingerly, Emily touched his cheek. Val's coldness frightened her more than a hundred demons ever could. "I'm so sorry. Forgive me."

No need. His eyes closed.

It's my fault you've been injured. Let me help you. Drink from me.

I cannot.

He was as stubborn as any mule. Action was required. Gingerly, Emily settled her body atop his, pulled back her hair and bared her throat. *I know you would prefer somewhere else—breasts, groin, and the like—but I refuse to disrobe in front of him.* She glared at Cezar.

Val hesitated. Emily raised herself to peer down into his face. "Don't tell me you are shy!"

His pale lips parted. "Are you afraid of nothing?" he said aloud.

"I'm afraid I won't please you. Val, let me give you the gift of blood."

Behind them, Cezar said, "Do it, *camarad.*"

A moment passed. Then Val's fingers moved to the neckline of Emily's dress. He tugged the material aside, wrapped one hand in her hair and drew her head back. She felt his lips, his teeth; cried out when his fangs sank into her flesh. The smell of copper flooded the air.

Pleasure rolled over Emily, Val's pleasure in tasting her, in taking her blood. Her own pleasure, raw and sensual, as she felt her heat and warmth pulse through his veins. And then his hunger was upon her, sweeping like a sweet narcotic through her veins. *Open to me, Emily. We feed on emotions as well as blood.*

Her body sang with strange sensations. Bright colors danced behind her eyes. Emily knew nothing but a deepening velvet darkness, heard not even the hammering of her own heart.

Chapter Twenty-Seven

Of two evils choose the least.

Val was dreaming. Of Emily.

She sprawled on top of him, her small body burning hot. She felt like all he would ever wish to know of heaven, sweet and soft and unbearably innocent. He longed to taste her flesh, to feel her thrum with anticipation; to drop his head to her breast, lick her belly, and the inside of her knees; to tease her with his tongue until she gasped and wept and moaned, and screamed out her satisfaction at the end.

But slowly, slowly. Val would not rush her pleasure, or his own. His hands caressed her as he bit gently at her lower lip, kissed the pulse beating at her temple, breathed her in. She pressed closer, as if she wished to crawl inside his skin. Well, then, he would let her. Val pressed his teeth to the tender junction of neck and jaw—

He wakened abruptly, to find himself alone in one of several stone-walled chambers kept for the use of the Brotherhood. Val had never before had need for one of these small rooms. He was unsure why he did now. He moved, and grimaced as he felt the soreness of his ribs. His body healed quickly, but not overnight. The fresh scars on his body would fade in time.

Scars? Broken bones? Val raised his hands to his head. He felt as he had in the old days after celebrating the feast of Dionysus.

Val no longer had use either for liquor, or chewing ivy leaves. The sole thing that could affect him this way was overindulgence in blood.

He touched his tongue to his lips. So vivid had been his dream that the scent of Emily still clung to him. He could taste her in his mouth. Her purity had been intoxicating. No wonder he felt drunk.

Val reached out for her. He should have been able to sense her emotions, her response to the dream; should have been able to feel the aftermath of pleasure curling through her, lazy and sweet. Having once tasted her, he should be able to touch her mind, to know her thoughts, to hear her heart beat.

He felt nothing. She had again closed herself to him. Val swung his legs over the side of the bed and walked unsteadily into the main meeting room. His Stăpân was there, addressing a golf ball. Judging from the other balls scattered around the room, his efforts today had not met with much success.

Cezar glanced up at Val. "Our ancestors believed that a corpse found with one eye open and one closed is in the process of transforming into a vampire."

Val squinted at the bright light of the candles. "'What does the Romanian like? Fresh bread, old wine, and a young wife.'"

Cezar directed his attention to his putter. "Zalmoxis taught that men don't die, but go to a place where they will live forever and have all good things." The ball rolled off the shank of his club and bounced into a wall. "Like I do."

Cezar was in a strange mood, mentioning old Dacian gods. Val noticed a teapot sitting on a table, and poured himself a cup.

Cezar retrieved the golf ball. "Andrei is keeping Lisbet occupied. He may soon supplant you in her affections before long."

"He may have her with my blessing." Val needed tea no more than wine, but the beverage's pleasant taste left him feeling revived.

Cezar moved in that sudden way that vampires have, which was of no use whatsoever to him in the game of golf. The ball rolled forward a few inches and came to a stop. "How much do you recall about the events of yesterday?"

Val put down his teacup. "I went to the sorcerer's shop, which is now in the hands of a man named Abercrombie. I questioned him about Michael Ross. He didn't know much. Then I realized Emily was in trouble." He closed his eyes. "Did I really do battle with the Darkness?"

"Miss Dinwiddie sent him home. It was all very polite, other than the fact you lost."

Val experienced an unpleasant premonition. "Tell me I didn't drink from her."

Cezar set aside his putter. "Very well. You didn't drink from her. You didn't enjoy drinking from her so much that you refused to stop. You didn't attempt to break my neck when I tried to stop you. I wasn't forced to summon Andrei for assistance. Nor did it take both Andrei and I to get you here. Yes, it was all a dream."

"What have you done with Emily? If you dared switch her memories around—"

"I've done nothing. Miss Dinwiddie is your responsibility. I suggest you don't delay much longer. Not, like I said, that it's any of my affair."

No? That was not Val's impression. It seemed to him that Cezar had a large stake in this 'affair'. "I'll ask you once more. What have you done with Emily?"

"And I'll tell you once more, I've done nothing. Come with me. See for yourself." Cezar led the way down a dim hallway and into another cell.

Val entered the chamber. Emily lay on her back on a narrow cot. Drogo was stretched out beside her. At sight of Val, the wolf lifted his head and growled.

Val moved closer to the bed. Emily was motionless, her tangled hair spread out on the pillow. Her eyes were closed. One hand rested limply atop the blanket. There was dirt beneath her fingernails, dark stains on her gown. Her skin was unnaturally pale.

Unease stole over him. Unnerving, to see Emily so still, so quiet, as if she had no more life force than a stone.

Life force? Memory crashed over him. Memory of Emily's body sprawled atop his. That had been no dream.

Val clasped her dirty hands. Her fingers were like ice. Still, he felt a faint heartbeat. *Emily.* There was no response.

He felt Cezar behind him. Val said, grimly, "You let me take too much."

"Since when am I your conscience? At any event you were in no condition to heed the voice of reason, as I have already pointed out.

I did warn Miss Dinwiddie, if you'll recall, that she was likely to be your next meal."

Val touched his fingers to the bloody marks on Emily's neck. She had trusted him, and he had failed to protect her, despite his vow to keep her from harm.

"The responsibility is not entirely yours," said Cezar. "Miss Dinwiddie would not be swayed from her path."

"You attempted to do so? How unlike you, then."

"I did not. It would have been futile. She was determined that you should drink from her." Drogo looked anxiously from one of them to the other. Cezar touched the wolf's head. "And you did."

Val chafed Emily's hands. This was not the way the stories went. The hero was not supposed to require that the heroine make a blood sacrifice of herself. "You could heal her," he said.

"I could, but then she would be mine. You don't want that, I think."

What Val wanted was his existence as it had been before Emily arrived to turn him lunatic. Cezar added, "You must make a decision. She hasn't much time left. Don't glower at me. I didn't make the rules."

"No, but you enforce them. I don't suppose you'd care to turn a blind eye."

"No. However, she risked her life to save you, knowing full well what you are. That sort of courage is rare. Too, the Dinwiddie Society has collected a great many secrets over the centuries. I think our little wren must not be allowed to fly away from us just yet."

"*Our* little wren?"

"Are we not comrades?" Cezar pulled out a silver knife and slit his wrist. "Now, will you remedy the situation, or shall I?"

Val took the blade. Impossible to know the consequences of feeding a mortal their mingled blood. What would it do to Emily? What would it do to them? Such a thing was so far beyond the rules that the mere thought was staggering.

If Cezar chose to share the repercussions of this forbidden act, so be it; but it would not be Cezar's blood that Emily tasted first, not Cezar's blood that forced the bond. Val slashed the vein on the inside of his elbow. With all his force of will, and Cezar's will behind him, he focused his mind. *Emily.*

Her eyes fluttered open. He felt a great sorrow at the emptiness he saw there. *Emily, drink.*

Chapter Twenty-Eight

Honey is sweet, but the bee stings.

Emily opened her eyes to find herself in a small stone-walled room. A rather crowded stone-walled room, which contained Cezar and Val, and Drogo stretched out beside her on a cot. The terrible gash in the wolf's flank had completely healed, leaving only a smooth scar.

She surveyed her Spartan surroundings with a degree of disappointment. "Is *this* the secret meeting place of the Brotherhood?"

Cezar moved to the foot of the bed. "Not all of us are sensualists like Val."

Emily glanced back at Val, whose auburn hair tumbled loose over his shoulders. He had removed his ruined clothing, and wore only a pair of breeches, in which he looked even more delicious than Mrs. MacCamish's Paradise Cake.

He was watching her watch him. Emily felt most unlike herself, doubtless because of what she'd done. Or what had been done to her. "I take it I'm still alive."

Drogo snarled softly as Val sat down on the bed. "You are."

"And I'm not a vampire?"

"No, elfling, you are not." Val's bare skin brushed against hers, and little sparks fizzed up her arm.

Animal magnetism. Magnetic friction. Emily had previously been privileged to glimpse Val's chest. To see him in almost a state of nature— "Um."

Cezar was holding a golf club. He gave it a gentle swing. "Nor are you merely mortal, because both Val's blood and mine have mixed with yours. Which leaves you, Miss Dinwiddie, somewhere betwixt and between."

Emily contemplated the coverlet. *Both* of them! The ultimate intimacy, indeed. She wished she could remember more of the experience.

"I don't," murmured Val.

Colors were brighter. Sounds were sharper. Emily raised one hand, wriggled her fingers, touched them to her lips. "What *am* I, then?"

Cezar's smile was ironic. "You are yourself, Miss Dinwiddie, and a good bit more."

"But what does that mean?"

"I truly do not know. We will have to wait and see."

See? Emily's eyes widened. "I'm not wearing my spectacles, and yet you're not just a blur."

Cezar exchanged a glance with Val. "Miss Dinwiddie may hold other surprises in store than merely sending the Darkness away."

Emily blinked, but the bright colors didn't fade. "Don't talk about me as if I wasn't here. By the Darkness, do you mean Samael? It was pure luck that I happened on his name."

Cezar rested his golf club on his shoulder. "Samael is leader of the Fallen Ones. Otherwise known as the Venom of God. If you had not been wearing Marie d'Auvergne's amulet, we would not be having this conversation, for all your demon-banishing skills."

Emily touched the pendant, quiet now against her breast. Her first demon, and she hadn't had a chance to interrogate him. *Drat!*

"You are undeniably your father's daughter, Miss Dinwiddie." Cezar resumed his putting stance.

"You knew my papa?"

"By reputation only." Cezar swung.

Val settled more comfortably, his thigh inches from hers. "Samael wasn't merely out for an early morning stroll. It might be helpful if you could tell us who might seek to do you harm."

Emily leaned against him. "Not Michael," she said. "He would have no reason, even if he possessed the power to call up demons, which I take leave to doubt. I had agreed to marry him, thereby giving him access to not only the Society's resources but also mine, neither of which he would have if something happened to me before we were wed. After we married he would, of course, but since I've no intention of marrying him, that is a moot point."

Came a brief silence while Cezar and Val seemed to be having a silent conversation. Emily mused upon the possibility that she might grow fangs. Develop a craving for raw meat. Become irresistibly charming. The whimsy made her smile.

You are already irresistibly charming, little one. Val's voice in her mind was a caress. *You charmed me on our first meeting, with your umbrella and your garlic and your assorted talismans.*

Now Ravensclaw was emptying the butter boat over her head. Emily had never in all her life charmed anyone. She narrowed her eyes at Cezar. "The literature claims that vampires can strike one dumb, rob one of one's strength and beauty, and steal milk from nursing mothers, although I don't know why you would. Your senses are so heightened that you can hear a liar's heartbeat, and smell the faintest fear. I wonder how you can prevent yourself from eavesdropping."

Cesar glanced up from his imaginary golf ball. "Val didn't mean *you* were a bothersome detail. Bothersome, unquestionably, but much more than a detail."

Emily stroked Drogo. "That was rather more than eavesdropping. I hope this doesn't mean that now I'll have *you* in my mind."

No, little one. Nor will Cezar invade your dreams. Val took her hand in his.

Emily sighed. "I fear I've been less than diplomatic. Again."

Cezar murmured, "I will leave the two of you to your own devices. Drogo?" The wolf growled softly and refused to budge. "It seems you have acquired a champion, Miss Dinwiddie. Or a chaperone."

Emily remained silent until Cezar had left the room. "I hope he's going to search for the athame."

Val rubbed his thumb across her knuckles. "More likely Cezar is going to rescue Andrei from Lisbet. Or practice his golf swing."

Emily wished Cezar might practice his golf swing on Lisbet. "Are you going to scold?"

Val wound his fingers through hers. "Would you listen if I did?"

"Papa used to say the same thing." Emily stared at their interlaced hands. "I *must* find that athame."

"We will." Val put a knuckle under Emily's chin and tipped her face up to his.

She felt as if she were drowning in his eyes. "Just how closely *are* we bound together now?"

So closely that I feel your heart beating as if it were my own. His fingers brushed her breast. "As Cezar, Andrei, and I are bound to our maker, you are bound to Cezar and myself. Not as strongly, certainly, but if anything happens to one of us, you will not remain unaffected. And the opposite, as well."

Curious as Emily might have been about Val's maker at another time, she was in this moment appalled. *Cezar knows what we are doing now?*

It's not so close a bond as that.

Emily lowered her gaze to Val's bare chest, the faint traces of dried blood.

He stiffened. "You don't want to be like me, Emily."

She wanted to be *with* him. For eternity. As his *ailaltă*. Which was something he clearly was not prepared to hear.

Emily wriggled around and thrust her hand into her pocket. Val winced. She retrieved the dirty crumpled note that had led her to Samael and handed it to him.

Val studied the note. Emily wondered if his preternatural senses were at work. Did some of the writer's aura cling to the paper? Some scent?

He remained silent. "Well?" she demanded, after several moments passed.

"I was trying to decipher the handwriting."

Emily snatched the note from him and read it aloud.

"That's ambiguous enough," Val said. "How could the writer be so certain you would take his bait?"

Emily tucked the note back into her pocket. "Papa used to say I have the curiosity of a cat combined with the good sense of a pudding. I fear it's true."

Val didn't argue. "I wish you would stop scaring me half out of my wits."

Emily felt so astonishingly unlike herself that she grinned at the notion Ravensclaw might become a nitwit, too.

Val cupped her face. *I am forever in your debt, elfling. You risked your life for me.*

You and I and Cezar— I've never heard of such a thing.

I will never forgive myself for taking too much from you.

Emily drew back. *There is a way you may repay me. You did say you'd let me do things.*

You are determined to drive me mad, aren't you? So be it. What would you like to do to me?

Where to begin? Words failed her. Emily slid her hands up his muscular arms to his strong shoulders, and tugged.

Val's resistance crumbled. Passion flared as his mouth touched hers. He spread a line of teasing kisses along the curve of her cheek, sampled the taste and texture of her earlobe. Her breath caught in her throat as Val's teeth grazed her neck. *Yes. That.*

He kissed her, really kissed her, then. Need quivered deep in her belly as his tongue twined with hers.

Emily was afloat on a river of sensation. She shivered as Val's fingers lingered on the marks he'd left on her throat. She wanted— Emily didn't know what she wanted, but she wanted it ferociously. She pressed against him, her fingers digging into his shoulders, her hands fisting in his hair.

Drogo growled. Val froze. Emily opened her eyes to see Ana levitating above the bed and bit back a shriek.

The ghost looked cross. "So here you are, and doing what you shouldn't. You pledged yourself to me until death did us part, remember, Val? And though death did, it didn't, so you're stuck with me until—"

Enlightenment dawned. Emily gasped, "It's not your house that's haunted, but you, Ravensclaw!"

Ana drifted closer. "What's happened to you? Really, Val, you should take better care of her. Although, as I recall, you didn't take very good care of me."

"He didn't?" said Emily.

"I did so," retorted Val.

"Then where were you when Oko stuck me in that burlap sack? Nowhere to be found, that's where."

Now Val was contemplating violence. Fascinating, this glimpse of married life. Equally enlightening, Emily's own desire to strangle Ana with one of those flimsy veils.

Veils? Burlap sacks? "You were a concubine?"

"I was an odalisque," Ana informed her. "A favored one. The sultan liked my way with the *dance du ventre.*" She struck a pose, and began to undulate.

Never could Emily have conceived of anything like this. Or anything like Ana, for that matter. She wasn't accustomed to seeing a female so scantily dressed. True she couldn't see Ana as much as see through her, but there was no question that Ana wasn't wearing much. Her meager garments were in constant movement as she jiggled and writhed, rippled her belly and contorted her body, dropped to her knees and bent backward until her hair swept the floor. Every muscle and both shoulders quivered. She concluded with a final suggestive wriggle of her hips, and a two-handed finger snap.

"Astonishing!" said Emily. "I wish I could do that."

"No you don't," retorted Ana. "Being fancied by the Sultan wasn't all that great a treat, particularly when he was in the mood for the Fixing of a Nail, because he wasn't *perky*, even with the help of a special paste made of forty-one different spices, honey, and herbs." She looked reflective. "The eunuchs, on the other hand—"

"I beg you," interrupted Val. "No more."

Ana plopped down at the foot of Emily's cot, on top of Drogo, who snapped at her. "Have you found my spell?"

Val said, "We've been a little busy. Abercrombie did inform me that if I burn acorns, mistletoe, and oak bark, at the same time murmuring my ardent desire for you to do so, you might leave."

"No!" protested Emily. "She might be able to communicate with my papa. Maybe he is still present, too."

Ana adjusted her veils. "I don't think we stay around without good reason. I wasn't here myself until Valentin called me back."

"I *didn't* call you back," Val reminded her. "That was Emily. In case there's any doubt, I would rather you weren't here."

Ana's lower lip quivered. "This, after all those vows you swore to me? Does it not matter to you if you break my heart?"

Val snorted. Emily poked him with her elbow. "Where were you before we called you back?"

Ana was still sulking. "I don't know. Somewhere *other*. I also don't know why you're not trying to find a spell to make me solid, because the sooner you find it, the sooner you can tup yourselves." She frowned. "That didn't come out right."

Though the notion of tupping oneself was intriguing, albeit somewhat perplexing, Emily was more concerned with matters more immediate. "*Can* you contact other spirits?"

Ana pouted. "I'm sure I don't know."

Chapter Twenty-Nine

Never choose your women or your linen by candlelight.

Dusk had darkened into night by the time Val escorted Emily up the stair to his front door. That portal was opened by Isidore, who so forgot himself at sight of them that his lips formed a faint approximation of a smile. Isidore's reaction was shared, rather more enthusiastically, by the other members of the household, Mrs. MacCamish even becoming inspired by Miss Dinwiddie's return to prepare a Cullen Skink. Jamie summed up everyone's feelings when he said, "Lor', Miss Emily, ye gie us an awfu fricht!"

Once assured of Emily's well-being, Zizi, Bela, and Lilian rushed off to prepare her a hot bath, and a fresh change of clothes. Jamie scurried to fetch his master a sustaining pot of tea. On, then, to the drawing room, where Machka marched up to Drogo and swatted him on the nose, then twined herself around his legs with a rumbling purr.

Lady Alberta sat in an upholstered chair, on the table beside her a stack of books. She wore a gown that flattered her, and so it should have, considering the cost. Not that Val begrudged a penny. Lady Alberta was worth her weight in gold, a weight that had noticeably increased since she'd taken up residence beneath his roof.

She watched Drogo settle on the hearth. "I don't believe I've noticed that scar before."

"It is of fairly recent origin." Machka was twining about his own legs now, and Val picked up the cat. "Nothing to concern yourself about"

Emily nudged him. *Due to Cezar. He's a healer, isn't he?*

Val placed Machka on his shoulder and took Emily's hand in his. Cezar was indeed a healer, a gift rare among the Breaslă. Impossible to tell the long-term effects of what they had done.

Emily seemed quite lively at the moment. So lively that, had Val not known better, he might think she'd been into his port.

Lady Alberta did not know better. She eyed him disapprovingly. "I don't know what's going on with the two of you—and I beg you will not tell me!—but there's definitely something in the air."

Emily grinned. "I suspect it's me."

"Whatever it is, it seems to agree with you. Have you lost your glasses, dear?"

"I have. But it doesn't matter. I don't need the silly things." Emily snatched up a small volume and began to read aloud.

"'From my grave to wander I am forc'd/Still to seek The Good's long sever'd link/Still to love the bridegroom I have lost/And the life-blood of his Heart to drink...' What drivel." She tossed the book aside.

Lady Alberta regarded her with interest. "Johann Wolfgang Von Goethe's *Bride of Corinth* is drivel?"

"The heroine is a ninny," Emily responded. "A lovestruck young maiden who dies when her parents refuse to allow her to marry her paramour, then returns from the grave to consummate her love, as beautiful as she was in life mind you, only to end up burning on a funeral pyre."

Val paid little attention to the conversation. He didn't know what to make of this hey-go-mad Emily. What he wished to *do* with her was simpler. He wanted to give her slow, sweet kisses until her toes curled.

Emily tugged him down on the sofa. Val tucked an errant tendril of hair behind her ear. Machka leapt down from his shoulder to curl up in his lap.

Val dropped his hand to the cat's soft fur. Somehow, when he wasn't paying attention, Emily had stolen past his guard.

Or had crawled under his skin. Damned if it didn't feel like she was inspecting him from the inside out. From the inside of his elbows to the outside of his knees. His shoulders to his thighs. His—

Emily's body grew warm. Her heartbeat speed up. Val's own body warmed apace until Machka growled and bit his hand, and Val recalled that they were not alone in the drawing room.

Emily. Stop staring at my mouth.

Lady Alberta rapped her knuckles on the table. "It seems I must be blunt! Whatever else the two of you have been doing, Val, I trust that you haven't given Emily the Kiss."

He had given her any number of kisses. Val found himself at a loss for words. Emily said, "What a very vulgar question. Lady Alberta, I am shocked."

Lady Alberta was briefly distracted by the arrival of Jamie with a tea tray bearing Tantallon cakes, border tarts, and raspberry buns, sent from the kitchen to sustain them until more hearty fare had been prepared. After informing them that Isidore had said that an army of stags led by a lion would be more formidable than one of lions led by a stag, Jamie was persuaded to depart.

Once she had performed the tea-pouring ritual and in the process snatched several delicacies for herself, Lady Alberta returned to the attack. "Don't be obtuse, Emily. I was referring to *the* Kiss. The Dark Kiss. The Kiss of Souls."

Emily took a bite of border tart. "I didn't know kisses had names."

"Oh, but they do, my dear! The basic sort include the Peck, which I think of as the Chicken Kiss, the Lip and Nip, the Neck Nibble, and the Butterfly. Among the more advanced varieties are the Buzzing Kiss, and the Tickle Kiss, and the Reverse Lips."

Emily said, "Hmm."

Val sipped his tea. She would require a demonstration. Miss Dinwiddie's thirst for knowledge was unquenchable.

As had been Val's thirst for her. Emily was making him remember what it was like to have life, and be in love. Although love as Val remembered it had been a simple emotion, nothing like the complex muddle of feelings he felt now. Did he regret the complicated tangle Emily had made of his existence? Val decided he did not.

He *did* regret his appalling lack of control.

Lady Alberta had not stopped talking. "Not that I should be speaking to you of *that!* Mr. Ross came to call during your absence.

He was most unhappy when I informed him that not only were you not here, I had no notion where you'd gone."

Emily licked cake crumbs from her fingers. "Lady Alberta, do you believe in the undead?"

"The Celtic Dearg-dhu, the Red Blood Witch, supposedly rises once a year from her grave to seduce men into her embrace and drain them dry of blood. Personally, I consider once a year entirely too seldom for any creature to feed." Lady Alberta gestured toward the stack of books at her elbow, which included *Dissertation on the Appearance of Angels, Demons and Spirits; and on the Revenant Vampires of Hungary, Bohemia, Moravia, and Silesia,* written in 1647, and *The Tibetan Book of the Dead.* "I have been reading all sorts of curious material, since I had to do something to distract myself from worrying about you."

Emily looked startled. "You worried about me?"

"Of course I worried. As did Isidore. Jamie and the girls scoured the town in search of you." Lady Alberta's hand hovered over the remnants of the Tantallon cake. "Why do you find it such an odd notion that someone should be concerned on your behalf?"

"I suppose because no one ever has been." Emily selected another raspberry bun. "Oh, Mama worried that I would behave inappropriately, with some justification, I admit. But she never worried about *me.* Papa simply refused to let me do anything that might have become worrying. Lest he be distracted from his experiments."

In that case, the Professor must be spinning in his grave. And if he were not, Val might give him a good shove.

Lady Alberta sat up straighter. "I see! As I was saying, my own efforts at distraction led me to reading, and I have consequently discovered that there are apparently a great many more things than hitherto dreamt of in my philosophy. I know now that if a gentleman pricks an orange all over and sleeps with it under his armpit, then presents it the next day to the object of his affections, and if the lady eats it, she will return his regard, unless instead she eats lizards dipped in urine. It hardly requires a leap of faith to also credit the existence of Mr. Polidori's vampires." Lady Alberta reached for the teapot.

Not for the first time, Val wished Polidori to perdition. Emily licked jam off her lower lip and he squelched an all-too-mortal urge to turn her tap-salteerie and acquaint every freckle on her little body with the Besotted Vampire kiss. Instead he gave Lady Alberta a brief, expurgated summary of recent events, to wit that Emily had been set upon and rescued in the very nick of time, omitting any mention of demons and ghosts lest he try her newfound tolerance too far.

Lady Alberta clasped her hands together. "How very romantic! You rescued dear Emily in the nick of time."

"How very paper-skulled, you mean. Emily could have been killed."

Emily twinkled at him. "But I wasn't killed, was I? Because of you. My hero."

Damnation. If not for the presence of Lady Alberta, Val would have had his wicked way with Emily there and then. And then he remembered that he mustn't have his wicked way with her then or ever, and was suddenly cross.

And about to become more so. Steps sounded in the stairway. Isidore's irritable tones intertwined with familiar sultry tones. Val cursed as he rose from the sofa. Emily's hands clenched into fists. Machka padded across the carpet to curl beside Drogo on the hearth.

Lisbet pushed past Isidore and into the room, elegant in a gown of embroidered silk gauze with a sarsenet slip and very likely nothing underneath. Her hair was drawn up in an Apollo knot. Around her shoulders she wore a velvet mantelet trimmed with white swansdown. "*Mea amant,* I could not imagine what had become of you. You do recall that you are engaged to me tonight, for the theater and after, Val?" She linked her arm possessively with his. "*Zau!* Lady Alberta, you have grown quite plump. My dear Miss Dinwiddie, has the cat got your tongue? You will forgive my plain speaking, but you look like something that creature dragged in."

Lady Alberta spoke before Emily could respond in kind. "Least said, soonest mended! Dear Miss Dinwiddie has been having an adventure, but we shan't bore you with that, not being at a loss for manners, unlike some I could name... What an interesting gown you are wearing, ma'am, but I fear you have left part of it behind. It is unwise to bare your chest in this climate, lest you catch your death of cold."

Never had Val been so grateful for Lady Alberta's chatter. *Elfling—*

Emily turned her face away from him. *Go to the devil, Ravensclaw!*

Chapter Thirty

Good words cool more than cold water.

The sun was shining on Auld Reekie, a rare occasion at this time of year. The streets of the Old Town were crowded with pedestrians: children escaping orphanages and the slums beneath the city; street vendors selling everything from herbs to hardware; perambulating pickpockets and prostitutes; judges in their satin robes; dissolute lordlings staggering home to their beds.

Among those savoring the sunlight was Lady Alberta. She beamed with approval at the cerulean blue sky. "What a lovely day! For once the rain isn't pouring down like cats and dogs. Wherever did that expression come from? No matter how hard it may rain, I cannot imagine miniature Drogos and Machkas descending from the heavens. Why not ducks, or perhaps, frogs?" Neither of her companions commented, though Jamie might well have, had he not grown fond of the auld bletherskate. Didnae Miss Emily look bonnie without her spectacles, and wisna he the lad o' pairts in his finery and with the knife tucked in his boot, Miss Emily being set on going out, and Lady Alberta being equally determined not to let her go out alone.

Lady Alberta pointed out places of interest as they strolled along the High Street: Brodie's Close, home to a Town Council member whose penchant for midnight burglaries climaxed in an abortive armed raid upon the Excise Office in the Royal Mile, and who was consequently hanged; John Knox's House, near its door the street well which at one time had been the only source of water in the neighborhood; the spot that had once marked the end of Edinburgh, the Canongate having been a separate town envied for its gardens and orchards. Jamie added his own observations, of a more ghoulish nature, concerning Fleshmarket Close and Coffin Lane; Greyfriars Cemetery where a mountain of corpses, executed Covenanters and plague victims, had been dumped to rot in unmarked graves.

Cemeteries were, in fact, one of the reasons Emily had been so determined to remove herself from under Ravensclaw's roof, in spite of addlebrained assailants and the bedamned athame. Canongate Kirk, and its surrounding kirkyard, stood facing the Royal Mile. The Kirk was architecturally interesting, with its Dutch-style end gable and curious, doric-columned portico. The cemetery was even more so. Various notable personages were said to be buried there, including David Rizzio, the Italian courier stabbed to death in the presence of Mary, Queen of Scots.

Lady Alberta trailed after Emily into the older part of the cemetery. "Might one know what you are looking for, my dear?"

Emily bent over to read the inscription on a tombstone. "Dirt from the grave of an innocent."

Lady Alberta sighed. "I had to ask."

Some little time passed while Emily poked and peered among the lichen-covered monuments—*Here lye the mortal remains of John Frederick Lampe whose harmonious composing shall out live Monumental register,* at the base of the stone a skull and two crossed bones, at the top two figures holding a small book. Jamie aided in her efforts, while Lady Alberta wandered off to inspect the Coachman's Stone, which displayed a skull and the motto 'memento mori', and a relief sculpture of a coach and horse crossing a bridge. It was Jamie who at last found treasure, a lass who expired at seven years of age, and a hundred years earlier, most likely being unkenand. Emily scooped up some dirt into a twist of paper, and tucked it in her reticule.

Lady Alberta rejoined them. As they descended the steps to the street, she said, "You know he really doesn't care for Lisbet Boroi."

Emily didn't pretend to misunderstand the identity of that "he." Had she not lain awake all the night waiting for Ravensclaw to return home so that she could either kiss him, or kick him, or rip off his jacket and do both at once?

The marks on her neck were fading. Soon that entire encounter would seem no more than a dream.

Where *had* Val passed the night? Not in dirt from his native land. Emily could not help but ponder the various permutations of what Val and Lisbet might have done to one another during those dark hours, and wonder whether fangs had been involved. "Then why spend so much time with her?" she snapped.

Lady Alberta glanced over her shoulder at Jamie, who was pretending not to listen. "Sometimes gentlemen find it difficult to extricate themselves from their little entanglements."

Emily doubted Val would find it difficult to untangle himself from anyone or anything. She was a case in point. He might have disengaged himself from Lisbet with equal ease, had he so wished. Therefore she must conclude he *didn't* wish to extricate himself, which was most perplexing: Emily had the impression that Val didn't like Lisbet above half.

Maybe liking wasn't of importance in matters amatory. "I'm sure I don't care."

"Doing it rather too brown, my dear, but never mind." With an assessing eye, Lady Alberta surveyed Emily's ankle-length pelisse of grey shot sarsenet; the straw and muslin capote with a stiffened brim that framed her face and hid her curls. "Since we are out, may I suggest a visit to the shops? It's time you left off those somber colors and adapted a more dashing style."

Emily wondered how Val would react if she wore her gown cut down to her navel. Maybe if she was more fashionable, he would find it less easy to disengage. More likely he would not, but Emily wasn't eager to return to his house. Lady Alberta had been kind to her, and Lady Alberta had a fondness for shopping almost equal to her fondness for Mrs. MacCamish's Honey and Whiskey Cake, and therefore shopping they would go.

Thus informed, the older woman set out like a foxhound following a scent. Within moments, Emily found herself caught up in a whirl of shoemakers and woolen-drapers, modistes and milliners and manufacturers of fine lace; engaged in the acquisition of, among other things, a Kashmir shawl, not the sort made on hand looms in Edinburgh, or heaven forbid Paisley, but the genuine article woven in a twill tapestry technique with goat's fleece taken from beneath the coarse outer hair of the underbelly of wild central Asian goats, the result being a light, smooth shawl with a natural sheen.

Having declared he'd be struck down deid afore he set foot in a ladies' emporium, Jamie waited in the street outside, for which his companions were grateful, due to his tarry-fingert tendencies. In no time at all, Emily found herself in possession of a morning cap trimmed with white work embroidery, and an evening cap confection of colored satin trimmed with ribbons and lace; a fichu of fine sheer white muslin embroidered with a continuous band of purple flowers and shaded green leaves, the edges scalloped and embroidered with green silk; ivory satin garters to hold up her stockings; a pretty pair of slippers in robin's egg blue, another of green leather with blue-green silk ribbon trim and ties, and half-boots of brown kid leather embellished with silk rosettes at the toe. Jamie attempted to balance the pyramid of purchases, and muttered that since he was packed up like a donkey, the ladies might want to bewaur 'is teeth.

"Don't sham it so, you cheeky wee rapscallion!" Lady Alberta caught a package in mid-tumble and tucked it back under his chin. Her questing eye was next caught by a chemist's shop. There was nothing for it then but they must sample Improved Gowland's Lotion, Royal Tincture of Peach Kernels, and Olympia Dew. Did Emily know that the juice of green pineapples would take away wrinkles and give the complexion an air of youth, and that if pineapples were not available, onions would do as well?

Emily did not. Nor had she been aware that powdered parsley seed prevented baldness, or that grated horseradish immersed in sour milk would remove freckles. Of this latter, she remained unconvinced. If her recent adventures had left her freckles unaffected, then they were with her for life, in their vast numbers and various hues.

Their transactions finally completed—Emily having at the last minute been inspired, or coerced, to invest in some Pomade de Nerole for her unruly hair—the ladies returned to the street. Jamie's pile of packages now reached almost to his nose.

"Hsst!" He gestured. Outside the Penny Post Office, from which letters and small parcels were dispatched eight times a day to Leith, stood Michael Ross.

Michael threaded his way through the traffic. "Emily! I almost didn't recognize you without your spectacles. Have you broken them again?" He cast Lady Alberta a dark glance. "I must speak privately with you."

Lady Alberta drew herself up to her full height. "I trust you jest, young man. Anything you have to say to my niece may be said in front of me."

Emily winced as Michael grasped her elbow. Lady Alberta continued, "I trust I make myself clear. You may be as private as you wish with Emily *after* you are wed."

Michael didn't argue. He simply punched Lady Alberta on the chin. With a screech and a flurry of petticoats, she toppled over, landing on top of Jamie. Packages went flying everywhere. Passersby quickly gathered round to gawk and offer advice and try to snatch some of the scattered parcels. Jamie kicked one would-be thief in the knee and elbowed another in the cods and demanded to know what had given anyone the idea he was a chuntyheid? In the midst of the confusion, Michael hauled Emily with him down the street.

She snatched at her bonnet. "Do slow down, Michael, pray! I will accompany you willingly, if only you stop pawing me about." Or not-so-willingly, truth be told, but it was past time she discovered what the deuce he was about.

"You haven't gone anywhere willingly with me since you came to Edinburgh." Michael's fingers dug into her flesh.

Through a labyrinth of crooked closes he drew her, turning first this way and then the other, so that even if she wished she couldn't have found the way again. They came at length—if Emily's sense of direction had not entirely deserted her—to the warren of vaults formed by the arches of the South Bridge. Michael plunged through a crumbling doorway, down a dim passage so narrow that Emily could have laid a hand on either side, so steep that in bad weather the ground would be as treacherous as ice.

So this was the underground city she had heard so much about. The atmosphere was dense with open fires for heat and cooking, the stink of human excrement, the reek of fish-oil lamps that provided what little light there was. Loiterers littered the broken pavements, unkempt barefoot children, ragged men, women wearing tattered flannel petticoats and ancient tartan shawls. Some were sleeping, some were drunk. Some would never venture out into daylight. Michael grabbed a lantern and dragged her through a series of abandoned tunnels. Emily gasped for breath. The air was noxious, stifling. Michael was muttering under his breath.

Around one last corner, down a slippery incline. An ancient door loomed ahead. Michael inserted a key into the lock. A tomblike vault gaped open. He pushed Emily into the room. She tripped and fell to the ground.

The hard ground. Emily cried out as her hands encountered stone so rough it tore the soft kid of her gloves. Behind her, the door slammed shut.

She scrambled to her feet. The palms of her hands stung. Emily pulled off her torn gloves.

Michael had hung his lantern from a rusted hook set high in the old wall. Laid out on a rickety table, a collection of instruments gleamed in its sickly light. Spring-loaded lancets, fleams, a scarifier with a series of twelve spring-driven blades that when cocked and released would cause many shallow cuts, a sharp curved sword—

The room stank of fish oil, and worse. Pungent herbs smoldered in a brazier. What was that, tossed so carelessly into a corner? Emily choked back bile. From the grisly stack of severed heads came the stink of rotting meat.

Ravensclaw would have *her* head for putting herself in this position. If only she had her pistol, lost in the encounter with Samael. Or even her umbrella, which Lady Alberta had insisted be left behind, because to carry it in such lovely weather would seem odd indeed. At least she had the pendant. And her necklace of charms.

She couldn't just stand here, quivering like a trapped rabbit. Emily attempted to sound stern. "What is this place, Michael? Why have you brought me here?"

"You left me no choice." Michael pressed one palm against his temple. "Deuce take it, Emily, why are you so determined to be a thorn in my flesh?"

Was it the headache that caused him to appear unwell, so feverish and gaunt? "How?" Emily asked.

Michael looked confused. "How what?"

"How am I a thorn in your flesh?"

He glared at her. "You shouldn't have come to Edinburgh. All this is your fault."

"How can you say that? I'm not the one who broke into the Society's vaults. Were you also responsible for Papa's accident? Was it you who sent those men to snatch me? Who summoned Samael?" Emily almost wished the demon would pop up now. She would rather bargain with Samael than with Michael, which gave rise to the question of which was the greater fiend.

Michael wrinkled his brow. "Summoned who?" he said. "The gull-gropers had got their talons so deep in me I thought I'd never manage to row myself out of the River Tick. But then the professor— You know how he went on! He was waxing enthusiastic about Jean Baptiste Lamark's theory of *Transformisme*, and not paying me attention, at least I thought he wasn't, and so I grasped the opportunity to pocket his keys. Unfortunately, as it turned out, he may as well have had eyes in the back of his head. I meant him no harm, I swear it. If you weren't so damned unreasonable you'd admit I had no choice." If Emily had been unreasonable, it was in giving this horrid man the benefit of the doubt. "Of course you had a choice. You could have chosen *not* to murder Papa. Michael, you must give me the athame."

"I must, must I?" It was as if a stranger stared at her through his eyes. "What I *must* have is your pendant. Now."

Emily felt the amulet flare to life. "I'm not wearing it today."

"Liar." Michael raised his hand. His sleeve fell back. Lamplight gleamed on leprous flesh, glittered off the sharp edge of a blade.

Independence and so forth were all well and good in their place, but it was clearly time to call for assistance. Even though she wasn't speaking to him. *I'm sorry! I'm a peabrain! Please help me, Val!*

Michael started toward her. Emily edged away from him, stumbled over something lying on the floor. A large something, lean and muscular, with chestnut hair half-hiding a harsh, scarred face. She knelt beside him, saw no obvious injuries. "Mr. Torok?"

"It is not so difficult to snare an old fox. Give me the pendant, or I will take it from you." Michael raised the knife.

Emily didn't doubt he'd try. Fluttering her eyelashes, she said, "Does this mean you no longer wish to marry me, Michael?"

Chapter Thirty-One

Curses, like chickens, come home to roost.

Val would have been first to admit that he was very old. Just recently he had attempted to reckon his own age, using human lifetimes as a measuring stick: if he counted four generations to a century, he could be Emily's grandfather how many times removed?

The resulting answer caused him to swear off higher mathematics. Val and Emily weren't May and December, they were this century and the dawn of time, and why was he tormenting himself? He couldn't have Emily, and that was the end of the matter. He couldn't let her have him. And he would be eternally damned before he allowed anyone to do her harm.

Not that he wasn't already eternally damned. And damn Lisbet as well for showing up before he'd found an opportunity for explanations and then keeping him with her until well past dawn.

He'd left her now, and without a word of explanation. Let Lisbet make of that what she would. She was already displeased with his performance, or his lack thereof.

Emily was frightened. Val experienced her emotions as if they were his own, and with them a great rage. Emily was his—well, not really, but if he wasn't what he was she damned well would have been—and if anyone was going to frighten her, it should be him.

He didn't wish to frighten her. He *did* wish to shake her until her teeth rattled in her head.

She served as his beacon. In less than the time it took to think his angry thoughts, Val was in the vaults beneath the South Bridge.

Into the gloomy abandoned tunnels, where his keen eyesight and heightened senses guided him more surely than any light, around one last corner, down a treacherous pathway— Emily's presence was so vivid Val could almost touch her. Her voice came to him through an ancient barred door.

She sounded calm, all things considered. "You can't get your hands on all my lovely money unless you marry me, Michael. And you can't marry me if I'm dead."

Val paused, poised to break down the door, as Michael spoke. "You shan't tell me what I can and cannot do! Anyway, I'm not the one who wants you dead."

"Then who?"

"I can't say."

A moment's silence, while Emily ruminated. Through her eyes Val saw the small stone chamber, the table with its grisly instruments, the grim corner display—and Andrei? What was Andrei doing here? Emily appeared to be in no immediate danger, so Val waited to hear what she would say next.

Which was, "Do you remember the Phantasmagoria, Michael?"

"The Magic Lantern. Adjustable lenses and ventriloquism and moving slides. I remember everything, Emily." A pause. "Almost."

"Then you may also remember that people believed the forces of darkness and sorcery were responsible for the lantern's ability to project images where none had been before. Which was so much twaddle. Whatever *you* believe, Michael, the athame must be returned to the Society."

Val felt the athame, stronger now than he remembered, even more dangerous. It was the nature of the thing to feed off the person who wielded it. Michael Ross was no longer the young man who had courted Emily.

"The knife belongs to whoever holds it, and I'm holding it now. See how it gleams in the lamplight, Emily." His voice was almost pensive. "Feel how sharp it is."

Val felt the sting of the blade as it pierced her skin. Furious with himself for delaying, he kicked in the door.

Emily glanced at him. Her wrist was bleeding. *I apologize for wishing you to the devil. Thank you for coming anyway.* Michael took advantage of the distraction to slip his knife under the clasps of her pelisse. They melted like soft butter, exposing the pendant to view.

He reached for it. Emily clasped her hand around the ruby and backed away.

Marie d'Auvergne's athame and her pendant in one place at last. The air throbbed with unfocussed power. Val felt as if his feet were mired in sludge.

He couldn't move. Not only power, but something else had him in its grip. Burning in the brazier were pungent herbs. As Val tried to identify them, Michael spun and sprang at him, athame upraised to strike.

Val! Emily hurled herself in front of Michael. He shoved her aside. She slammed against the instrument-laden table. It collapsed, taking her with it to the floor.

Val recognized the unfamiliar smell then, as his limbs refused to obey him. "Adder's tongue," said Michael Ross. "So much for vampiric powers. You walked into the trap, just like your friend." The young man feinted and jabbed, putting Val in mind of a whirling dervish he had seen lifetimes ago.

Mr. Ross was fortunate that Val couldn't move, else he would have snapped the bastard's neck. He stood frozen while Michael slashed at him with the athame, and the sharp blade drew blood.

One hand emerged from the table wreckage, then a leg. Emily was swearing, viciously, in his head. *What in all the hells is the matter with you, Val?*

The herb burning in the brazier. It renders us helpless. See if you can rouse Andrei.

Michael paid no attention as Emily scrambled out from under what was left of the table. Her scalp was bleeding now, as well as her wrist.

The adder's tongue hadn't affected Val's vision, or his ability to appreciate the sight of Emily's sweetly upturned bottom. If this was to be his last sight, it was at least a pleasant one. He regretted both his prudence and his forbearance, now that it was too late.

Over her shoulder, she scowled at him. *Never did I think to hear such drivel from the great Ravensclaw.* As Michael brought down the knife again, she jerked open her reticule, uncorked her vinaigrette, and stuck it under Andrei's nose. The sharp scent of vinegar mingled with the other odors in the room.

Michael danced around, slicing and chanting until Val felt like a maypole being wound about with ribbons of blood. "Stinking motherwort grows upon dunghills. Moonwort will open locks and unshoe horses. Dead nettle— I forget what dead nettle does, but it will come back to me."

Emily said, irritably, "Stop this foolishness at once!"

Ignoring her, Michael pricked Val again with the athame. "How do you like your adder's tongue, Ravensclaw? The juice of the leaves, drunk with the distilled water of horse-bait, is a singular remedy for all manner of wounds. The leaves, infused with the oil of unripe olives, set in the sun four days, make an excellent green balsam. Not that either will help you now."

There was something wrong here, Val realized, beyond adder's tongue and lunacy. He concentrated all his effort on holding the madman's attention fixed on him as Emily reached stealthily for the sword and Andrei climbed unsteadily to his feet.

Emily propped Andrei up, shoved the sword at him, and pressed the vinaigrette into his other hand. He looked disheveled and disreputable, and no whit less dangerous for the vinaigrette held to his nose. Flickering lamplight lent his scarred face a diabolic cast as he stared Val in the eye and smiled. Andrei's smile at the best of times was chilling. In this moment he resembled the Grim Reaper responding to a bad joke.

"What do you think, Emily? I could pour boiling oil on him, make a paste of his flesh and feed on it, cut off his toes." Michael's feverish gaze was still fixed on Ravensclaw.

Emily edged closer to them. "Cook his heart with vinegar, oil, and wine? Prevent him from straying by stabbing nine spindles into his grave? You are carrying this too far."

Michael reached out for Emily. "If you drink the lifeblood of your enemy, you will gain his powers. You and I should drink the blood of Ravensclaw."

"I already have. It was quite tasty." Emily raised her hand and threw the contents of a paper packet into Michael's eyes.

"Gaaah!" Blinded, he lowered the athame. Emily dropped to her knees as Andrei swung the sword.

Blood sprayed as metal shredded flesh, shattered bone. Michael screamed and fell. Dragging his useless arm, he crawled toward the broken table of instruments. Andrei swung the sword again, and once more for good measure. Michael's head rolled to rest among the others stacked up by the wall.

The fresh air—'fresh' being a relative term in a place like this— had begun to sweep away the poisonous smoke. Val found that he could speak. "You can open your eyes now," he said weakly, as Andrei, still holding the vinaigrette to his nose, extinguished the brazier and carried it into the passageway.

Emily snatched up the athame, dropped to the floor beside Val. She had lost her bonnet, and her hair stuck out in all directions, and she was the loveliest thing he had ever seen. "You have rescued me again, elfling. What was that you threw into his eyes?"

"Dirt from the grave of an innocent. I had fetched it for another use, but it turns out to be very handy stuff." She frowned at his numerous cuts. "You're not healing."

"It's the adder's blood."

Emily pulled her sleeve away from her still-bleeding wrist. Val tried to turn his head. She threaded her fingers through his hair and made him look at her. "Yes, I know. You don't trust yourself to take me again without taking me too far. Well, *I* trust you. Don't be so stubborn, Val."

Val had meant to keep Emily safe, at least until he was certain she suffered no ill effects from her misadventures. If Val were honest with himself, he wanted to keep her safe longer than that. For Emily, forever wouldn't be enough time.

But he didn't have forever. Or if he did, Emily did not. What she did have were both the d'Auvergne athame and its matching pendant. Val could no more have resisted her than the earth could have refused to orbit the sun.

Not that he wanted to resist her. *This is becoming a habit, little one.*

A pleasant one, I hope. She drew him closer. *Pleasure me, Val.*

Her skin was sweet against his lips. Her scent rolled over him. Val pressed his mouth to her wrist, and drank. She sprawled atop him, her head resting against his chest.

The adder's tongue had worn off. Val could have moved, had he the inclination. Emily's riotous curls were tickling his nose.

He knew he should stop. He didn't want to. She moaned.

That little sound undid him. Rules be damned. Val would take Emily home and make love to her as she deserved. Flesh to flesh. Heart to heart. He would introduce her to all the forms of loving that he knew, and then make up some more. He would—

She thumped him in the ribs. *Val.*

He groaned. *What now?* If Ana had interrupted them again he'd find a way to make her corporeal long enough that he could wrap his hands around her throat.

Andrei's ruined voice roused him. "The Stăpâna, Valentin."

All the warmth drained from Val's body. He set Emily aside and rose.

Lisbet stood in the doorway. *"Iubiera ca moartea e de tare.* I warned you, *baĭat."*

Chapter Thirty-Two

Women are the devil's nets.

Lisbet threw back the Persian shawl she wore draped over her head. Her pale skin glowed in the lamplight. Dark hair tumbled loose over the shoulders of her muslin morning gown. "What a cozy gathering. All we lack is Cezar. How very vexing of him to refuse to rise to the bait."

Val stepped forward to face her. Andrei bowed his head. Emily slid the athame into the small pocket of her pelisse as she climbed slowly to her feet.

Tension lay thick in the room. Tension and dark energy.

Lisbet prodded Michael's lifeless body with her toe. "A faulty tool, but useful for a time." She fixed her eyes on Emily. "Troublesome chit, you have been playing with my toys."

Emily was feeling more than a little vexed herself. "Your toy has been killing people. Was that your intent?"

Lisbet moved closer. "You misunderstand. I was speaking of Ravensclaw."

Emily glanced at Val. His mind was closed to her, his face as cold as the stone walls. He said, "Lisbet. Let her go."

"No." Lisbet's tone bit like a whip. "You disobeyed me. To take your little English miss away from you would be a fitting punishment, I think."

Val was trying to protect her, Emily realized. He didn't want Lisbet to learn of their shared bond. She said, "You consider Ravensclaw your toy?"

Lisbet circled Andrei. He made no move of protest when she trailed her hand along his arm, took the sword from his hand. "Val,

Andrei, and Cezar. Pretty, are they not? A pity they are equally flawed. Cezar's failing is arrogance, Andrei's pride, while Val cares for nothing but himself and his pleasure." Lisbet snapped the sword in half and tossed it aside. "I wonder, Miss Dinwiddie, how well he has pleasured you."

Not well enough, not yet. Emily didn't dare look at Val.

"Don't try and deny it." Lisbet ran her finger along the sword's sharp blade. "Val has set his mark on you. Cezar might have stopped him, but he did not. Andrei appeared to remain loyal to me but is nothing of the sort. I would have dealt with them before this, had not other matters taken up my time." Blood welled from Lisbet's finger, dripped down her hand.

Val hadn't stirred. Andrei stood impassively. Emily felt like a rabbit cowering in a forest of tall, motionless trees.

Lisbet raised her bleeding finger to Andrei's lips. "I grow weary of this conversation. You will give me the pendant now."

The sight of Andrei licking Lisbet's blood was beyond unsettling. "The phrase 'over my dead body' comes to mind."

Lisbet threw back her head and laughed. "You think to challenge me?"

Emily thought someone should challenge Lisbet, and she appeared to be the only one so inclined. Brave little bunny that she was. Her body hummed with the combined power of the pendant and the athame. "It seems I don't have a choice."

Lisbet stepped away from Andrei. Her dark, bottomless gaze pulled at Emily with tangible force. Emily stared back, caught up in that slumberous, seductive spell. Lisbet's dark eyes were mysterious, mesmerizing—

As bottomless as the pit, came Cezar's voice in her mind. *And as dangerous. Draw back, Emily. Now!*

Emily blinked. Lisbet stood so close she could feel the heat of the other woman's body. Emily hadn't seen her move.

Lisbet stroked a cool finger down her cheek. "Give me the pendant, child."

Emily almost wished she could. The thing was searing her flesh. She reached out for Cezar, and struck out with all their combined mental strength.

Lisbet recoiled. The force of her fury sent Emily to her knees.

It was like being buffeted by a storm. A very angry storm that shrieked and raged with a force strong enough to peel her skin from her bones. Emily squared her shoulders and opened her eyes.

There was nothing to focus one's concentration like staring at a set of fangs. Lisbet's fangs, to be precise.

"Stupid girl!" hissed Lisbet. "I am Val's Stăpână. His mistress. Do you understand?"

Emily had thought she did. She was no longer sure. Speechless, she shook her head.

Lisbet's fingers dug like talons into her shoulder. "I made him, you stupid girl. I made them all. Now they are grown so ungrateful as to try and find a way to escape my hold. *Proşti!* There is none."

Emily felt like she was drowning. She sensed Cezar in her mind, and less clearly Andrei and Val. They all seemed to be telling her she must do something. *What?*

It was Cezar who responded. *Don't give her the pendant.*

She wasn't such a ninny. Emily snatched up a piece of the broken table and thwacked Lisbet on the knee.

"*Tâmpita!*" Lisbet flicked her hand across Emily's face, a movement so quick that Emily barely saw it coming before she tasted blood. "Cease this foolishness. I know you have the pendant, and the athame as well. I can feel them. I *will* have them. Cease wasting my time."

Emily slipped her hand into her pocket. Herbs no longer burned in the brazier; why, then, were Val and Andrei so quiet and still? According to the literature, a vampire could not kill its maker. She could only hope this was not an occasion on which the literature was proved correct.

Lisbet struck Emily another sharp blow. "Give them to me and mayhap I will let you live."

Emily believed that no more than she believed in flying pigs. "No."

"Then I shall simply take them." A concussive surge of current, and Lisbet stood transformed into a creature straight from nightmare, all fangs and claws and dead black eyes.

What *was* she? Lamia? Empusa? Some new sort of monster altogether? Emily hoped she survived long enough to make an addendum to the Dinwiddie list.

At the moment, it seemed less than likely. Lisbet was like a magnet, drawing the athame. Emily dug her fingernails into the handle of the knife.

She needed to break Lisbet's concentration, but how? "Goodness, but you're ugly! You should do something about that skin. I'm told that the juice of green pineapple takes away wrinkles and imparts the air of youth."

Snarling, Lisbet leapt. At the same time, Val stirred. In a blur of speed, he placed himself in front of Emily. He, too, had changed, into the fanged, clawed creature Emily had seen once before. But he was no monster. He was simply Val.

Lisbet swung the sword at him. Val leaped aside. She rocked back, lunged for his throat. He swept her arm aside and clamped his hands around her neck. She jammed her elbows between his and reached for the hollow where his jawbone met his skull. He flung her away from him.

Emily started forward, toward the discarded sword. Andrei caught her wrist. She struggled to jerk free. "What are you doing? Let go of me!"

His hand gripped her like a steel band. "*Sst!* Do not distract me unless you want to see Val harmed."

Emily didn't want to see Val harmed. Or anyone else. Unless it was Lisbet, and that she longed for fervently.

Val caught Lisbet's arm and snapped it. She slammed him to the ground. He sent her sprawling with a kick to the jaw. She picked up the sword and flew back at him, knocking him off balance. He struggled, but she hacked and slashed until she was straddling him, one hand fisted in his hair to pull back his head, the sword pressed to his flesh. Emily wrenched away from Andrei with strength that surprised both of them, and flung the athame.

It struck Lisbet in the throat. "Jesu!" she cried, and clasped her neck. Val shoved her off him. Emily pulled out the athame, leaving a gaping wound. She reached for the pendant and, as an afterthought, her necklace of charms.

A flash of light, the sizzle and stench of burning flesh. Lisbet spat and cringed.

Emily stared at her crucifix. "Why did it work this time?"

Andrei replied, huskily, "Because she believes."

If temporarily distracted, Lisbet was far from defeated. Before anyone could try and stop her, she sketched strange symbols and chanted an incantation in a foreign tongue.

The air filled with mist and smoke. When it cleared a great winged creature stood in the middle of the room. Emily grasped the pendant in one hand, and the athame in the other. "Samael, angel of death, prince of the fifth heaven, genii of fire, demon who tempted Eve—"

"Stupid girl!" Blood spewed from the gaping hole in Lisbet's throat. "The Darkness is mine."

"Not for long, unless he wishes to be." Even as Emily spoke, Samael changed from a large snake with scales of metallic green and blue, a bald head, and multicolored eyes into a great hulking mound of black-charred flesh and muscle, fingers and toes that ended in deadly sharp talons, and several rows of razor-sharp teeth; and finally a rather pretty goat with cloven hooves and eerie yellow eyes. "That was a most impressive display, but could we leave off the theatrics, Samael?"

The demon reverted to his manlike form, and shook out his wings. "I had so hoped to impress you. And no, I *don't* wish to be."

Lisbet shrieked and rushed forward. Samael bowled her over with a lazy flick of one great wing.

"Pray take Lisbet away, and keep her there." The pendant had grown almost too hot for Emily to hold. "Somewhere *other,* so she will bother us no more. Incidentally, you won't bother us anymore, either. Do you understand?"

"Perfectly." With his wing, Samael held Lisbet pinned to the ground.

Emily raised both the pendant and the athame. "Samael, angel of death, prince of air, leader of the angels who married the daughters of men, I command you in the name of Yod, Cados, Eloym, Saboath, and Yeshua the Anointed One to return from whence you came."

Thunder cracked. The floor, the walls around then shifted and shook. When the dust settled, both Lisbet and Samael were gone. Emily thanked the heavens that her papa had made her memorize her abjuration spells.

Val turned to her. "Put down the athame."

Was it the athame he had wanted all along? Had Emily misjudged him, too?

So be it, then. She dropped the knife.

Val reached out, and drew her close. Emily hugged him tightly, not minding in the least that he was covered in a great deal of blood. Val said, into her hair, "I had wanted you to be aware of the beast that is part of my nature, though not so graphically as this."

Did he expect her to run away shrieking from him? Privately, Emily admitted that this episode had given her pause. When everything was said and done, the most charismatic vampire in all existence remained a vampire.

"That was *very* interesting!" Ana hovered in midair. "If a waste of good graveyard dirt. I found your papa, Emily. He was arguing with Albertus Magnus about an ever-burning lamp, and said he didn't have time for mortal nonsense, but that you're a clever girl and will figure it all out."

A clever girl, was she? The hereafter hadn't changed her papa one whit. And his opinion of her was higher than Emily had realized.

Andrei shook himself as if emerging from a trance. Or a state of shock. "Sister? What are you doing here? Why are you dressed like *that*?"

Ana said, "Oh, rats."

Chapter Thirty-Three

No herb will cure love.

Lady Alberta and Cezar sat in the drawing room, a tea tray on the table in front of them. Val recognized the skeleton of a plum cake. Cezar held a teacup. Lady Alberta pressed a towel filled with melting ice to her bruised chin. "Good gracious!" she said, as Val and Emily walked into the room. "Speak of something the cat dragged in. My dear, you really should take better care of your clothes."

True, Emily resembled something Machka might have dragged in. Val fancied he looked even worse for wear. He said to Cezar, "You're drinking tea?"

"Brandy." Cezar watched Emily drop into a chair. "We finished off the tea some time ago. I assume you'd like a fresh pot?"

"Isidore is bringing it."

Cezar said, sardonically, "Isidore informed me upon my arrival that an ass was an ass, though laden with gold."

Lady Alberta reached for the brandy decanter. "We were just discussing the *Historia Rerum Agticarum*. The author, William of Newburg, refers to 'certain prodigies' who sallied forth from their graves to wander about wreaking terror and destruction." She poured herself a generous libation. "Mr. Korzha, of course, doesn't acknowledge the existence of such things."

"Of course." Val leaned against the back of Emily's chair.

Cezar saluted them with his teacup. "The eagle has been vanquished, Miss Dinwiddie. I congratulate you both."

"But for how long, I wonder," Emily said.

"I have discovered a most interesting recipe for a love philter," offered Lady Alberta, her tone somewhat garbled due to the towel she held against her chin. "One powders together the heart of a dove, liver of a sparrow, womb of a swallow, and kidney of a hare. I dislike to be vulgarly inquisitive, dear Emily, but the last time I saw you that dreadful Mr. Ross was dragging you off somewhere. Fortunately, Mr. Korzha arrived in time to rescue Jamie and me from that mob. As Ravensclaw rescued you, I credit." She eyed Val, and his bloodstained appearance. "Or perchance you rescued him."

Emily smiled up at Val. "It was some of both."

He added, "Mr. Ross will bother Emily no more."

"Then you did give him his bastings!" Lady Alberta beamed.

"Rather," murmured Emily, "Andrei baked his bread."

Lady Alberta fanned herself with the damp towel. "Ordinarily, one hesitates to speak ill of the departed, but in this case—"

Emily shifted in her chair. "Lisbet Boroi has left Edinburgh."

"Was, er, her bread also baked?"

"No. Although I wouldn't be surprised if Samael took some sort of revenge."

"The angel Samael?" Lady Alberta held up her hand. "Forget I asked!"

Emily glanced around the room. "Where are Machka and Drogo?"

"They were both here earlier. I'm sure I don't know."

Cezar rose to leave, bowed over Lady Alberta's hand. She blushed like a young girl. Val said, "There's something I neglected to tell you. Ana has returned."

Cezar's poise briefly deserted him. *"Ana?"*

Emily explained, "She's haunting Val. Demanding to be made corporeal so she can be tupped."

Lady Alberta echoed faintly, "Tupped?"

"That is what she called it, among other things. The beast with two—"

Lady Alberta fanned herself more briskly. "Never mind!"

Cezar murmured, "Secrets, Val?"

Val walked with Cezar to the stairway. Secrets were but one of the tools he had employed to survive. All three of them would experience some malaise as a result of Lisbet's banishment. Andrei would suffer worst. Lisbet's claws had sunk deepest into him.

"Whereas you will suffer least," said Cezar. "I give you my blessing. Take advantage of it before I change my mind."

"And the consequences?"

"Miss Dinwiddie is your *ailaltă*. She has met the *provocare*. Even the Council cannot naysay you now." Cezar touched Val's arm. "Go, be happy, *camarad.*"

Val stood in the doorway as Cezar descended the stair. When he turned back into the room, he found both women watching him. Emily's mind remained closed.

Having polished off the last of the plum cake, Lady Alberta shook crumbs off her skirt. "I believe it's time that I retire."

Emily studied her dirty hands. "Leaving me alone with Ravensclaw? How very broad-minded of you."

Lady Alberta tutted. "It would be remiss of me if this were the first time, but since it is not, forbidding you would be like locking the barn after the horse has bolted." She rose from her chair.

Emily sat up straighter. "My business in Edinburgh is done, and I will soon be going home. I wonder, Lady Alberta, if you would care to return to England with me. I can offer you a comfortable home, and would be glad of your company."

"What a lovely invitation, and so generously extended. I will consider it, my dear." Lady Alberta left the room without meeting Val's gaze.

"I will take Jamie, too, of course," Emily announced.

Val folded his arms across his chest and uttered not a word.

She got to her feet. "And now I shall also retire."

Val stood in his empty drawing room. He felt as if he had been flattened by a gaggle of stampeding geese. A pity brandy no longer served him, or he would have been tempted to down a gallon of the stuff. In no mood for further conversation—not that anyone appeared eager to converse with him—he withdrew to his own bedchamber.

Tea awaited him there. Val picked up the pot and flung it into the fireplace. His feelings—feelings, for God's sake! Shouldn't he be beyond such stuff?—in no whit improved by this demonstration of temper, he stared at his reflection in the looking-glass. Torn and bloodstained clothing... He looked like the walking dead.

Hell, he *was* the walking dead. Scant surprise that Emily wanted no more to do with him. She had seen him as he truly was, and no amount of glamour would erase that from her mind. Val would not try to sway her. Even if he could.

He had once thought himself content, before Emily forced her way into his life and turned his comfortable existence upside down; had reminded him of all these unsettling mortal emotions he had long forgot. It wasn't blood that Val needed now to survive.

He *would* survive without her. He had no real choice. If Emily was so disgusted as to walk away from him, then Val must let her go.

It wasn't as if he hadn't known from the beginning that this moment must arrive. Val tore off his ruined clothes and approached the copper tub of hot water Isidore had left for him, scrubbed savagely at his skin. Self-scourging didn't ease his misery, but at length he felt clean. As he was stepping into a pair of breeches, Emily walked into the room.

She closed the door and leaned against it. "Now, where were we?"

You were tossing me back into the sea like an underweight haddock, thought Val, but only to himself, as he pulled up his breeches and fastened them. Because Emily had previously demonstrated interest in his bare chest, he left off his shirt. "Andrei has gone to Mr. Ross's lodgings to retrieve the remaining stolen items."

"You read Michael's thoughts?"

Difficult not to do so when the man had been so close, and a true cesspit his mind had been. "I did. Abercrombie bought your books. I'm sure he can be persuaded to return them to you. For a fee."

Emily was carrying a small earthen bowl and a candle. She placed them on a table and set the mixture alight, then moved to the hearth. "Do you want me to return Marie d'Auvergne's necklace to you?"

What the devil was she wearing? It was frilly, frothy, shockingly low-cut. And startlingly flimsy in the firelight. "Would you return it if I asked?"

She pursed her lips. Val said, quickly, "Never mind. You will know what's best done with the necklace and the athame." What in Hades was she burning? He smelled acorns, mistletoe, and oak.

Emily remained silhouetted in front of the fire. "Lady Alberta chose my negligee. She seems to know a great deal more about such things than she should."

'Such things?' Val's curiosity was piqued. Before he could pursue that intriguing topic, Emily spoke again. "Some of this might have been prevented, were I not so hesitant to take up my duties as overseer of the Dinwiddie Society."

"Don't be absurd." Val crossed the room to her. "The fault is mine. I was unable to keep Lisbet from knowing how I felt. And then I gave you the amulet. You would have been in little danger otherwise." Her scraped palms were already healing. He started to turn away.

Emily caught his arm. "I would have been in *worse* danger, because I would have come in search of the athame and Lisbet would have squashed me like a spider." She touched the scars forming on his chest.

Val shuddered. "Emily—"

She pressed her fingers to his lips. "Shush! I have decided to be blunt. That fight with Lisbet—"

Val couldn't bear to hear the words. "I understand."

"No, you don't. It was the most stimulating thing I've ever seen."

Val stared at her, bemused. "You are partial to stimulating sights?"

"I think I must be." Emily appeared to be considering the matter. "However, I hadn't seen any until I met you."

Could she mean what he thought she meant? "What are you saying, Emily?"

She looked up at him. "It was the strangest thing, feeling Cezar in my head. I didn't like it much."

Val was pleased to hear this, jealousy being one of the all-too-mortal feelings he'd been experiencing of late. He was less pleased when she drew back and said, "How *do* you feel about me, Val?"

Why must women ask such questions? *Touch me, Emily.*

Like this? She laid her hand on his heart.

Val wanted very much to touch her in turn. "You would be wise to leave now, elfling. Vampires don't have hearts."

Piffle. You have mine.

He froze. Emily swatted him. "I won't die of love, you know."

"I know." Thanks to that abominably provocative bit of nothing that she wore, however, he might well die of lust. "What do you want from me?"

"I want you to make love to me. Heart to heart. Flesh to flesh." She colored fiercely. "To teach me the Buzzing Kiss and the Reverse Lips. And most of all—"

"Most of all—?"

Emily rose on tiptoe. "Most of all," she murmured against his lips, "I would like to experience the Fixing of a Nail."

Chapter Thirty-Four

All meat to be eaten, and all maids to be wed.

He lowered his lips to her throat. Pleasure hummed through her veins. His teeth found her pulse. A melting sensation, a growing warmth...

Her hand clutched his shoulders as he traced her mouth with his tongue, teased her with feather touches until she opened for him, her hands fisted in his hair. He laughed and kissed her breasts, her belly, and the inside of her knees; covered every inch of her body with slow, merciless caresses; loved her with long slow strokes of his tongue. His fangs scraped the inside of her thigh.

Her body burned. She whispered, "Val."

He looked up at her. And then—

"Hah!" said a familiar voice. Emily opened one eye to find Ana perched on the foot of the bed. The ghost appeared irritated. Emily said, "Too late."

"Too— You didn't!" Ana bounced indignantly.

"I did." Emily savored the recollection. "Several times. And what a revelation it was. So you see it does you no good to try and stop us now. I already know what happens next."

Ana tsk'd. "Times have not changed for the better. I would have been shocked right out of my garters to find another woman in my husband's bed. Val *is* my husband. You can't get around that."

"Stuff and nonsense!" Emily sat up. "He *was* your husband and you aren't wearing garters. For that matter—" She paused as strong warm fingers moved under the mound of covers to wrap around one bare leg. "Neither am I. Ana, I need to speak privately with Val.

Will you leave us if I promise to find some more nice graveyard dirt?"

"I don't know that I shall ever leave. I am feeling cross." Ana put her foot on the lump beneath the covers, and attempted to give it a good shove. "Burning acorns and mistletoe and oak to keep me away. That should be against the rules."

"I'm not sure there *are* rules for things such as this," said Emily. "If there are, I don't want to know them, because I suspect it's far better to make them up as one goes along. Now shoo."

Ana folded her arms beneath her shapely bosom. "I won't."

"You will, else you make *me* cross." Emily attempted to look stern, no easy undertaking in light of what those strong, warm fingers were doing to her leg. "If I can banish demons, I can surely get rid of one pesky ghost."

Ana thrust out her lower lip. Emily raised her hand and began to chant. "Air, Fire, Water, Earth—"

"Oh, very well!" Ana disappeared.

The lump beneath the covers stirred. "Did you really get rid of her?"

"Temporarily."

Val sat up, caught her hand, and raised it to his lips. "Miss Dinwiddie, you are remarkable."

"No, I rather think you are, after last night. I had no idea... Well, I may have had a little, because Lady Alberta explained certain things. How Lady Alberta knows what she does, *I* don't want to know, but she was almost prescient in predicting the effect of the negligee." Emily glanced at that item, whose remnants lay in a frothy puddle on the floor. Val pulled her back down beside him on the bed.

She peered uncertainly into his face. *You won't send me away?*

Why would I do that?

Some idiotic nobility of character?

Vampires aren't noble. Didn't your literature tell you that?

Emily wondered who wrote those silly books. Val had been so concerned that she'd turn away from him after seeing his other form. She might have been annoyed with him for so misjudging her, were she not in such a splendid mood.

"It wasn't so much a matter of misjudging you," said Val. "As the inescapable fact that I am *vampir*."

"So? I'm freckled. It is much the same."

"*What* did you just say?"

He was going to be difficult. Emily exhaled. "You are *vampir*, I have freckles. It's what makes us different. I, for one, don't believe that being different is necessarily a bad thing."

"Your logic astonishes me. It is also beside the point." Val rolled her over on top of him. "I won't do it, Emily. I won't make you like I am." A pause, then he said casually, "You mean to leave soon?"

Emily rested her head on his shoulder. "That depends. Vampire you may be, but you're *my* vampire, and I'm not going anywhere without you."

Val smoothed his hand down her slender spine. Perhaps the events of the past few days had scrambled his brain. With his own excellent ears, had he not heard Emily invite Lady Alberta to return with her to England? As well as demand to take Jamie? "You can't mean to abandon the Dinwiddie Society."

"I've no intention of abandoning anything or anyone." Emily's voice was muffled by his chest. "I suspect there may be some other items of interest to you in our vaults."

Val pulled her upright so he might see her face. "Not another amulet."

Emily didn't meet his gaze. "We could spend part of the year in England, and the rest anywhere you like. I haven't forgotten that you promised to show me your dungeons." She paused. He remained silent. "*Must* you make me say it? Very well. I need you, Val."

"No, you don't. Not really." Val couldn't help but feel a little sad.

Emily pinched him. "Impossible creature! Maybe I don't need you to manage the Society, but I *do* need you. Prodigiously pushing as it may be of me to say so, I think you need me, too. How dare you smirk at me like that?"

Val wasn't smirking, not really, just looking very fond. Since Emily was also feeling fond, some time elapsed before the conversation resumed, at which point Emily was lying half on and half off the bed.

She straightened herself. "I dislike to point this out, but if you don't bring me over—what *do* you call it?—you will stay all ripe and juicy while I shrivel up like an old prune."

Emily sounded sublimely unconcerned. Val wasn't deceived a bit. "It is most unlikely that you'll shrivel. You have Cezar's healing blood."

"What does that mean?"

"We will have to wait and see."

Emily was exceedingly tired of being told she must wait. However, Val had said 'we.'

He had also reminded himself that he wished to count Emily's freckles. Val had just reached two hundred when they were interrupted by a knock on the door.

Emily grabbed for the sheet. Val said, "There's someone I'd like you to meet."

Emily looked down at her naked self. *"Now?"*

"Enter!" He tucked the sheet up under her chin.

Jamie stepped into the room, gaped, clapped his hands over his eyes. "Crivvens! I shouldna be seein' this."

Emily squirmed about until she sat upright with the sheet clutched tightly to her bosom. "It's all right, Jamie. Ravensclaw is coming back to England with us, so you might as well get used to such shocking sights."

Beside her, Val stiffened. Emily nudged him with her elbow. *Aren't you?*

He looked down into her determined little face and gave up the struggle. *It would seem I am. You are my ailaltă, Emily.*

She was his *ailaltă?* Emily flung her arms around Val's neck. Jamie slipped away to the kitchen, there to inform the rest of the household, who had gathered to enjoy Mrs. MacCamish's oatmeal bannocks, that Ravensclaw and Miss Emily were as comfortable together as an auld pair of slippers, and furthermore it was his considered opinion that Miss Emily was no longer unkenand.

The sound of a clearing throat came from the doorway, reminding Emily, barely in the nick of time, that she and Val were not alone. She snatched up her sheet, which during the exchange of adorations had become considerably disarranged.

Val watched her fondly. The die was cast. His fate was sealed. *I will accompany you to the edges of the earth,* he told her. *And beyond.*

Edges of the earth?

Flower petals are involved.

Emily's toes curled. She was very curious to learn more about those flower petals. But first—

She turned her attention to the man and woman who had entered the bedroom, and had waited patiently through this silent exchange. He was compact and muscular, with light brown hair and high cheekbones and strange yellow eyes. She was plump and black-haired with a triangular face and a pouting mouth. Neither seemed at all surprised to find Emily in Ravensclaw's bed.

Val murmured, "Allow me to present my friends, Vasile Dragomir, also known as Drogo, and his wife, Michaela. Drogo and Machka were additional victims of Lisbet's malice. With her departure, they were freed." Drogo made an elegant bow. Machka yawned.

Forgetful of the sheet, Emily sat bolt upright. "Shapeshifters! Why didn't anyone say? Will you please tell me what it's *like* to be a shapeshifter? There are any number of things I would like to know!"

Drogo sat down on the edge of the bed. "Ask away, Miss Dinwiddie. We are in your debt."

Machka leaned against his shoulder. "So we are. No more fleas."

Already deep in questions, Emily reached for Val's hand. *Ravensclaw?*

Um?

I love you, too.

***

And so, a short time later, after various negotiations were concluded, and mysterious documents signed, Miss Emily Dinwiddie and Count Revay-Czobar wed in a simple ceremony performed by Cezar Korzha, who was among other things a Dacian priest. The ceremonies were enlivened by the bridegroom's previous wife, who in honor of the occasion performed a dance of veils that was no less astonishing for her semitransparent state.

Young Jamie served as ring bearer, and filched not a single thing.

Zizi, Bela, and Lilian attended, in great good spirits, for it had long been obvious to them that Miss Emily was the master's *ailaltă*, and they were pleased that he finally had realized it himself. Drogo and Machka were also present, the latter becoming so moved by the occasion that she rubbed herself all over the former in a manner startlingly reminiscent of a cat in heat. Mrs. MacCamish prepared a special nuptial feast, in honor of which Lady Alberta left off her stays. Andrei Torok stood guard at the door.

It fell to Isidore to propose the wedding toast.

Nimic peste putinta la dragoste se-ntelege.

Love will find its way.

A Brief Dictionary of Romanian Words

Ailaltă—other

baĭat—boy

Breaslă—guild, brotherhood

Bună seara—Good evening

Bună—hello

camarad—comrade

cătea—bitch

Consiliu—council

Damnatiune!—Damnation!

Dudevite dracului!—Go to the devil!

Fraternitae—fraternity

Iubită—lover, sweetheart

La dracu!—Damn!

Dragul meu—my dear

Locotenent—lieutenant

Mea amant—my lover

neisprăvit—do-nothing, scamp

nelegiuit—evildoer

nefinistat—unfinished

pisică—cat, wild cat

proşti—fool

provocare—provocation, challenge

puşti—boy, lad

Roscat—redhead

Stăpân—master

Strigoii—undead

Tampită—fool

Trădător—traitor

Vampir—vampire

Vrajă—charm, talisman

Zau!—really